GOT A LIGHT?

BURN

JESSICA LYNCH

FOREWORD

Thank you for checking out *Burn*!

This is a dystopian romance set in a fictional part of New Jersey at the end of the world, following an event where one-third of the US population Turned into ravenous zombie-like creatures known as lurkers overnight. Their assault on the remaining population decimated it. At least half of the country perished in those early days, leaving the remainder a scrappy bunch of survivors fighting to make it through the rough ones that follow.

There are themes of grief and lost loves in this book, as well as adventure, determination, and graphically detailed descriptions of violence (specifically toward the lurkers who, as the title states, must burn). This book also has a romantic subplot that weaves its way throughout the entire story, and while it's a slow burn (pun intended), you can expect a couple of open-door intimate scenes in *Burn*. Because this is a dangerous, dystopian world, there will also be a dubcon scene (when the MMC and FMC are forced to be together, though it gets cut short—and the guy who does the forcing gets what's coming to him). Plus, you know, lurkers are zombie cannibals, so there's that, too.

It also is reminiscent of a post-pandemic world (while I'm completely aware that we're still living through one), and I don't shy away from the anti-government views that are commonplace in a dystopian book—or very timely, considering the state of the world today. I wrote the initial draft of *Burn* more than a decade ago, waiting for the right moment to release it, and if I continued to wait, it would never be live.

But now it is, and I hope you enjoy it!

xoxo,
Jessica

PROLOGUE

Once upon a time, zombies weren't real, true love existed, and the world wasn't on fire.

I liked those stories best.

— Hallie Holden

There are three steps to exterminating a lurker.

One: the stare.

Sounds kind of foolish, and maybe it is. No one knows what the hell a lurker sees with its soulless black eyes; they can't talk so they'll never be able to tell us. But if you can stomach it to look one of them dead in the face long enough, the power of a survivor's stare can freeze it.

Not for long. Never for long. But if you're experienced at the hunt, it's long *enough*—

Hallie is standing two steps behind me. I'm crouched in the dirt, head bowed while she keeps watch. We're on the edge of Ridgemond Street—a once busy thoroughfare in our suburban city—both of us tensed and ready in case the lurkers attempt to breach the boundaries again tonight.

The empty glass bottle in my hand thuds as I tap it anxiously against the cracked asphalt. Out of the corner of my eye, I catch Hallie chewing on her thumbnail. Every ten seconds or so, she allows herself to blink.

The old traffic lights on the corner of Ridgemond and Grove have been out for months, but the street lamp just above my head must have recently gone dark. By the time Kevin and Chase discovered it during their early evening patrol, it was too late to do anything about it.

Darkness rushes toward the Grave, and with the dark, the lurkers. We need the brightness of the remaining street lamps to keep them back. If even one of the bulbs winks out, we're fucked—and we all know it.

Tonight's watch is up to us. I'm here because no one else has as many kills as I do. Hallie's my backup because of that freaky way she can sense the lurkers approaching before anyone has eyes on them. Together, we're the perfect team.

I've long given up trying to convince her to stay back at the Holden safehouse once the sun sets. God knows that Chase has pleaded with Jack too many damn times to take Hallie off of a hunting team, but if anyone on this shell of what was Earth should know better, it's her devoted—and admittedly overprotective—fiancé.

But Hallie… she's too stubborn, just like me. When I'm out on a hunt, she's going to be right there beside me, and if I can't talk sense into her hard head, I wouldn't want it any other way.

Her long hair hangs like a curtain in front of her face.

The pale blonde strands gleam more like silver in the weak moonlight. I yank my matching waves back, tying the mess tight with a rubber band so that they won't get in the way as I lay out tonight's supplies: a glass bottle, one small gas can that is maybe half empty, a folded piece of cloth, and a cap full of motor oil.

Everything I need to make a firebomb.

I glance up. The nearest working street lamp is about thirty feet away. Despite the faint amount of light it offers, I'm used to the dark. I can make out the copse of blackened trees that beckon in front of us. Charred and carrying the scent of smoke, I'm reminded that there are signs of fire everywhere these days. This part of the Grave is no different.

Hallie shifts her weight from one foot to the other, her whole body radiating anxiety and nerves. I tap the glass against the ground a second time, harder than before to catch her attention.

She stops fidgeting immediately.

For a second, I think she realized just how distracting her movements were—but only a second since, with the next, I pick up on the sound of her breath catching in her throat. I'm instantly alert.

I know exactly what that sound means.

"How many?"

Hallie concentrates as I stay low, prepared to pounce depending on her answer. I'm not like my twin. I don't know how many lurkers are near until I actually see one of the bastards with my own eyes. To be honest, whenever she tries to explain what it feels like to sense them, I almost have to refrain from accusing her of fucking with me. She's never been wrong, though. I trust her, and there's nothing I can do but wait until she can get a read on her feelings.

"Two," Hallie says before correcting herself right away. "No. No, it's three… Three." She pauses before adding hesitantly, "At least I *think* it's three."

Three's not too bad. We can handle three.

I start to uncap the gas can, then stop. It's not just that I don't want to start a fire we can't control. Like the other hunters, I have to make sure I'm not using any more gasoline than necessary. There's still an abandoned gas station inside the borders of the Grave, but one day it will run out and we'll have to figure out another way to kill the lurkers with what we have left.

I don't want that day to be today.

"Okay. You think it's three. I'm ready, but you tell me when you're sure."

My sister shivers behind me.

"I am. It's three," she confirms, and I start measuring out the gasoline into the glass bottle. "They're heading right this way. They're not too far off, either."

I don't have to tell her to keep her eyes on the trees. Trusting Hallie to do her part of the hunting mission, I start to prep the firebomb.

The second step is the most important of the three: the fire.

Guns don't work on lurkers; not unless you're a sharpshooter who can hit one right between the eyes after you stared them into momentary submission. Within twenty-fours of infection, the monster's cells regenerate too quickly for any other injury to cause death. Knives don't make a dent against the high density of their skin. Their otherworldly strength makes it impossible to strike them down, crush them, *hurt* them.

But fire... not even a lurker can protect itself from the impetuousness and speed of a hungry fire set right on its path—

"Got a light?"

Hallie stops biting on her thumbnail though she keeps her eyes on the trees. Brushing her hair behind her ears, she pats her pockets. The right one. Then the left. Then the right one again with a little more intensity.

My temper sparks, beginning to flare the same way as the gasoline will as I grit my teeth; already so close to the surface these days, it's all I can do to keep from snapping at Hallie. Bringing the matches separate from the other materials is the only other part of the job I trust her with and... and I let out a sharp huff of relief when she gasps under her breath, then pulls the pack of matches out of the back pocket of her worn jeans.

"Ah..." Her laugh is breathy and fast. The nerves always get the best of her, the closer the lurkers get. "Here they are."

She moves to hand them to me. However, whether it's from her nerves or the way she's still focusing intently on the trees, she misses my palm by a few inches. The matches hit the dirt with barely any sound at all.

My expression softens as I swallow back my frustration. I reach for the matches before Hallie gets the chance.

Scooping them up, I shake the dirt off the matches and set them on the ground by my knee. Before I do anything else, I shrug off my heavy jacket. Since it's unseasonably warm out tonight, I don't really need it, but I always wear it—until I'm ready to fight the lurkers with fire. After the first time my sleeve nearly caught and the leather started to shrink and char, it's become a habit of mine to remove Rory's old leather jacket whenever I prep my firebombs.

Hallie waits for me to finish before taking it. Without tearing her gaze away from the half-burnt trees, she folds Rory's jacket neatly. Neither one of us will risk anything happening to it so, quickly and with only the smallest of stumbles, she places it blindly on the asphalt ten feet behind me. It should be safe.

If only we were.

I might not be able to sense the lurkers the way Hallie can—and hell if I can see perfectly in the dark like a lurker —but my eyes usually adjust enough that I'm not blinded out here. Underneath the waning moon, the shadows begin to move. The ragged black cloaks each lurker covers themself in waft in the evening breeze making it seem like they're swimming between the dying trees, sharks screaming after a single drop of blood.

Even so, my ears catch the sound of steady, plodding footsteps crackling against fallen, brittle tree branches. The air turns sour and cloying, and I begin to breathe through my mouth as shallowly as I can without letting the old, familiar panic rise.

The rotting scent of dead meat is almost too overpowering as the three lurkers move closer to where we're waiting for them.

They're coming.

And I'm *ready*.

Once the fire's lit, all that's left is the burn.

Lurkers are supposed to be indestructible. That's why they were made. The Injection was created to erase any and all human vulnerabilities but, then again, no one counted on us being so desperate to survive that we'd resort to setting fire to creatures that used to be our family and friends.

It's amazing how quickly they catch. As flammable as dry kindling doused in oil, all it takes is one spark, then stand back. Just watch the monsters burn away until there's nothing left except for a pile of smoldering ash and the fervent wish that, with each and every one we destroy, the world could just go back to the way it was be before the Turning—

"They're getting closer," Hallie whispers. From what we can tell, a lurker's hearing doesn't seem to be any better than a survivor's, but she whispers anyway. We all do. "I can see the one in the lead. The other two are right behind it."

I haven't finished with the rig yet. I still have to look.

She's right.

Lurkers aren't very fast—their top speed is about half that of an active survivor—but they're very strong and forever hungry. The creatures will keep on coming, only stopping to feed… unless we put an end to them first.

We have to kill them, and all those like them. I won't run from a lurker again.

I turn my attention back to the firebomb. I've made so many of these simple rigs in the last five months, but it's essential that I'm careful, that I take my time. That doesn't mean that it isn't tedious, or that I don't get frustrated easily. I do. These handmade bombs work best when they've been built to the specific needs of the mission: How many lurkers? Is there anything that might catch fire with the creatures? Dead trees or dried brush that could catch light and blaze out of control? Any forgotten gas lines that might go up with that one spark? Our community wants to kill any of the white-skinned, black-eyed monsters lurking at the edge of the Grave, but the territory must be protected at all costs.

It's all we have left.

"I'm almost finished," I announce, my head down. "Keep your eyes on them."

"I won't blink," she promises.

Practiced fingers finish tying the knot on the makeshift wick. I can't forget that single dab of motor oil on the tip so that it catches and catches *fast*. One quick shake to make sure that none of the gas can spill and I'm satisfied. The matches are where I left them. I yank two from the inside of the book, placing the head of one against the strip. I won't strike it until Hallie gives me the signal.

"Done," I tell her. "Can you see their eyes yet?"

"Almost."

As far as we can tell, their eyes are the only weak spots they have. The Injection made it so that the recipients had perfect vision and, like everything else, it backfired on the monsters. Even the smallest amount of light blinds them once they Turn; like the cockroaches they are, the lurkers scatter and hide in the dark. That's why we rely so desperately on keeping the street lamps functional.

The burnt-out light hanging over my head is a mocking reminder of just how important they are. I refuse to look at it again so, instead, I squint and strain my eyes toward the trees. I hardly breathe, waiting for that first flash of waxy skin peeking out from under the shadow of their heavy hoods.

As quiet as it is in the Grave after sundown, my ears are trained for this ominous task. I make out the continued sound of their steps, each one in rhythm because they're of the same mind.

Food.

That's all they're thinking about. It's all a lurker *ever* thinks about. We're not a pair of twenty-three year old women to them anymore, just like they're no longer our friends and neighbors. Once a lurker Turns, it's an *it*—and the first time you forget that, you're a *meal*.

Hallie makes a small whine in the back of her throat.

My chest tightens, but I have to ignore it. No matter how many missions we've partnered on, she still hates the idea of killing the lurkers. She knows we have to, and she knows how much I'm relying on her unusual ability, but I can't get her to stop pitying them.

I wish I could give her a hug and comfort her the way I've done all my life, but I can't. My head goes down again, my hands poised to light the match, my reflexes ready to throw the firebomb.

One step, two steps… no step. The monsters have paused, frozen like weathered, warped marble statues. Frozen from Hallie's stare.

"Now," she whispers.

I have maybe ten seconds to do this. Fifteen tops since they're a trio that Hallie's staring down. I only get one shot.

Gritting my teeth, I strike the match. The flame blossoms on the head before leaping down to the gas-soaked rag poking out of the top of the rig. Thank goodness for the motor oil. It catches immediately, leaving thick black smoke to trail behind it like a snake's tail.

Without climbing off of my knees, I straighten up just enough to pick out the unnatural shadows on the edge of the normal ones. The outline of their ratty, hard-worn cloaks fade into the color of the night, their hoods up and hiding most of their ghoulish faces from view.

The lurkers are about ten feet away from us. The one on the left is already struggling to break out of the stare. There's no time to lose. I lob the sparking firebomb at the horrific trio and pray it smashes at their feet.

And in the light of the blaze as it arcs toward the first monster, I see the rainbow haze in a flash and I realize what I've done.

We found out about the dead street lamp with barely enough time to plan a proper mission. We arrived in position right as the sun disappeared for good. There hadn't been any time at all for recon, or for a backup team in case the lurkers broke through Ridgemond. No time even to check for the simple safety measures we all take for granted.

Gas, I think. Somewhere there's a gas leak. And I just threw a Molotov cocktail at it.

The scream rips out of my throat—

"Hallie! Get down!"

It's no use. I know in an instant that I'll never get to her in time. But that doesn't stop me from diving toward my sister, trying to bring her down and out of reach of the fire's rebound.

It isn't enough. I hit the ground hard and Hallie... innocent Hallie, worried Hallie, petrified Hallie... she's still standing there, her normally soft green eyes suddenly dark and wide and utterly terrified as the pupil eats up the iris. She doesn't move. I *can't* move. I just look up at my twin and, for the first time since the world Turned, I pray.

In the moment before the gas ignites and the fireball comes back at us, Hallie's lips form one soundless word. *Xandra.* She might even have said my name out loud. The explosion bursts outward, leaving me deaf and flat on my belly on the asphalt. The force finally knocks Hallie on her back, even further out of my reach. The flames engulf us both.

And, I hope, the three monsters that we're burning for. Did the glass even get the chance to smash? I guess I'll never know.

The pain comes, the pain and the absolute certainty that I'm dying. But it's nothing, it doesn't even compare to the overwhelming horror of knowing that I did this. I killed Hallie. It's my fault. I've killed somebody else that I love—

Fire really is the only thing that can fully kill a lurker. Probably because the two aren't all that different. The lurkers are incapable of remorse; fire doesn't care if you're good or bad—so long as you can burn, you're a target. Both are unstoppable, bringing nothing but death and destruction and *agony* if they aren't snuffed out first.

Not only that, either. Give the hungry flames a chance and, like a lurker, they'll devour *everything.*

PART ONE
STARE

We got our name by accident.

A community huddled around the broken remains of Grove Avenue, we were the Grove the first months after the attack.

Later, someone called us the Grave. I don't remember who.

It doesn't matter.

It was fitting, and it stuck, and that's all that *does*.

We're the Grave now, and there's no escape.

- Alexandra Holden

CHAPTER 1

It's not the first time I've woken up screaming.

My reaction is the same as always: I shove my fist in my mouth, the tangy taste of blood landing on my tongue as I reopen another one of the cuts on my knuckles. It doesn't stop the screaming, but it muffles it until I can shake the last vestiges of my nightmare from my mind and get some kind of control.

It's pitch-black around me, the unfamiliar room full of nothing but too-haunting memories. The screams have stopped as my breathing turns frantic; the same terror that I've gone blind in the night makes it hard for my lungs to function the way they should. It's suffocating, like someone has sucked all of the oxygen out of the air. I start to choke.

My legs kick at the sheets already so hopelessly entangled after another night of restless terrors. I want to run, I want to break free, I want to get out and kill any lurkers I can find before they get me.

A cold sweat breaks out on my forehead, on my neck,

down my back. I have to get the hell out of here, but to where? I have no fucking clue.

I yank my hand out of my mouth. Fingers clutch at the sheets, fisting them, grounding me. I suck in another breath. Pushing myself up on my elbows, I blink a few times, looking past the impenetrable dark. It fades, letting the shadows in.

For a split second, I'm still lost. My bed never faced this way before. When I had a TV that worked, it was mounted on the other wall. My closet door was in front of me, not to my left, and I used to enjoy sleeping by the window. Waking up in the winter, rolling over to see the snow… it was one of those little pleasures in life.

But it's not worth the risk of a lurker breaking through the Grave and smashing the glass. This bed is positioned as far away from the blacked-out, covered windows as it can be.

Oh, and it's not my bed.

It belonged to Stacey Finch. I went to school with her younger brother, Tom. They lived with their parents in a complex of pretty pricy condos called Oak Grove. When the survivors abandoned their homes, moving closer to local high school, Jack brought my twin and me to take over one of the empty condos. We've lived here ever since, and if I still wonder whether Stacey fled, she was lurker food, or Turned herself, I try not to obsess over it too much. The Finches were gone when the Turning was done, leaving their house ripe for the pickings, and that's all that matters.

At least, that's how Jack explains it, and it's easy to just agree with him.

Does that mean I want him to know that I'm having

another nightmare? The master bedroom is down the hall. If he was home to get a couple of rare hours down himself and he heard me, he'll never get any rest.

Worrying about Jack is enough to help me slowly get my ass under control. My throat is raw from screaming and the strain of choking on my breath. My eyes have adjusted enough for me to finally remember where I am, and at the very least, I know I don't have to run.

Not yet, anyway.

I'm safe. I'm alive.

I'm *alone*.

All of a sudden, the panic gives way to a heavy weight pressing against my chest. It feels like someone just dropped a rock on me. I lay there, paralyzed for a moment, all the fight in me simply gone. Angry, hot tears appear in the corners of my eyes, but I pretend not to notice them. I fool myself into thinking it might be the sweat dripping from my brow that's causing my eyes to sting. I don't care. Besides, I'm used to it.

Instead, leaning over, I start groping around the edge of the bed. My emergency pack of matches must be somewhere near. My lighters are never too far away, either.

My hand closes on something poking out from under my pillow. It's rectangular and sleek and cool against my palm. The relief is sudden and sweet. I finally feel like I can breathe again at last.

It's my phone.

I know it's silly, especially since most of the survivors got rid of theirs when we eventually gave up on any hope of cell service returning, but I still keep my old phone charged whenever we can spare the power. All of my games and contacts and photos are long gone—no technology means no cloud and our devices went kaput months ago—but it still has its uses. Tapping the screen, I squint at the bright display. A makeshift glow-in-the-dark clock, even when the electricity is off.

It takes me a second to read the screen. When I do, I groan. It's eight o'clock in the morning. If Jack's here, he let me oversleep.

Again.

Before the Turning, my concept of passing time was a hazy blur at best; past or future, it was either coming or gone. I was twenty-three. Fresh out of college, working a shitty retail job while I waited for my history degree to put me on the map, I was carefree. Having fun. The future could wait—and then, suddenly, it was January, the Turning happened, and, like everyone else, I was forced to change, too. That's when I started to think of everything as "ago", as in nine months ago the world turned to hell. It's only gotten worse since.

Ago—

Two months ago, I still had my twin sister.

Seven weeks ago, I didn't.

Seven weeks ago… it seems like a lifetime, but it's only been seven weeks since the accident. Just seven weeks since I woke up in the triage area at St. Matthew's, just like I've done nearly every morning since: panicking, afraid, and, no matter who was home, completely on my own.

I couldn't remember anything at first, but everyone knows they only keep you in the church when they want you as close to God as possible. I saw the weathered wooden crucifix hanging over my head, witnessed the memory of the blazing fire coming back at us in my mind's eye, and I instantly knew what had happened as certain as if I had seen Hallie's ghost hovering next to my bedside. Sometimes I imagined I did.

I survived the explosion. Hallie didn't.

Five weeks ago, I came home to an empty condo. Not entirely empty because Jack still calls our stolen condo 'home', but I hardly ever see him—and, well, that's not really his fault.

It's nothing like the two-story house my family shared about a fifteen-minute walk away from Oak Grove. From the layout to how narrow it is, the condo is just... *wrong*. After all these months of living in it, I'm still not used to that, and maybe I was still dazed after they let me leave St. Matthew's, but after I accidentally, forgetfully, *stupidly* walked into the room Hallie claimed—Tom Finch's old room—my first night back, I took a hammer to the door-knob and mashed it in. I left it the way it was, a shrine to my twin and maybe my old schoolmate, too, and I know one thing: it's a room I won't ever enter again.

Four weeks ago, I decided it was time to start hunting again.

As much as it hurts, as much as I still feel like I'm only partially whole without Hallie by my side, I've never been the type to grieve and mope. All I wanted then... all I want *now* is to get to take out my anger and pain on as many lurkers as I can. Not even in Hallie's memory will I spare them any mercy.

But, damn it, Jack won't let me.

He seems to think it's safer if I stay in at night when the threat of the lurkers is at its peak. He won't come out and *say* it, but he's already rearranged all of the patrols so that I'm not needed for any of them. Whenever there's a new mission and he calls for volunteers, he never sees my hand. If I try to head out with my gas can and a bottle, one of the other survivors always escorts me back to the front porch.

I'm fucking twenty-three and the whole community is treating me like I'm a kid.

I hate it. I absolutely *hate* it. It's driving me crazy. I tried to sneak out once, to prove myself, but when Camden skipped his patrol to bring me back home and Liza nearly got bit by a youngling, I promised myself that I wouldn't do anything so foolish again. I won't let anyone else get hurt because of me.

So now I'm nothing but a reluctant prisoner until Jack decides to let me be useful. Seeing as how he seems to think it's best if I sleep my life away, I doubt that will happen any time soon.

Leaning over, I grab the bat lying under this side of the bed and bang it twice against my floor. If Jack's still home, he'll turn the fuses back on so I can get ready. We've got to be an example, he says, to show the other survivors that we can get along without electricity in case it disappears like the television and the phones did months ago.

So he turns the fuses off purposely every night to conserve it, I guess, and I'm left to wake up blind every morning. Sometimes I wonder why, when everything else went to hell when the world Turned, we still even have power, but Jack tells me not to question it so I don't.

In the beginning, I used to torture myself with *why*'s. Why did this happen? Why did everyone take the Injection? Why did the supposed miracle cure backfire, leaving most of the population little more than ravenous monsters? Why now?

Why *me*?

But now all I think is: Why worry? Why wonder? I know firsthand it doesn't help. All it does is cause heartache and grief. Fuck knows we already have way too much of that in the Grave.

It'll take a few minutes for Jack to go into the cellar and reach the fuse box. I busy myself with picking clean clothes out from the mounting piles of soiled ones scattered on the floor. Laundry day was three days ago, but I haven't gone to the community center where we're encourage to share washers—and socialize—in two weeks. Eventually I'll run out of fresh clothes—plus those that a spritz of perfume can't cover up—and I'll have to face the gossiping women that work there. Rifling through the clothes, I'm determined that won't be today.

When I find a shirt that doesn't make my eyes water, I throw it onto my bed for later, then head into the bathroom.

The power isn't on yet. That's nothing new. Sometimes Jack has an early meeting, or someone in the Grave needs him… they *always* need him, and he's always on duty. Oh, well. I've gotten used to taking showers in the dark. It doesn't really bother me anymore. It's only Jack's concern that I might fall and hurt myself that keeps me from always leaving the lights off.

As long as the bathroom mirror remains hanging over the sink, I'll take a hundred showers in the dark if it means I can avoid my reflection.

There are no mirrors in the bedroom. Once they let me out of St. Matthew's, I took one look at the wall mirror upstairs and punched the glass. After that I smashed every mirror I could find except for the bathroom; and that was only because I was bleeding too much to work up the energy to take on that one. Jack didn't say a word about my breakdown, not even when he had to bandage my hand up himself. He spent three hours picking shards of glass out of my hand, three hours when I'm sure he was needed elsewhere, and never asked me why. In return, I never explained why I lost control like that. I still think it's obvious.

How can I stand to look in the mirror when all I see is Hallie staring back?

CHAPTER 2

The lights come back on when I'm in my room, halfway dressed.

It's not all that difficult to get ready in the dark. I never really cared about my appearance before the Turning, and these days I basically wear the same kind of clothes every day, almost like a uniform: A pair of black jeans. A white tank, or light grey if the whites are all dirty. My hiking boots. And, most importantly, Rory's jacket.

I finish tying the laces on my boots, then quickly run a brush through my damp hair a few times. Leaving it loose to air dry into messy waves, I head downstairs to look for Jack. If he's still here, I know where I'll find him.

Jack Holden is the leader of the Grave, of our people. At forty-eight years old, you'd think he's too young to be a widower, though with his salt-and-pepper hair, sad brown eyes, and chiseled jaw, it's no secret that he has plenty of female admirers amongst the survivors in our community. But he still wears his wedding ring religiously, and seems oblivious to their attention. In the before times, he used to be a firefighter—the last one left in our side of town who never had the chance to accept the Injection when it was offered to his firehouse—and, in a world that runs by fire, that was the only qualification he needed in order to take charge of us all.

He's also my dad which makes my position as difficult as it is. As my dad, it's easy for him to be overprotective, especially after what happened to Rory and Hallie. As our leader, he can get away with making changes to the Grave's routines. No one dares argue with him.

I certainly can't. Even if I call him Jack to respect his new title, instead of Dad, I know that that's exactly who he'll always be to me.

He's in the kitchen, just like I suspected. A cup of coffee is set before him, but he isn't drinking it. Instead, Jack is staring into space, lost in thought. He jerks when he sees me enter the room and he stands up quickly—but not so quickly that I don't see the worried expression that flashes across his face.

Even though his mug is half-filled, he picks it up and turns toward the sink.

"Allie!" he calls out, voice rough. That, coupled with the deep circles under his eyes, tells me it was another long night for the hunters. "Good morning, honey. Sleep well?"

I twitch at the name Allie. I can't help it. Before I decided I wanted to go by Xandra when I was twelve, it always used to be Hallie and Allie, the Holden twins. But ever since Hallie's death, Jack has started to call me Allie again. I don't have the heart to ask him to stop, even though it's like a prickly splinter every time I hear it, nagging and annoying if essentially harmless.

"I guess I slept okay," I lie, taking the seat he emptied. The nightmares come at night which means sleep rarely does. I'm sure the matching bags under my eyes are a big enough clue. "I know I slept past the six o'clock patrol. Any news this morning?"

Jack keeps his back to me as he dumps the coffee down the sink, taking his time to wash the mug out. I count to ten, waiting to see if he'll answer me. Figuring he must not have heard me, I try again.

"How were the patrols?"

"Hm? The patrols?"

"Yeah."

"What about them?"

Something isn't right. No matter how tired or busy he is, Jack's never *this* distracted. I watch as he grabs another mug from the cabinet only seconds after dumping his first cupful of coffee. He won't even look over his shoulder at me. It's as if he's avoiding my question.

What doesn't he want to tell me?

My stomach tightens. I'm not ready for bad news—I don't know if I ever will be—but I absolutely refuse to remain ignorant. In our new world, that's too dangerous.

So, swallowing back my unease, I raise my voice as I call out for him: "Jack!"

There's no way I don't see how the edge of his jaw goes hard when he hears his name. It's a habit I picked up after the Turning, after he took over as the leader of the Grave. He doesn't mind when we're around other survivors, but I know he hates it when I call him Jack when we're alone.

He turns slightly.

"Why don't you have some breakfast? Mrs. B brought over some of her pancakes this morning," he says lightly, gesturing to a plate piled high with the fluffy cakes sitting on the side counter. I don't know how I didn't notice them before. "There's fresh syrup on the stove."

Jack is as transparent as one of my glass bottles: I can see right through him. But he knows me nearly as well as I do him, and we're both aware that there's not much that can sway me from hunting. Food—especially Mrs. Baker's pancakes—might be the only thing.

I'm not really hungry this morning, but I still remember how terrible those first days were after the Turning, once we realized that there was no going back to the way things were; no help from the world outside of the US, either. We went weeks with empty bellies, eating whatever food we could scrounge before the Grave banded together and it became an *us* versus *them* situation rather than everyone fending for themselves. I never turn down food now—and Jack knows it. I'm climbing out of my seat and moving toward the dish cabinet at the word *pancakes*.

I give up on asking about this morning's patrol. Somehow, I don't think Mrs. Baker would be bringing over breakfast if Jack had somewhere else to be. It must've been a routine check, no lurkers reported. I'm probably just overreacting, and Jack's just tired.

I know I am.

"How's Mrs. B?" I ask, reaching around him for a plate and a fork. "And the baby? They're all right, I hope."

Mrs. Baker is a kind-faced, cheery woman in her mid-thirties. A math teacher from before, she spends her days teaching the young children in the Grave, and that's when she's not baking treats for Jack. Her husband was considered one of the first victims—someone who died on

January 1st when the first lurkers Turned and were initially vulnerable—and he left her with two kids and a third on the way. When she went into labor a few months later, Jack was right there to help deliver the baby boy. She comes by at least once a week to give him something to show how grateful she is.

As I help myself to a small stack of pancakes, Jack's eyes brighten and, look at that, he finds his voice. He tells me all about baby Jackson and how Mrs. Baker's daytime classes are going, pausing only to pour himself that second cup of coffee and add a heaping spoonful of sugar to it. I think he's glad to have something safe to talk about, something that doesn't revolve around hunting lurkers.

Then again, he's always been something of a gossip. My mom used to tease him mercilessly about it, but he always said it had something to do with spending most of his time at the firehouse. Now, though, as our leader, it seems most of the juiciest gossip comes straight to him. And since I'm all but under house arrest nowadays, he feels like he has to tell me all about it.

"This weekend we have six birthdays to celebrate," he says, and that at least makes me feel a little more hopeful. I'm allowed to go to the daytime affairs if I want to. I haven't in ages, but it's nice to know there's something to celebrate in this terrible world. "Mrs. B already agreed to bake the cakes," he continues, "and I'll have some of the boys spruce up the decorations down at the school. We're going to need it, too. I heard from Charlie down at the corner that his boy Scott wants to marry Pamela Ascher as soon as—*oh*."

My fork falls from my hand, clattering against the

wooden tabletop. My mouthful of pancakes suddenly tastes like sand. I have to force myself to swallow.

Jack clears his throat, obviously uncomfortable as we both realize he won't finish his sentence. He takes a small sip of his coffee, despite the smoke still swirling above the mug, if only to have something to do. I'm silent as I hesitantly pick my fork back up.

I don't take another bite.

He looks down at me as if wondering what to say next —or if he should even attempt to say anything else at all. He should've known better, or maybe I shouldn't be so sensitive. Who knows? His brow furrows and, while I'm not happy about it, I'm also not surprised at the turn the conversation takes—

"Speaking of..." He shakes his head, frowning. Wrong start. "I mean, I almost forgot to tell you. Chase stopped by the house last night. I told him you were sleeping."

He doesn't add the *again,* but it hangs there at the end.

I bite down on my bottom lip, trying to fight the frown. "What did he want?"

My unsaid *now* joins his *again.*

"He just wants to talk. He misses Hallie."

"He's not the only one," I mutter.

Jack sets his coffee down on the countertop. There's that set to his jaw again. I'm not getting out of this lecture. It's pointless, though. I could probably mouth it along with Jack, I've heard it so often. It's not going to change anything.

"Listen, honey—" It's always *honey* when Jack feels sorry for me. It stings almost as much as *Hallie.* "I miss her, too. I'd give anything to get her back... your mom, Rory...

I would sell my soul to have them with us again. But we have to understand that we can't—"

"I know that. Don't you think I know that?" My heart starts beating a little faster. I shove my pancakes away from me and climb out of the chair. "I'll eat these later. Leave 'em here, okay?"

"Allie, stop." Jack sounds tired, defeated. My blood is racing, my pulse pounding, but I listen to him. He's my dad, after all, and he's lost just as much as I have. More, really, if you count me… "I'm doing the best I can."

"Yeah? Well, we all are. It's called surviving." I'm sorry, but I can't stay in the kitchen any longer. I can't stand the sympathy in his eyes, and the pain etched into every premature wrinkle on his face. I have to get the hell out of here. "Bye, Jack."

"Where are you going?" he calls after me.

I huff under my breath, scowling as I peer back at him. "Does it really matter? How far can I really get?"

Jack's sigh is like a knife to my heart. I know I'm taking all of my frustrations out on him because he's the only one around, and I also know it's not fair.

Too bad I can't find a way to stop myself.

And then he says absolutely the wrong thing, and it only gets *worse.*

"If this is about Chase—"

Inside the sleeves of Rory's jacket, my hands clench into tight fists. "I've told you before," I say through gritted teeth, "it's got nothing to do with him."

He doesn't believe me. And he shouldn't. We both know that I'm lying.

Jack covers his cheek with his hand. "I know it's hard, Allie, but you're going to have to face him eventually." His voice is shaky as he takes a deep breath before exhaling roughly. "You can't avoid him forever."

That's what he thinks. I know all of Chase's patrol schedules. Avoiding him is one of the only things I *can* do.

***

If only to get into the sunshine and out of my prison cell, I'd planned to take a walk over to the old high school after breakfast. It's only about a half-mile trek from the Oak Grove Condominiums, and one of the few places where they leave the lights on all the time. I like to disappear into the depths of the library, not because I find any real joy in reading these days, but because it's quiet and hardly ever occupied.

After my argument with Jack, I changed my mind, choosing to return to 'my' room instead. I have to. The Reynolds' two-story house is directly across the street from Madison High, and though Chase is the only one living there now, I refuse to risk the chance of running into him.

Not today.

Not with the scene from breakfast so vivid and clear… and the memories still way too fresh.

Chase Reynolds is—*was*—Hallie's fiancé. The three of us had gone to school together since kindergarten; Chase and Hallie were inseparable from that time in fourth grade when they would play pretend-husband and pretend-wife on the elementary school playground. Everyone thought it was inevitable that they would get married and, when the lurkers appeared and tomorrow wasn't promised to anyone, Chase didn't hesitate in throwing away their life plan—college first, working their way up at their prospective jobs, saving for a downpayment on a house—before impulsively proposing.

Not surprisingly for a world gone to shit, their February wedding kept getting pushed back. Something seemed to happen every day that made the two of them feel as though their getting married would be selfish compared to all the hardships in the community. Chase has always puts the needs of the Grave before his own, and Hallie was just as selfless. At last count, my twin had set the simple wedding for the second weekend in July, but I'm absolutely positive something terrible would have caused another delay.

Why did it have to be Hallie's death?

I don't blame Chase for his reactions. Apart from me and Jack, he took her death the hardest. I know how he felt—we both lost our second half. Of course he would think it was my fault that I survived and she didn't. It *is* my fault. He was the only one Jack allowed to visit me at the church, and though my memory of those first few days after the accident are hazy, I pointedly remember him sitting there with bone-dry, frantic eyes as he pleaded with me, demanding that I bring Hallie back.

But then something happened. Something changed. When I was able to go back to Oak Grove, he, well, *chased* me there. He'd visit every night before I began to purposely avoid him. At first he said he just wanted to talk, and I felt guilty enough to encourage him to open up to me about his grief. The first time he called me Hallie, I told myself that it was a slip. When it happened again and again, I wasn't so sure.

And then, before I shut the door on him for good, I did the unthinkable—

Three weeks ago, I slept with him.

It was a mistake. If I'd had two words with him since, I'm sure he'd agree. Between mourning Hallie and sharing half a near-full bottle of whiskey he snuck over while Jack was on patrol, we drowned our sorrows in forbidden booze, bitched about how it wasn't fair that Hallie was gone, and then… one thing led to another.

That's how it always goes, right? In the right light—or maybe because my better sense was clouded by alcohol, plus the fact that I've always been a lightweight—Chase looked tempting. No denying what he saw when he looked at me. Hallie. He wanted his lover, and I wanted comfort.

So I fucked him, then panicked when it was over. Before Jack returned to our borrowed condo, I kicked Chase out, and now I can't face him. It's impossible. Every time he looks at me, I don't know if he's seeing Hallie, Hallie's killer, or her replacement, and that scares me more than anything else in the world. At least I know how to take care of the lurkers.

I don't think fire is the answer when it comes to Chase.

CHAPTER 3

T he scraping of my penknife against glass is like a lullaby to me. No matter how anxious or angry I am, the repeated motion, the soft yet harsh *scrape, scrape, scrape,* it always manages to calm me down.

There's probably about thirty bottles in the bedroom. They're lined up against the molding, stashed in empty dresser drawers, covering every inch of the fancy wooden desk in the corner. I used to spend my days with Hallie, scavenging old recycling bins, looking for anything that might work as a container for one of my firebombs. Some of the other survivors would save them for me when their rations ran out so that, before long, I always had a steady supply.

Of course, that was all before the accident. Things are different now, but that doesn't mean I've given up. I keep my bottles ready just in case Jack finally changes his mind. My gas can is full and perched expectantly on our back porch, the pockets of Rory's jacket are stuffed with matches, and I keep scraping the labels of our old lives from the bottles. Somehow it just doesn't seem right to throw a firebomb that still says Heinz ketchup on the label.

It's September in New Jersey, and before I got to work, I dared pulling the blackout curtains away from the windows, cracking them open just enough to let in a breeze. The sky is a pretty blue out there. The remnants of a brutal summer are definitely holding on, despite being so early in the afternoon. I can't wait for fall. Making our way through three months without AC was rough, and even if it's still warm out, at least it's not that humid out...

Small victories, Xandra. Celebrate what you can.

It was winter when the Turning happened. Those early days were cruel, too, especially since we had the worst winter we've had in years. When we discovered the power of fire, the snow either melted into puddles or lingered, covered in ash blown in from another lurker hunt. Us Holdens—the ones still standing—stayed in the family home through mid-January. Halfway through the first month, it became clear that huddling behind locked doors on our own wouldn't save us.

A community might.

The Grave—once known as the Grove due the name of the throughway that stretches through this part of town— was formed by the end of the first month, with Jack its de facto leader, and our surviving neighbors closing ranks.

When we left our old house on Firestone and moved into Oak Grove, most of the condos were already long abandoned. Except for the traces of blood left behind and signs of fire everywhere, it was as if the people living here simply disappeared right in the middle of their ordinary lives.

Jack and some of the other men who agreed with him

spent close to a week checking the complex for any lurkers —or lurker victims. The condos that were completely uninhabitable were marked with an "X" in red spray paint. Jack and the others moved half of the Grave into the rest.

It was easy for me to recognize the owners of our condo. The Finches had pictures of Stacy, Tom, and their parents all over the first floor. Jack quietly took them all down. He didn't want the reminders that this wasn't really our house, or that we only have it because the Finches couldn't.

My dad didn't put up any pictures of our family, either. Even then, it was easy to tell he couldn't handle the reminders. I struggled, too, throwing myself into hunting lurkers and keeping the Grave safe. Sure, I might have to live in the condo now, but it wasn't home.

My home was smack dab in the middle of a lurker nest, barely a mile away.

That didn't stop me from holding out hope that we might figure out a way to defeat the hordes of monsters instead of just taking out the stray ones that test our boundaries. Nine months in, I have to accept that we never will.

I can't. My mother… Rory… they haunt the old house as much as Hallie haunts this one. Ghosts follow me everywhere. I might as well stick close to the other survivors while I can.

The truth is that, sometimes, I think about leaving this place behind, maybe even abandon the Grave, but here I am. Sitting in another ghost's room, *scrape, scrape, scrap*ing another label off the glass.

To leave… it would be both selfish and foolish. I can kill a lurker better than nearly anyone else in the Grave, but I know I could never survive outside of the community on my own; especially when I don't have my twin watching my back. Leaving would be a suicide mission, and how the fuck can I do that to Jack when I'm all he has left?

So here's some more *scrape, scrape, scrap*ing as I sit on the floor, and shower in the dark, and prepare empty firebombs for the day Jack decides I can take all my pain and frustrations out on the monsters that stole everything that I ever cared about from me.

As I work, I purposely keep the door open. When Jack heads out for the day, I want to know.

He's trying. It can't be easy, watching each and every member of his family get picked off one-by-one while knowing he has the fate of the entire Grave on his shoulders every minute of every day. He didn't ask to be leader—the role was just thrust on him during the early days of our people coming together—and he's doing the best he can. It's just... sometimes I wish he would try a little less when it comes to me.

My nerves are showing as I grab another bottle and attack the label with my knife. In the back of my mind, I hear a *tsk*, then Hallie's worried whisper telling me to be careful. At that exact moment, I swipe the glass harder than I should. The blade slips, finding skin. The blood seeps out of a slice on my finger about two inches long before a sharp pain hits me.

I wince, muttering a curse under my breath.

The glass bottle and knife both fall to the floor, forgotten.

Shit.

The cut isn't deep enough that I have to go to St.

Matthew's for help, but it's definitely too deep for me to ignore it. Jumping up to my feet, I'm out of the room, halfway to the linen closet for an old washcloth when something catches my attention.

I stop dead in my tracks.

A couple of voices filter up the steps. Though they're too low for me to tell who's talking, I know for sure that Jack's not alone.

I can't hear what's being said. The conversation is muffled because whoever Jack is speaking to is keeping their voice down. Jack's not giving me anything to work with, either. The fact that they're being so quiet is a clue that I'm not supposed to know they're talking at all.

Which, of course, means that after I grab the washcloth and twist it around my finger, I quickly tiptoe over to the top landing. I strain to see if I can make out what's being said yet. It's still just a hum and, taking care to avoid the creaky step that would give me away, I start downstairs.

The voices are coming from the kitchen. They're still talking in an undertone.

A narrow hallway cuts through the first floor, leading to the kitchen. With my back to the wall, I move toward it. A second later, I'm rewarded when I get close enough to catch Jack saying, "And the auditorium is a go for noon, Eddie?"

Ah. Eddie.

Eddie Collins is Jack's right-hand man. Whenever Jack can't do something by himself, he relies on Eddie for help. Well, crap. I should've figured he'd be the one downstairs.

"It's all set," Eddie grunts in answer. I can just see him scratching the grey scruff along his jaw. "The boys sent out the word already. The whole of the Grave will be waiting for you, just like you wanted."

"Good. He's at the church right now, getting checked out. He seems like someone we can trust, but... Stranger." *Stranger*? "After the Turning, it's better to be safe than sorry."

He's not wrong, but that's also my cue. I stride down the rest of the hallway, entering the kitchen as if I haven't just been listening in on their conversation.

"Sorry about what?" I ask. "Hey, Eddie. How've you been?" Without waiting for an answer, I glance over at my dad. "What's going on, Jack? I miss something?"

If the whole of the Grave is waiting to see Jack at the auditorium at noon, and the clock over the stove says it's eleven-thirty now and *I* wasn't invited...

I raise my eyebrows.

The two men take turns watching me, Eddie's mouth clamped shut like he suddenly knows he's already said too much while the vein along Jack's temple starts to pulse as he frowns. So absorbed by what they were discussing, it's clear that neither one of them was expecting me to pop my head in.

I wait.

Jack jerks his head at Eddie. He murmurs something under his breath, just loud enough that his second hears it —and I don't. With a quick nod in my direction, Eddie scuttles out through the back door leading off from the kitchen without another word.

Once he's gone, Jack spins around, his arms outstretched, his eyes deceptively innocent. "Allie! I thought you were napping, honey."

"It's only like eleven-thirty. Why the hell would I be

napping?" Remembering the washcloth on my bloody finger, I fist the soiled material before hooking my thumb oh-so-casually through the belt loop on my jeans. "So… what were you and Eddie talking about?"

I thought I was slick, but I forgot for a moment that I'm dealing with my father. His eyes lock on my fist… and the bloody washcloth I should've left upstairs.

He moves forward. "You're bleeding," he says, reaching for my hand. I shake my head, warning him back. I'm not about to let him use a silly little slice as a distraction, but Jack's concern is regrettably genuine as his expressions sags. "Oh, honey… not another mirror."

My stomach twists.

"It was just a little nick with my knife," I tell him, "and nothing to worry about. I'm fine. But you… what's going on? The auditorium? Why is there a meeting of the Grave at the high school?"

And, again, why didn't I know about it?

He shakes his head. "It's nothing, Allie—"

Bullshit.

My jaw goes tight. "Daddy."

It's a manipulation tactic, and I'm not afraid to admit that. He hates it when I call him by his first name, but when I call him 'Daddy' like I'm a kid again instead of a hard-earned twenty-three, he's putty in my hands.

Especially when I add, "You're not hiding something from your own daughter, are you?"

It's not an unfounded suspicion. For weeks now, I can't shake the feeling that I'm out of the loop. That there's something everyone knows… except me. It's an intangible belief, like catching the wind in the palm of your hand: I feel it, I almost have a grasp on it, but it isn't there when I look for it.

Except for now.

A fleeting expression of pain flutters across Jack's tired face, there and gone again before the guilt can really creep in. Fucking shame that he hurriedly rearranges his features into a look I know all too well.

His "leader" look.

The one that says that not even I'm getting around it.

"What? That? Eddie's helping me set up another one of those boring meetings we're always having." He waves his hands, dismissing the meetings though I'm well aware that the only reason Jack is always going to meetings at the high school is because he insists on them. "There weren't any lurkers sighted last night, but some of the boundary boys think that we could be in trouble tonight. Like the beasts are biding their time." Considering lurkers are too brainless to do anything but hunt to feed, I doubt it. I don't get a chance to tell him that, though, before Jack is adding, "We're weighing the benefits of doubling up patrols to make sure there's always a pair of sensors"—someone with Hallie's unique ability—"and hunters on duty after nightfall instead of leaving some of our borders unprotected. It'll put a strain on our sensors, but the boundary boys think it's worth the risk. A debate like that could go on for hours, sweetie, you know how it is."

"And that's all?" I know how it is—and I also know that can't be all. "What about 'he'?"

"'He'?"

As a hunter who knows their place in the Grave, I'm not usually so curious about the day-to-day running of the community. I trusted Jack. Relied on my father. Give me a mission, a rig, and a match, and I'll protect our people the only way I can.

But, nowadays, I'm on the bench. If Jack's trying to shut me out of hunting, he should've expected I might turn my attention elsewhere.

Like, oh, a called meeting with a *stranger*.

There are no strangers in the Grave. If you were a survivor in our community when we closed ranks, you're one of us. If you're part of the outside world, you're a target for the lurkers. We protect our borders. We don't let anyone in or out.

At least, I didn't think we did.

"Yeah," I say pointedly, "you said 'he'… 'he' might be trusted. 'He's at St. Matthew's. You called him a stranger, Jack. Who's 'he'?"

Jack blinks once, twice, three times before he visibly relaxes. "Oh. I know what you're talking about. You must've misheard. Eddie and me… we were talking about Oliver. You know him, don't you, honey?"

Oliver. He was a sanitation worker in the old days. Now, he fancies himself a hunter, even if he—like Hallie—gets his worth in that ability to sense when a lurker is lurking. In all of the Grave, there's about forty people who can. That's only about ten percent. Jack appreciates his skill, though he won't let the tall, lanky, klutzy man in his early thirties anywhere near a flame.

I narrow my gaze. "Yeah. I know Oliver."

He's definitely not a stranger—and I definitely heard Jack use that word.

My dad still tries to play it off like he didn't. "He has

this cockamamie idea that he should take a group of survivors past our borders, see if there's anything we can salvage for our stores. Eddie sent him to Audrey so the doc can talk some sense to him."

Audrey Monroe isn't a doctor. Not really. A second-year nurse who worked at a hospital an hour away, she's one of the other survivors with any medical training at all. She's also a kind soul with a good nature, and though Doctor Wilson—a surgeon before the Turning—did the most when it came to my recovery and healing, it's Audrey you can find at St. Matthew's at any given hour of the day.

That would explain why Jack mentioned 'he's at the church. If Oliver is acting *strange*-ly, maybe *that's* what I heard. I bite the corner of my mouth, wondering if I could buy that. His story rings true and yet—

"Whatever. Anyway, I was thinking about going to the library today. Maybe I can grab a snack for lunch, then I can walk with you over to the school."

I know in a second that I've got him. Jack has this habit of fiddling with his wedding ring whenever he's feeling super anxious. And now? He's turning it and turning it until it slips off his finger, landing on the floor with a soft *clink*. He picks it up and jams it back on again.

"You don't have to do that," he tells me while I inwardly smirk. "In fact, it would probably be better if you stayed home. Put a bandage on your finger and get back to prepping your bottles. You might need them soon."

Oh, you *dick*. I love my dad, but when Jack goes "leader of the Grave" mode, he can be a real dick.

Distract me with the prospect of returning to the hunt? Why not?

I decide to go along with it.

"Really? You mean it? You're really going to let me back on patrol?"

"Well, you heard Eddie and me talking about it, Allie. If the Grave decides to double up on the protections we already have, it would be selfish of me to keep you home when the threat out there is only growing. At the end of the day, it's all about keeping our people safe."

All of them, not just his sole surviving family member.

"In that case," I reply, "I should probably get some of my rigs together."

"I— yes. That's a good idea, honey."

He edges closer, squeezing my shoulder in a wordless gesture before he absently pats my bicep.

It was hot in the condo. I shrugged off Rory's jacket while working on my bottles, and the tank top I have on does nothing to hide the large scar on my upper left arm. Surprisingly, the apple-sized second-degree burn was the only visible injury I suffered in the explosion that didn't completely go away. As it was, it took three weeks for it to heal enough that I could call it a scar, but while it stopped peeling, the raw pink skin is a reminder of what one stupid fucking mistake cost me.

Jack's breath catches in his throat, a sure sign he's thinking the same damn thing that I am.

I answer his suffocating grief with a fleeting smile that doesn't quite reach my eyes. As Jack adjusts his wedding ring again, I go back upstairs—but I leave the glass bottles right where they are. Instead, I hurry over to the open window just in time to see Jack slipping through the front door beneath me.

Using my phone as a clock again, I wait until Jack's

been gone for five minutes before I grab Rory's jacket from the back of my door, run down the stairs, and stroll after him.

CHAPTER 4

There are three different housing complexes called the Oak Grove Condominiums, lining up on one side of Grove Avenue until it meets Oak Street. Ours is the middle one, parked in the center of the street. Even in the before days, you can get nearly anywhere if you follow Grove through Madison, and since we formed our community, there's always someone out on the sidewalk.

Today is no different. For a second, I'm afraid that one of the other survivors will see me and tell me to go back home, but that was a pointless worry. Multiple groups are traveling down Grove, heading toward Madison High. Eddie was right. He had his guys round up the rest of the community, and now, more than ever, I'm pretty fucking sure this sudden meet has shit to do with border patrol.

It's grown hotter out. Still not humid, but the sun's a scorcher. I'm already baking under Rory's jacket, but I refuse to take it off. Sure, it makes it easy for anyone to spot the scowling blonde in any crowd and know it's

Alexandra Holden, but between showing off my burn or feeling like I have my older brother with me, it's a no-brainer.

Still, as I follow a trio of school-aged kids toward the intersection of Oak and Grove, I shove up the worn leather sleeves if only for a little bit of relief. I recognize Mrs. Baker's eldest child in front of me, a girl of about nine or ten named Annabelle. It must be something really important, I think, if the call for this meeting includes even the youngest members of the Grave.

That makes my pulse pound a little, my head throbbing as a familiar stress headache starts brewing. What the fuck, Jack? Sure, he's my dad, but he's also in charge of the Grave. Excluding me is just wrong, and I'll make sure he knows it after the meeting.

In order to get to the local high school, you can cross over Oak, continue down Grove, then turn into the school's long driveway. But if you're walking—and we all walk in a bid to save the remaining gasoline lingering in the pumps of the only gas station in the Grave—you can take this hidden path that cuts nearly a quarter-mile off the trip.

Even if it wasn't a shortcut, I'd still go that way because it means that I won't have to pass the Reynolds' home—

"Hey! Hey, Ha—Xandra!"

Fuck.

My heart skips a beat at the sudden sound of my name rising up above the hum of the other walkers. That, and because of the familiar voice that called it.

I can't help it. I glance up, tracking the echo, watching

him come jogging out from the shortcut on this side of the path.

And there he is. Chase Reynolds.

There's something about him that reminds me of the sun. Bright and warm, I'm drawn to him whenever he's near, like a sunflower always tilting its face skywards. But I can't stare at him for too long before my eyes start to tear, and I feel like I'm burning up from the inside out...

Chase is more than a head taller than me so that I feel as if I'm *always* looking up at him. Though he spends most of his time on patrol late at night and early in the morning, he's still no stranger to the outdoors. His healthy, glowing tan is proof of that.

He wears his sandy-colored hair short on the sides, long in front, and it's impossible not to see how vibrant and alive he is when you get a glimpse of his warm hazel eyes and his dazzling white smile. Though it's been years since we graduated from Madison High, he hasn't lost his lean, muscular quarterback build. Constant boundary checks and lurker patrols have a way of keeping us all in excellent shape.

I never really thought of him as anything other than Hallie's boyfriend for so damn long that it came as a huge shock to me when, two cups into that whiskey, it hit me just how attractive he is. I blame my mistake on the booze, but I wouldn't have slept with him if I didn't feel some kind of pull toward him. Sometimes, when he surprises me or when I least expect him, I still feel it.

I'm hot for my dead twin's fiancé, and if that isn't a reason to keep my distance, I don't know what is.

It sucks. It really fucking sucks. Especially since there's so much of the accident, plus its horrifying aftermath, that

I don't remember. Like how did I survive the blast? Who found me and pulled me from the flames? How did I get to St. Matthew's with scrapes on my skin, the fresh burn on my arm, and smoke in my lungs?

Was Hallie's final word really my name before she died?

Chase, though… Chase always at my side in the church, Chase yelling at me, crying with me, begging with me to give him his Hallie back… I can't forget *that*.

Stupid, Xandra. Fucking *stupid*. I was so worried about going by his house and seeing him when, if he knew me at all, he'd have to guess I'd take this path to get to Madison High… and, whether Jack hid this meeting from me or not, Chase would bet on me showing up anyway.

He's right.

I don't want to be a coward. No way in hell can I pretend not to see him, and turning tail to head back to Oak Grove just means that Jack wins. I'll miss the meeting.

Suck it up, buttercup. It's just the last guy you had sex with. If I avoided everyone that Alexandra Holden banged in town, there are at least three other survivors in the Grave I'd have to duck. True, I haven't seen any of them since the accident, but I'd smile and nod and pretend like I didn't know what their dick size was.

Or that, when I try to remember what it was like fucking anyone but Chase, it's as big a blank in my mind as the accident itself…

I shake my head, shoving my loose hair out of my face. "Chase. How are you?"

He's there. Right there. Lost in my thoughts, he closed the gap between us, digging the tip of his shoe into the yellowed grass on the edge of the path when he stops short.

Aware he has my attention, he sticks his hands in the pockets of his jeans, casually leaning on his heels. The sun catches his hair, making the longish front strands seem blonder than usual.

As calm and casual as he appears, I notice a strange gleam in his hazel eyes. It's a hunger, a desire, a *need* to look at me as though he's trying to will Hallie into my place.

I swallow back the uneasy feeling—other than attraction—that being around Chase gives me. I've stopped wondering if it's regret or remorse or something else entirely. I just know I don't like it.

He gives his head a little shake of his own, like he's realizing that he's doing it again, watching me with that intense way he has. A small chuckle escapes him, an attempt to diffuse the awkwardness. "Can't complain. You?"

I shrug.

He leans forward, inching closer. "You know, it's really good to see you."

I take a step back. "Okay."

Undeterred by my short answer, he tries again. "I've been stopping by after my patrols to say 'hi', but seems like my timing never's right. Jack always says you're sleeping."

I don't say anything to that. There's no accusation in his tone, only earnestness; he seems to genuinely believe that it's only by coincidence that he's missed seeing me these last few weeks. The truth is that I'm never sleeping when Chase knocks at the door, but when Jack cuts the power and I lie there with a blanket over my head until it comes back on, I can pretend.

A wrinkle creases his brow, his handsome features going taut. I used to tease Hallie that Chase was like her very own puppy dog. Eager to please and forever there, forever following her at her heels, there's something very golden retriever about him.

Now? Putting up a wall, shielding him from getting any closer to me… I feel like he's sitting there with his tail drooping in despair.

"Hey," Chase says again. "Is everything okay?" He reaches a hand out, like he's about to tuck my hair behind my ear or maybe stroke the height of my cheek with his thumb.

Forget taking a step back. I fucking *jump*.

He frowns. "Xandra?"

I should be grateful he knows my name. Glad he uses it. Not my twin's, not my childhood nickname, but the reminder of who I am… I need that.

I don't need the pleading in his eyes as his lips part.

I swallow roughly. "I'm fine, Chase," I lie.

Does he believe me? He bites down on his bottom lip— I fist my hands, trying to erase the way that simple gesture twists my insides—before exhaling softly. "I'm glad to hear it. When Jack said you weren't feeling up to going to today's meeting, I was…" He runs his fingers through his hair, his eyes still worried and sad as he admits, "I was worried about you."

I feel myself frowning, and I'm not sure if it's because of what Chase just confessed—or because he thought I would purposely miss this meeting I had no clue about. "Wait. You talked to Jack? Today?"

"Of course." His brow furrows even deeper, leaving lines etched there. Worry lines. Shit. If there's anything I hate, it's having *anyone* worry about me. But Chase… "Didn't he tell you I had coffee and pancakes with him this morning after my patrol?"

Not really, I think. Jack said something about seeing Chase last night, but nothing about this morning. I do, however, remember the mug of coffee on the table he didn't touch—and how he didn't have any of Mrs. B's pancakes with me, either.

I grit my teeth, trying to conceal the fact that I'm both angry at Jack for lying to me *and* at myself for not expecting something like this. Not even just how he's protecting me. But having breakfast dates with the man who would be Hallie's widower if they'd managed to get hitched?

"It must've slipped his mind on account of the meeting."

Chase brightens a little. "It doesn't matter now anyway. We can both go to the meeting together." He reaches out a second time and, before I can react, he smooths the edge of my collar. "Walk with me to the school?"

He's bold. I freeze under the gentle caress, and he shifts his hand. His fingers brush absently against my neck. It tingles where our skin meets, traveling like a current all the way down to the soles of my boots.

I jerk in place like I've actually been shocked.

"Sorry," I say flatly. "Can't. I just remembered… Jack needed me to grab something from the condo for him. I forgot it. I've got to go back."

"No problem. I'll go with you."

No fucking way. "That's alright."

"Xandra—"

I firm my jaw. "No." I feel like I kicked a puppy, the way his face falls, but I… I can't.

"But don't you want to talk—"

About what happened three weeks ago on the living room couch? "I'll see you around, Chase."

"Will you? Really?"

Sometimes I wish that Chase wasn't so candid and honest and open. Hallie used to love that about him. He's the kind of guy who never keeps secrets, and who always told her exactly how he felt. You never have to worry where you stand with him. When he was my sister's boyfriend and just another guy in our friend group, that didn't both me.

But that's not all he is anymore, is it?

What makes it worse is that Hallie was always just as honest and forthright with Chase—and that's why he expects it from me. I wish I could just tell him what I feel… but that's impossible.

My smile is rusty and feels out of place as I call it to my face. I keep my hands balled up and inside of Rory's jacket so that, when I place my sleeve on his arm, I'm not actually touching him.

Though I know it's wrong, I use his insistence that I'm just like her to my advantage—

"Promise. Look, why don't you head over to the school and get ready for whatever Jack's got going on. I'll be right there. Save me a seat?"

—because I can lie straight to his face and he'll never see it coming.

Hope. Hope fills his expression, and he answers my

smile with a dazzling one of his own. "Of course. I'll make sure it's the one right next to me."

He stands there for a second more, staring at me as if there's something else he'd like to say. Whatever it is, though, he changes his mind and waves at me before jogging off. He joins a group of guys our age that we both went to school with heading down the path, diving into their conversation as easily as if he were jumping into a pool.

It's easy for him.

It's never been that easy for me.

I watch him for a moment before deciding that, if I'm going to pretend I have to go back for something for Jack, I should probably start heading up Grove again. Once I cross over Oak Street, I bend down and untie one of my hiking boots. I count to five, re-tie my bootlace, then double-back toward the high school.

I don't stop thinking of Chase the whole time I'm doing this. And I wish I didn't know why.

All of our lives, there were people, places, and things that we shared, that belonged to the Holden twins together. Going ice-skating together at Mirren Park. Bowling with our old friends over in Randolph. Shopping at the mall before the lurkers turned it into a nest that got burned down last February.

Then there are those that belonged to me, or were only Hallie's. Camping used to be my thing. Hallie had cheerleading. I spent weekends going hiking in the mountains upstate with Rory, and going out with a different guy every couple of months.

Hallie? She always had Chase.

Chase is Hallie's, I remind myself. And I won't ever forget that.

I *can't*.

CHAPTER 5

nce we were a street. Grove Avenue. Just one street in a pretty stuffed New Jersey town of about one hundred thousand people.

Now, during our weekly roll call, our community can barely top four hundred. Babies are born and people die. Some can't cut it living in our secluded community anymore. Lurkers eat the rest.

Of course, having such a small population does have its advantages. You know everyone, and usually everyone's business, too. We have to rely on each other so trust is absolutely essential. That also means that there's no violence in the Grave, and no crime; when the alternative is being abandoned to the lurkers, it's surprising how well the threat turns us all into law-abiding citizens. We don't have any concept of money. Each week we get our rations from whatever non-perishables are left at the grocery store located in the old shopping center on the corner of Ridgemond and Grove. Some of the survivors are growing fruits and vegetables in the grounds behind the church. Others make bread and sweet cakes out of the flour and sugar stores. No one goes hungry.

Some people are hunters and border patrol—like I am, and Chase—whose job it is to kill the monsters. Some are sensors, those who send out warnings to the hunters when they sense lurkers; that was Hallie. Jack's our leader. Mrs. Baker teaches. Eddie and his group of boys are our version of law enforcement, keeping the Grave safe while extending the boundaries and securing any supplies from abandoned houses that we absorb into our settlement.

We all have our jobs here, we all have our purpose.

All of us together are the reason why we've survived so long. I just… I just wish Jack would let me be useful again. I'm not so naive to believe his words back in the kitchen this morning are anything but a ploy to keep me in line.

That's what I'm thinking about. As I walk alone into the old high school, I'm stewing over how I've been nothing but a drain since the accident.

My eyes dart upward as I pause just inside the front doors. The motto scrawled in paint is still visible in the anteroom: *enter to learn, depart to serve.*

Huh, I scoff. If only.

Most of Madison High is closed off, big metal gates blocking the paths that lead further into the school. No one with access or keys survived the Turning, and we only managed to break in and disengage the alarm with the help of a couple of hammers and some wire cutters.

It was worth it, though, because there are still four main areas in the center of the school that are not blocked off and very useful: the library, where we can go for peace and quiet and a good book; the gym, which doubles as an indoor playground during the day, and a place to sleep at night for those who feel safer inside; the cafeteria, where we took all of the non-perishable food and are stockpiling it for the future; and, lastly, the auditorium, the only room large enough in the Grave for everyone to assemble for meetings.

By the time I get inside, the auditorium is nearly full. I cast one quick glance around, exhaling when I can't pick out Chase right away. Thank fucking god. I looked, don't see him, and now I can use that as an excuse for finding my own seat.

I take one on the aisle behind the last full row. A handful of survivors follow after me, providing me with enough cover that it's not so obvious I'm sitting on my own. I sink low in the chair anyway.

Sorry, but I'm not just avoiding Chase. I know better than to let Jack spot me before the meeting starts, either.

There's no sign of him yet. The stage up front is empty except for a podium and two folding chairs waiting for occupants. One of our precious bottles of spring water is perched on top of the podium.

That catches my attention.

Who are we waiting for? Who deserves such a gift?

Who is 'he'?

Lucky for me, we don't have to wait long to find out.

Jack is the first one to come out on the stage. He's alone, and he approaches the podium slowly, his shoulders hunched as if weighed down already.

Bracing his hands on the podium, he leans forward, speaking into the microphone. "Good afternoon. I want to thank you for all coming out on short notice—"

Someone upfront starts to applaud. Someone else calls

out a question, asking what's so important they got yanked off their boundary check. Jack quiets them with a sharp jerk of his head. "Let me speak. What I have to tell you… it concerns all of us."

It does?

I lean forward in my seat.

"For close to eight months now we've come together, worked together, lived together. The Turning was hard on all of us… we've lost so much… but, as a community, we survived. That's all we can do. However, I know I'm not alone when I say that I wonder what's really going on out there. Past the lurkers, in the rest of the state. Hell, in the rest of the country.

"Is there anyone left to help us?" he continues. "Does anyone need *our* help? Today, I can say that I have the answer to at least one of those questions. Early this morning, a stranger from outside of the Grave made it through our eastern borders—settle down, everyone," Jack says gently yet firmly because nearly the entire auditorium has burst into conversation at the news. "He checks out. He's a survivor, just like us, only he came with a proposition and, well, I think I'll let him tell you all about it."

Jack starts clapping, and because he is, we all join in. It's half-hearted and off-beat because most of the survivors are more concerned with turning to their neighbor and discussing in feverish whispers what Jack has just told us.

Not me. I'm still staring at the stage, waiting for my first glimpse of this stranger.

As soon as we realized what parts of Madison had been taken over as lurker nests, creating our borders and enforcing them with fire, we basically closed the Grave off from *everyone*. Since then, we've had one—*one*—survivor manage to make it through the nests and reach our borders. He was a nineteen-year-old boy that Jack was ready to welcome into our community… until he noticed the blood seeping through his hoodie and realized the boy had been bitten.

It takes twenty-four hours for a lurker to Turn. If he'd made it to the Grave an hour earlier, we could've saved him. Hell, if he'd admitted his injury instead of hiding it, he still might've had a chance.

But he didn't. And when his eyes bled to black before anyone could help him, Eddie put him down behind the church, burning his remains. Like all lurkers, he went up in smoke instantly, and there hasn't been another stranger in the Grave since.

Until now.

At Jack's signal, a strikingly handsome man in his mid to late-thirties strides out onto the stage. His dark hair is dusted with grey, his features rugged and weathered. He has a pair of shrewd brown eyes and a thin-lipped smile.

The stranger is wearing all black, though the fabric has faded from its time in the sun. He's got on a pair of black hiking boots like the ones I remember Rory wearing, right down to the flecks of mud covering the toes and the frayed laces; the worn soles thunder against the dull wood of the stage, each step a slap until he takes his place in front of the podium.

A five o'clock shadow covers his sharp jaw as he casts a stare over his assembled audience. As Jack takes a seat in one of the chairs onstage, the stranger clears his throat. He seems at ease up on the stage, and I suddenly wonder how many other times he's faced a crowd of survivors like this.

"Thank you, Jack. And thank you for giving me this

chance to speak. Hello. Let me tell you about myself. My name is Maverick Brooks, and I'm just like you. I'm a survivor. We've all done what we had to do to make it to this point. That makes us the lucky ones. You see, I come from a small town in Connecticut that doesn't exist anymore. They didn't survive."

The auditorium is so silent, you could hear a pin drop. No one is talking. Captivated by his rough voice, the way he demands your attention... we're all listening to this stranger.

To Maverick.

"I've been out there," he says, and then he drops the bomb: "You're not alone. I can promise you that." He gestures wildly with his right hand. "There are dozens of settlements just like this one where"—he starts ticking them off on his fingers—"neighbors, friends, families... they've all banded together to make it on their own. Separate factions trying to live their lives... but it's a new life now." He slams his hand against the edge of the podium, gripping it tightly. "The lurkers are taking—no. They've *already* taken over. But it's up to us to take back our world. It's time to stop hiding. It's time to—"

Someone on the left side of the auditorium raises their hand. Maverick blinks, surprised, but whether that's because he's being interrupted or because someone raised their hand to do so, I can't tell. He turns behind him and murmurs something to Jack. Jack nods.

Maverick points toward the front row. A young woman in her mid-twenties stands up. She tucks one stray curl behind her ear, then waves at everyone sitting in the audience.

Audrey Monroe. Our nurse.

The moment she starts to speak, I feel like I'm back in triage again. There's something about her, how soothing her voice is, how earnest she sounds when she's trying to get her point across, that throws me back in time to those terrible weeks I spent at St. Matthew's after the accident.

The emotions return, crashing into me like a wave at high tide. The grief, the worry, the absolute devastation that came with learning that my twin was gone… my head is spinning and I have to remind myself where I am. What I'm doing here.

All at once I'm going under.

It's tough, but in the end I manage to pull myself together. I tread the water, pushing the feelings down in order to keep myself afloat as Audrey addresses the stranger…

"Hello," she begins, a little nervous giggle in her voice. "We met earlier."

Maverick nods. "At the church, yes. You helped me with my scrape. Thank you."

Audrey brushes off his thanks. Not surprising. If Jack sent the stranger to St. Matthew's, he wanted to have him there in case it was a repeat of that nineteen-year-old kid. Of course he'd ask the nurse to check out any injuries in case they were lurker-induced, and if he's here, he must've passed the test.

She nods, her expression a mix between her usual warmth and a hint of wariness. "I just wanted to let you know that I agree. And, yes, I get what you're saying. We all lost someone we care about during the Turning… My mom ate my father right in front of me," she says candidly, and no one blinks because that's not even the worst of the horrors that came out of that dark day, "and I'd leave the church and make a pile of lurker ashes of my own if they'd let me, but that's just it. The Grave can protect itself. We've never had a lurker make it past our patrols since before summer. We probably have one of the best hunters to exist—"

I slink lower in my seat. She has to be talking about me. Sure, I haven't been out on a hunt for too long now, but before that night when the street lamp went out, I had more verified lurker flamings than anyone in the Grave—

Leaning over, Audrey grabs her seatmate by the upper arm. She tugs, pulling him up, urging him to get to his feet.

Chase sheepishly stands up, holding his hand high as the audience applauds again.

I blink. Oh. Right.

Not me.

As the survivors rightfully cheer on one of their own, Maverick narrows his shrewd gaze on Chase, watching him with interest. He jerks his chin in his direction.

"What's your name?" he asks.

"Chase, sir. Chase Reynolds."

Chase isn't wrong. There's something about Maverick's bearing that just screams 'sir'.

"How many lurkers have you killed, Chase?"

His brow furrows. "I can't say. I mean, I don't count. I just do what I have to to keep us all safe."

To my surprise, Audrey squeezes his arm, beaming up at him. "Don't listen to him. He's just being modest. We've got a chalkboard set up over at the church, keeping track of all his kills since July. It's already up to thirty-eight."

Chase starts shaking his head as soon as she says July. The significance of that month isn't lost on me. Thirty-eight kills since Hallie's death. Seems like Chase got to take out his grief on the lurkers like I wanted to do.

Another round of applause breaks out among the crowd. I can't help but join in. There are one or two cheers.

With the arm that Audrey isn't still hanging onto, Chase raises his hand again, gesturing for us all to quiet down. "I don't do it by myself," he argues.

"See?" Audrey says. "Told you. So modest."

It's a quick kiss, and it's on the cheek, but I watch as the pretty nurse rises up on her tiptoes and kisses my sister's fiancé in front of the whole Grave. Chase turns bright red under all of the attention. He doesn't move away from Audrey or shake her off of his arm; instead, his eyes rove over the crowd, and I know with absolute certainty that he's looking for me, wanting to see my reaction.

I pause mid-clap, dropping my hands to my lap.

Fuck.

Chase and the nurse? When did *that* happen?

Maverick braces his hands on the podium like Jack did before, leaning in so that his lips are just about kissing the microphone. He clears his throat, drawing everyone's eyes back to him. Chase's head snaps forward again and he sits down, followed by Audrey. The applause dies down to a gentle roar, then nothing as we all listen attentively to what the stranger has to say next.

"I commend you, Chase. And I didn't mean to insult your people by assuming you weren't capable of fighting back. Just the opposite, actually. I was telling Jack when I first sat down with him this morning after my… welcome… that I thought I might've finally found a group of survivors that still had their backbones. And then I thought, maybe I've finally found the right people to help me at last. So you guys like to kill lurkers… how would you like to kill so many lurkers that his thirty-eight seems like nothing at all?"

He pauses there for effect. Another round of whispers erupts through the crowd. The stranger knows exactly what to say—and how to say it—to get a crowd of suspicious survivors to at least hear him out.

He continues—

"Listen. There's a nest. In my travels, I've heard too many people talk of it, whisper of it, speak of it with fear. But I'm not afraid. There's a nest, the biggest nest of lurkers on the entire East Coast, and it's not too far from here. It's the reason why we're plagued by so many lurkers to this day, why no matter how many we kill, they keep on coming. This nest breeds lurkers and provides for them and it needs to be stopped.

"I *will* destroy it. Whether I have to do it alone or not, I aim to set the biggest bonfire you've ever seen to this wretched nest, and I'll be damned sure I take out as many lurkers as I can along the way.

"So who will come with me?" he asks softly, the microphone amplifying his voice so that we all hear him anyway. As he goes on, his voice rises, "Will any one of you dare go beyond your borders? Will you kill the lurkers with me, watch them burn? Who will go?"

No one is saying a damn thing. Once again, it's dead quiet in the auditorium.

I know the people in the Grave. When we were still Madison, we stayed to ourselves. Living our own lives, ignoring our neighbors as we focused on ourselves. Now that we're a settlement, a community that relies on each and every one of us for survival, we haven't changed all that much. We've learned that we can only continue to exist if we look out for each other and take care of each other. No one else.

The Grave is all we have. Jack might have wondered what's happening beyond our border, but do we really care? After the Turning, no one cared about *us*.

They're going to say no. The silence is deafening. There are those who might think Maverick has the right idea, and others who, I'm sure, can't wait to see the backside of this insane stranger with his insane ideas—traveling *to* a lurker nest, risking your safety in a bonafide suicide mission—as he gets booted out of the Grave.

But no one is going to go.

And that's when I stand up.

"Me," I say, my voice echoing around the room. "I'll go with you."

CHAPTER 6

Everyone knows the story of the lurkers, and it begins with the Injection.

The Injection has a name, some long, fancy scientific name that nobody can pronounce and I can't remember. Everyone just calls it the Injection because, when it was first made available, the promise was that there wouldn't be a need for any other medicines after you took it.

Like, *ever*.

Think about it: one single shot that speeds up your metabolism so that, no matter your body type, obesity could be a thing of the past? One shot that would lead to an increase of lean muscle mass in place of body fat, making each prospective patient stronger? One shot that would enhance every process in the body on a cellular level so that injuries heal and diseases disappear and the projected life expectancy doubles, even triples?

At least, that's how it was advertised.

It came out of nowhere at the beginning of last year, a

rumor, a whisper, a myth. Everyone knew someone who had heard that the fabled Injection really existed—or maybe they knew someone who knew someone who'd actually been given it. Soon stories came out that it had passed all sorts of tests and it really was the miracle it was promised to be. They swore they would get it out to the public as soon as possible.

And they did.

First they started with the higher-ups. The president got his shot, his Cabinet, the war advisors, the Supreme Court justices, the high-ranking generals... basically everyone who was in charge, they got the first go.

Anyone with money had access to it next. Money talked in the time before the Turning, and if you were willing to pay, you got your Injection.

Civil servants came after. Doctors, teachers, garbage men, the sour-faced biddies who worked over at the DMV... and firefighters—

Last October. Almost a year ago now. That's when Rory was given his Injection. To this day I wonder why he took it when he was never heavy, never weak, never sick. Jack had been the captain of their fire department, and he passed on the shot in favor of giving it to Karen, the wife of his lieutenant who had a chronic illness; that's why he's with me today. I still wish Rory had also said no.

Then I wouldn't have had to watch him die.

It was no surprise when there was a shortage of the Injections. When the supply started to dwindle, they—whoever *they* are—they began to dole it out to those who needed it most: the elderly, the sick, the poor. Anyone who couldn't afford insurance, with the Injection they'd never have to see a doctor again. No Medicaid. No Charity Care.

Through the end of the year, you couldn't pass any senior center, any Medi-center without the telltale blue vans parked out front.

And then they ran out.

They promised us all that we would get our turn in the new year. Anyone who wanted the Injection would get it as soon as a new batch was created. But before it was… it didn't matter. On January 1st, the Injection went bad. It went wrong. No one knows why or how—but it happened.

Like a switch had been flipped, the influx of lean muscle mass turned one-third of the population into super strong creatures that could tear a human being from limb to limb. The increased metabolism turned them into ravenous monsters who would feed on anything—even human flesh, *especially* human flesh—in a frenzied bid to satisfy an endless hunger. Cells that repaired themselves immediately made them invulnerable until the accidental discovery that fire could do the job.

A severe aversion to sunlight, but a desire to continuously feed turned them into lurkers, always waiting until dark, always lurking on the edge, just waiting for the chance to eat every bit of flesh that they could get their hands on, before they wasted away and only a disfigured, skeletal figure remained.

No one could bring themselves to use the dreaded "z" word—even if that's what they are—and before the news stations went dead, thanks to the creative reporters and non-stop news coverage, we all were crying *lurkers* in our sleep.

On January 1st, the Turning began.

It's still not over yet.

Have you ever felt close to four hundred pairs of eyes on you at one time?

I'm suddenly aware that I haven't had a proper haircut since the beginning of the Turning; my hair is still singed and uneven from the flaming accident that cost Hallie her life. I lose my body in Rory's oversized jacket, trying to avoid their stares.

For the first time I think I might understand what causes the lurkers to freeze...

Maverick backs away from the podium before going around it and moving to the front of the stage. Jack is on his feet in the instant following my announcement, already shaking his head as he surges forward to stand right next to Maverick. Both of them are peering down at me.

I gulp, but that doesn't do anything to lessen my resolve.

"How long will it take?" I demand, jutting out my chin in defiance.

"It doesn't matter. You're not going."

I ignore Jack, waiting for an answer.

The stranger—Maverick, and what kind of name is *Maverick*—looks from Jack's set jaw to the way my arms are crossed over my chest and I can just see his brain working. There's enough of a similarity between us that it's possible we're related; there's enough tension to show that there's definitely a relationship.

He rubs the back of his hand across his mouth and shrugs. "I figure it's about 40 miles between this place and the bridge that will lead me into Manhattan." Manhattan. New York... I should've known that's where the lurker hotspot would be. "Without anything stopping us, it might not take more than a few days' hike to get there, then we'd have to find the nest, stake it out, then make our move. Me? I'm willing to take as long as I have to to burn this nest to the ground. I figure it'll be…" He thinks about it for a moment. "A couple of weeks at least… and that's without any trouble. Roads are closed, paths unsafe. Who knows? I might have to go a hundred miles out of the way. It could be a month or more—and I'm not even guaranteeing that anyone who goes on this journey will even come back."

Huh. Why do I get the feeling that Maverick has decided who he's backing and it isn't me? Like he's trying to convince me to change my mind… but that's not going to happen.

I'm sorry, but the way I see it, I found my escape from the Grave at last. I'm not going to let it slip through my fingers so easily.

"I'll take my chances," I tell him confidently. "It'll be worth it to be able to take out a nest like that."

Let him think I just want to pad my own kills. It's not *un*true. To get revenge for what happened to my family… I want every fucking lurker in the world to burn. And if I have my own ulterior motives behind wanting to take a break from the Grave?

Oh, well.

I'm doing it, and one is stopping me—

Maverick opens his mouth to say something but Jack holds out his hand, cutting the other man off.

—except, perhaps, my dad.

"Hold on," he says, and I can tell from the set of his jaw that it's taking everything Jack has not to forbid me from doing this. As leader, he can't—and we both know it. Doesn't stop him from trying, though... "This isn't a decision to be made lightly. We might not know exactly what's out there, but every one of us knows what the lurkers can do. I'm in charge here, and it's my job to make sure we do what's best for the Grave. And what's best for the Grave? It's *survival*. I won't let one of our own walk out into the woods if there's even the slightest chance she won't come back. We can't just throw a life away. I hope you would all agree with me on that."

A whisper runs through the auditorium. All around me people are nodding; one or two even start clapping again. Are you kidding me? Jack's playing *dirty*. He's not appealing to me as my father. Oh, no. He's turning to the survivors as their leader, trying to get them to side with him.

Well, two can play that game.

"You're right," I retort, my eyes locked on my father. "We all know what lives past our borders, hiding in the woods. *Monsters.* Every night there's the chance one of them might slip past our patrol and feast on the entire Grave—but most of us go to bed at night anyway. I don't know about you, but I would sleep a lot better if I know that there's a chance that a nest that big can be destroyed if someone's brave enough to light the match.

"Now, I'm not asking any of you to go with us. I just want the chance to be able to go out there on my own." My voice is shaking at this point, but I pretend not to notice. "Jack," and he's Jack in this moment to me and the rest of the Grave, "you said you hoped that we'd all agree with you... well, I don't. I'm not throwing my life away. If

I can kill even one of those bastards, I'll be *saving* lives. And I hope you'd all agree with *that*."

This time no one dares clap. There's a collective intake of breath because, while the stranger has no idea, they're all well aware that I'm Jack's daughter. His *only* daughter now.

And they're all watching to see what will happen next.

Before Jack can respond, Maverick returns to the microphone. "There's a very simple solution. We can find out exactly how this community feels." He shrugs. "You can always vote."

He says it in such a flippant way, almost off-handed, that it dawns on me that he doesn't expect anyone to take his suggestion seriously. I don't know what sort of settlement he's from—or if he's from any at all since he claims his town was wiped off the map by lurkers—but he obviously doesn't know the people of the Grave or how we do things here. Jack may be our leader, but everyone gets a fair say. We all know that.

I'm banking on it.

"A vote, Jack. I like it. What do you say?"

I know what Jack *wants* to say. I can just hear his lectures, only we're not at home. Here, in front of the whole Grave, Jack has to do his job. Good. I'd rather leave it in the hands of the survivors than my overprotective father.

"Fine," he relents at last. He definitely doesn't look happy about it. "Anyone here that's over the age of eighteen can cast a vote. Majority rules."

A couple of the children in the audience groan, and there's a flurry of argument coming from the few sixteen and seventeen-year-old survivors, but Jack just shrugs them off.

"I'm sorry," he says, "but I'd still like to think we're a democracy here. When you're eighteen, I'll let you vote. Until then we'll leave it to the adults. Are we ready?"

Murmurs of agreement ripple through the rows. I'm certainly ready.

Jack's frowning. "All right... hands up, everyone. Who here thinks that one of our own should be allowed to make the decision whether or not to accompany a stranger out of the Grave?"

My hand shoots into the air. Jack stubbornly keeps his hand at his side and, surprisingly, so does Maverick; his lips thinned when Jack called him a stranger, and I guess he figures that, as a stranger, he doesn't get a vote. Not so surprisingly, when I look for him in the front, I find that Chase has crossed his arms over his chest. Beside him, Audrey's hand is hesitantly lifted up.

She's not the only one. I don't have to count them to see that way more than half of the adults assembled are raising their hands.

It's settled then. There's nothing else Jack can do. The Grave has spoken.

The meeting breaks up almost immediately after that. Mainly because Jack and Maverick left the stage, and because no one else offered to join this suicide mission. Instead, the whole Grave moves quickly toward the back exit of the auditorium as though afraid that they'll be asked to come along.

I kind of feel bad for the stranger. I wouldn't be surprised if he's torn between taking me with him to have some sort of backup or taking his chances at the next settlement he arrives at. Knowing my dad, he's probably encouraging Maverick to leave before I can velcro myself to his side.

I'm going. I haven't felt so determined in ages. Finally, I have a purpose; or, rather, the same one as before. Kill lurkers. I can't bring my family back, but if there's a chance to eliminate a nest, I'll take it.

Maverick has to be a survivor. To make it as long as he has without a community to protect him, he might be able to pull off this insanity. Even if he can't, why can't I?

I have to leave the Grave. I think I've always known that I couldn't stay here. Not without Hallie.

Not with Chase wishing I *was* Hallie…

I haven't taken my eyes off of him. As soon as the crowd broke up, he immediately started toward me. Everyone's being careful to avoid me, almost as though they're already considering me gone—either out of the Grave, or another victim of the lurkers—but Chase…

He'll stop me. I can't let him.

So I bolt. At this point, I don't even care if it's obvious that I'm ducking out on Chase. The other survivors stop and step aside as I rush past and, in seconds, I'm already half-jogging out the front door.

I break into a flat-out run once I see the shortcut ahead of me. I don't stop until I've dashed across Oak, racing down Grove. I throw myself at the front door of the condo, struggling to get it open, then quickly locking it behind me once I'm inside.

In the Grave, where we have to have every trust in each other and crime has become a thing of the before days, this is the first time I can remember locking the door. But I have to.

I don't want to face Chase right now. Jack, either.

My every intention is to head up to the bedroom and pack a bag before Jack gets home. I need him to understand just how serious I am when I say that I'm leaving. And if he decides to go back on the survivors' decision, then I need to be prepared to sneak out of the Grave if I have to.

I had just found an old backpack in the downstairs closet when the first knocks come.

CHAPTER 7

My heart leaps up into my throat at the sound. I'm convinced that it's Chase out there, ready to talk me out of going. Which, after a minute of complete and utter panic, I tell myself is ridiculous. Why should he? He has to know that my leaving the Grave is the best thing that could happen to both of us.

It's easy for me to avoid Hallie's face just by getting rid of any mirrors. Every time he sees me, Chase has got to be reminded. And that's not fair to him.

The knocks are hesitant and soft and they don't stop. There's a break between tapping, but I get the feeling that, whoever's out there, they don't plan on going away anytime soon. It's not Jack. My dad would pound away so I'd let him inside. And Chase… no. It can't be Chase.

So who is it?

Setting my pack on the landing, I start toward the front to see who's out there when I notice that the sound is growing fainter.

I stop. It's not coming from the front door at all. It's coming from the *back*.

My curiosity is piqued; the Grave is not a back door community. Pulling the curtain aside, I peek out of the window that oversees the back porch and stare for a few puzzling seconds.

Huh.

Throwing open the door, I see a fragile blonde woman standing there, her big blue eyes wide with anticipation. Denise. She lives a couple of condos down from us—and it's actually hers from the before days—and is holding a bundle of black fabric held close to her chest. She's brought me one of her black hooded sweatshirts, saying that since we're both petite, it would fit me better than Rory's jacket. Plus, the hood is enough of a disguise in case I want to pretend I'm a lurker. She gives me a quick hug, then scurries away before I can say a single word to her.

I'm left standing there with my lips slightly parted, holding a sweatshirt that smells surprisingly of cotton candy.

One of Rory's old friends comes by soon after. Lisa has two empty bottles of vodka, and she tells me to add them to my collection for firebombs; they're not completely empty either, she confides, since one or two drops of the alcohol will add to the flame. I take them from her gratefully, knowing that I'll have to leave them behind. A bag of glass bottles will only slow me down, and who knows what sort of monsters I'll attract with the incessant clinking. But the thought's still there.

I just wish I knew *why*.

The knocks are never-ending after that, my neighbors all stealing up to the back porch with little trinkets and good wishes. Even Mrs. Baker brings me a plate full of chocolate chip cookies as one last treat before I go. None of them knock at the front door, almost as if they're afraid of coming face to face with Jack. I don't blame them, and I thank each and every one of my neighbors, not only for what they give me, but because it seems like it's all their blessing for me to go.

It doesn't take me too long to pack my bag, though the interruptions make it a tougher task than it should be. It's an old backpack of mine, from before the world Turned and I used to go hiking with my brother. Dark green and trimmed with black, it won't stand out in the darkness. It also has plenty of pockets and pouches to hold whatever I'm bringing.

A change of clothes, spare socks, a can of hairspray, a brush, a stick of deodorant, some mouthwash, and about twenty-five books of matches all go into the main pouch. I add eight lighters, a tightly sealed container full of gasoline tucked safely inside of two Ziploc bags, plus three ripped pieces of washcloth just in case the opportunity to make a rig comes up. On the off-chance I come across a random mirror and can't control myself, I tuck tweezers in with the lighters.

Lastly, I add a picture taken of my family last Christmas, right before the Turning. I don't really like to look at old photographs, obviously, but... I don't know. It just doesn't seem right not bringing one with me.

In a way, if I bring Mom, Jack, Rory, and Hallie with me, it's not like I'm really going out on my own for the first time...

I've just tugged the last zipper closed on my backpack when I hear the back door opening downstairs, shutting just as quickly. I freeze, barely even breathing as I listen—

"Allie?"

My stomach twists.

Shit.

Jack.

Hiding up in my borrowed bedroom is pointless. I have to get this over with anyway so it might as well be now.

Leaving my pack on the bed, I head right for the kitchen.

"Hey. You called for me?"

I expected to find Jack leaning against the counter like he spent our morning chat. Nope. He's sitting at the table again, though he isn't pretending to drink Chase's leftover coffee. He has a glass of water in front of him instead, plus a pair of brown pills. His hand is over his face.

I zero in on the pills. Aspirin from his private bottle, I recognize, guts twisting in guilt. Shit. He only dips into that bottle when his migraines are unbearable.

Me, I think. I caused this headache.

I bite down on my bottom lip, waiting for him to acknowledge me. I… I really don't want to do this. If I could just grab the pack, dash out the back door, and leave without having to see the fear and the worry he's struggling with, I would.

But I can't, and not only because he finally scrubs his palm down his face. He drops his hand to the table, showing me a pair of red-rimmed eyes and a shaky frown and, *fuck,* I should've taken the cowards way out after all.

"Allie," he says, his voice scratchy, "please, sit down."

Jack looks like he's aged ten years since this morning. Part of me wants to ask him why he tried to keep the stranger's arrival from me; the other part hasn't forgotten he had pancakes with Chase and hid that, too. I stay quiet. I'm leaving. There's no denying that. Why make my last conversation with my dad an argument?

Because it could be. My last conversation with him, I mean.

That unsettling thought overwhelming me, I grab a seat, yank it back, drop down onto it. I can't look at Jack. Suddenly, it's as though the grain of the wood on our adopted table is the most fascinating thing I've ever seen. I can't stop staring at it.

Out of the corner of my eye, I watch as he places the two pills under his tongue, takes a swig from his glass, and tilts his head back. His Adam's apple bounces as he swallows. He winces as if even the sound of the glass hitting the table is too much for him. This migraine must be terrible. I've only ever seen him get like this after Mom… I shake my head, pushing that memory roughly away.

"Jack," I say, and I murmur so that I don't aggravate his headache, "don't you think you should lie down? I can…" I gulp, but then I tell myself it's for Jack and I continue, "I can go get Eddie or… or Chase or someone, they can take over for you. You should rest."

Sleep is the only thing that really kills his migraines. Sleep and dark and five fucking minutes of peace—but I can't give him that, can I? Just like he won't let even his right-hand man know about his headaches.

He shakes his head gingerly. "Can't. There's not much time left. Besides, I, unh—"

He's wincing and, though the shade in the kitchen is drawn, there's enough natural light filtering in to make the pain worse. I know why he hides his migraines, suffering alone. They don't happen all that often, but the others might judge his abilities as the Grave's leader if they knew.

That, plus how anything that makes you seem more like a lurker than a survivor is always suspect. Lurkers are so debilitated by the tiniest bit of light that they can't step foot out of their dark dwellings until the sun has gone down. Flashlights slow them down almost as well as a survivor's stare, street lamps keep them from breaking into the Grave, and fire burns them to ash.

Right now, watching Jack gulp and wince and fight the light-sensitivity that comes with a migraine, I would be reaching for my lighter if I didn't know better.

"Okay," I relent, "then why don't you close your eyes? You might feel better."

He sighs. "I could, but then I wouldn't get to see you anymore. And if this is it, I'm going to treasure every last glimpse I have left."

My fingers flex. I grip the side of my chair, holding on tight. "Jack... *Dad*—"

"Humor your old man, honey. It's bad enough that I have to let you go. Just sit with me, let me spend some time with you. I never—I mean, it would be nice to be here together, Allie. Even for a few moments."

Back when he was a firefighter, it was always me and Hallie and Mom; Rory followed in Jack's footsteps and volunteered right out of high school. Rory would sometimes take me hiking and camping, acting the part of my dad because Jack was *always* working. It didn't get any better after the Turning. To help him grieve Mom and Rory more than anything else, Jack took over the Grave. It was usually just me and Hallie fending for ourselves.

I've seen more of him these last six weeks than in the last six years, and, yeah, I resented him for it, whether I'd admitted before now or not. That doesn't mean I'm not going to miss him. I am. Tears sting my eyes at that real- ization, and I swallow roughly, forcing them back.

Jack is the only one who can make my tough facade crumble. The back of my throat is burning. Fuck me. This is harder than I thought it might be.

"I have a gift for you," he says.

I can't speak. I just nod.

Jack gets up slowly and crosses the kitchen. There's a drawer at the end that we never use. It was jammed when we moved into this house, and when Hallie ripped the top of her fingernail off of her pointer finger trying to pry it open, he made us promise to leave it alone. We did… but now he heads right for it and, after playing with a catch on the underside, it pops open.

My lips part in surprise. I didn't know it could do that.

He grabs something from inside the drawer before closing it gently and re-engaging the lock. Then, wearing a wistful expression, he places it in front of me before taking his seat again.

It's a glass vial, about five inches tall and one inch wide, half-filled with a clear liquid. It's not water. It's too thick and gloopy to be, and it reflects the dim kitchen like a piece of glitter. A single cut of lilac-colored ribbon is tied in a bow around the lip. A piece of cork serves as a tight seal at the top.

I don't have to ask what this is. No wonder Jack kept it hidden. I've only seen one of these once before, when the initial delivery was made in the first few days following the Turning, but I've never forgotten what they look like.

An antidote.

"Jack, no… I can't take that." I shake my head, holding my hands up, warding the bottle away. "No. *No.* Put that thing back. I *won't* take it."

His jaw firms. "If you don't take it, I can't let you go."

He's dead serious, too, like he's going to go up against the whole Grave and tell them their votes meant shit, that I'm being grounded, all because I'm not selfish enough to take that bottle with me.

I have to make him understand.

"But we only have, like, fifteen of those for the whole Grave."

"Yes," he counters, "but I only have one daughter left."

And that's when I understand there's no way in fucking hell I can refuse his gift. Because I wouldn't be bringing it with me for me—I'd do it for Jack.

I reach for the vial. He places it against my palm.

"I'll bring it back," I promise. "I won't have to use it. I'll bring it back after I've killed off that nest, and when I do? I'll give it back to you."

A wistful smile tugs at Jack's lips. He doesn't say anything else, and neither do I. The silence, heavy yet content at the same time, says it all for both of us.

In a way, the antidotes are the world's biggest joke.

No one knows where they came from. The days directly following the Turning are a blur to many of us, hours of fright and despair and pure unadulterated fucking *horror* blending together so that it's impossible to remember one detail from the rest. To be fair, the survivors saw so many terrible things when the lurkers first appeared that it's probably a good thing we can't remember them all.

There are so many things I'd give *anything* to forget...

The antidotes were dropped from the sky, little wooden boxes filled with cotton, attached to a pristine white parachute that was meant to soften their landing. It happened one night when the lurkers were feasting outside and those who hadn't Turned were locked inside of their homes, waiting desperately for some news that this would all be over before long.

News that would never come.

I have no clue how many parachutes were dropped, but most of them were destroyed by the lurkers as they rampaged and fed. By the time we realized just how valuable those boxes were, there were hardly any left—and that was the only delivery.

Me and Jack and Hallie, we were some of the lucky ones. One box was dropped right in the backyard of our old house. It got stuck in the branches of a gnarled and twisted oak tree that took up most of the yard. Jack waited until sun-up one morning when the lurkers had fled from the light to grab the parachute. He used to be a big believer that the government could fix any mess; he hoped it was some sign from them that help was at hand.

In a way it was. At the very least, it was the only help those fuckers ever gave us.

Nestled beneath the cotton, four narrow glass tubes sat side by side. A thin strip of lilac ribbon was tied neatly around the stopper at the top; the end of each ribbon was stamped with a serial number. A clear liquid, more like syrup than water, filled the vials. A piece of card stock had one word written in a clear hand: *antidote.*

In my opinion, it was a little too little too late. Rory had already Turned. My mom was gone. I had no intention of letting one of those monsters get near enough to me that an antidote would be necessary. I remember looking down at the little glass vials and, for the first time since the Turning, I got angry. Red hot fury like I've never known swiped away all the fear and the self-pity I'd been wallowing in for days.

Before anyone could stop me, I grabbed one of those vials and smashed it on our kitchen floor. My twin gasped. Jack snapped the lid closed, moving the box out of my reach. He didn't say a word, and I didn't apologize for my reaction.

That was the beginning of the anger for me. It only got worse after that. Just the thought of the antidotes—the idea that we could've been saved before the Turning, but were helpless now—always seemed to make me want to do something rash and reckless.

As soon as the survivors discovered that lurkers burned, I channeled my bitterness and rage into fuel for my own personal fire. When I killed my first lurker, when I delighted in how easy it was to kill again, I decided that this was how I was going to survive—not by relying on a supposed antidote that came too late.

Now I regret smashing that vial. I threw away the one thing that could save a survivor if they ever got bit, so long as they drink the antidote within the first twenty-four hours. When the Grave banded into a community, the survivors all pooled together any antidotes that were recovered. Together, we managed to salvage about twenty antidotes. Jack took half of them and locked them away. The other half are hidden at St. Matthew's.

Those are the only antidotes we have, and probably the only ones we'll ever get. None of us know where they came from or why they arrived so damn late. All we *do* know is that they work—our people haven't had to use many, but the few ones that we've used have kept a survivor from Turning after a lurker attack—and that we should only use them in an emergency.

No matter what, I won't let myself be that emergency.

CHAPTER 8

ast night, I charged my phone while the electricity was still up, then set my alarm for seven o'clock. Pointless. I'm already wide awake by the time it buzzes loudly the next morning.

I spent the rest of yesterday with Jack, knowing that—despite my confidence—they could be our last moments together. Eventually, he told me that Maverick would be leaving first thing after he got a good night's sleep, bartered with other survivors for supplies, and had breakfast before the Grave all but kicked his ass out of our settlement.

He was a curiosity, but while we were willing to listen to a stranger, he was too close to being a rogue for Jack's liking. Either way, he was leaving today, whether he convinced one of us to accompany him or not. According to Eddie, he'd spoken to six neighboring communities in New Jersey over the last few weeks, but he couldn't find a single taker to join his suicide mission.

Until me, that is.

For those who don't want to dip into their rations, we have a basic meal rotation: three simple meals a day, served at seven in the morning, noon, and five in the evening. Breakfast, lunch, and dinner. While I scarfed down the last of Mrs. B's pancakes, my travel partner would be chowing down in the cafeteria with some of the other survivors.

His plan is to head out at eight. With the sun coming up around six-thirty, dusk sneaking in around twelve hours later, if we leave at eight, that gives us a good ten hours of sunlight to move without worrying about lurkers. They come at dusk which means, if we want to keep from Turning, we have to hunker down and be prepared to fight before then.

For now, I get ready to go. I rush through my shower, though I should probably be relishing it since there's a good chance it'll be my last one for a while. I double-check my pack one final time, cast a wistful look at my abandoned collection of glass bottles, and exhale softly, shaking my hands as if releasing any lingering tension.

There's nothing to be nervous about, I tell myself. I've killed plenty of lurkers and—no matter how the Grave voted—I know Jack wouldn't let me go if he didn't think I could handle this mission.

Besides, I have an antidote now.

The glass vial is wrapped up in a plastic bag, then tucked inside of a thick sock to protect it. I'd heard it's nearly impossible to shatter the antidote's glass case accidentally—it took a lucky hit and all my strength to smash the one I first found—but hell if I want to be the one to prove that it can be done. Besides, I know how valuable they are. I really don't want anyone—my new hunting partner included—to find out I even have one.

Jack is already gone. I'd begged him to do it, to leave the condo before I did. He'd fought back, determined to walk me to the borders before passing me off to Maverick, but I refused.

If he did, I wouldn't go—and we both knew that.

I need to go. I think, deep down, Jack knows that, too. That's why he gave in, promising not to make my leaving any harder than it's going to be. Because, no matter what he believes, this is the best thing for me. And maybe, when I do get back, things will be even better.

They certainly can't get any worse.

With Rory's jacket a comforting weight on my shoulders, I tuck Denise's sweatshirt under my arm and heft up my backpack and sleeping bag. I glance around Stacey Finch's bedroom one last time, promising that I'll see it again.

I will. I mean, if I could survive a flaming that stole my twin from me, I can survive any fucking thing.

I head out through the front. If I hadn't been anxiously nibbling on my thumb nail, already thinking ahead to my first steps out of the Grave, I might've realized that was a mistake. Going out the back might've been smarter. It's closer to Grove Avenue and more private, but the front door... that's just the one we normally use so that's what I did.

I don't realize my mistake until I tug in the door and nearly stumble into the back of a sandy-haired man sitting on the edge of my porch, knees up, arms hugging his legs as if warding off a chill.

My breath catches in my throat. My teeth click as my

mouth closes quickly. A heartbeat later, I swallow back a muffled curse.

It's Chase.

As the sound of the door closing behind me reaches him, my twin's fiancé rises up from his crouch. It's a slow wobble, nothing like his usual athletic grace. In fact, his legs nearly give out, hand reaching for the nearest post to steady himself, but I can't tell if he's weary, tired, or just took a wrong step.

Then he turns, searching for me, giving me a good look at his face. I suck in a breath. His eyes are bloodshot, red-rimmed and glassy; his carelessly tousled hair from yesterday is mussed and messy, like he'd spent hours running his fingers through the short length anxiously. There's the stubbled beginning of a darker beard along the edge of his jaw that makes it look like he forgot to wash some dirt off.

Overall, he looks like shit. More than that, he looks like he didn't sleep at all last night. And if he did? He did it while sitting on the porch, waiting for me to finally leave the condo.

I think back to yesterday. Shit. That's the same shirt he had on at the high school, isn't it?

Run, Xandra, I tell myself. Run back inside, dash out the back, escape the Grave—

Chase sighs. His gaze is locked on my face, sadness in his eyes. His voice is dry and cracked as he softly utters my name: "Alexandra."

It's my full name, too. *Alexandra.* Four syllables, and I feel like I'm in more and more trouble with each one. Who knows? Maybe I am. Closing my eyes for a moment, I take one shaky deep breath.

Why me? This… this wasn't supposed to happen. I made sure to say my goodbyes to Jack last night. He's the only one I owed that to. That should have been it.

And, fuck me, I should've known better.

"Chase." A gulp. A frown. My fingers tap anxiously against my jeans. "You shouldn't be here."

"I had to come."

Maybe he did, but he shouldn't have. "Don't try to talk me out of it," I tell him. Way I see it, there's no reason to beat around the bush. "I've made up my mind. I'm going."

"Xandra, don't—" He's quick, or maybe I'm too slow. Chase closes the gap between us in the time it takes me to glance away, grabbing my wrist in my hand as if he thinks *that* will somehow keep from me from leaving. "Don't go."

I swallow my sigh.

He's not demanding or forceful. The uncertainty is what makes it worse, that and the pleading in his voice.

"I have to. If I can kill that many lurkers, then maybe I'll—"

I stop there. My words fail me, or maybe it's the way he's standing so close to me. The heat from his fingers warm me up from the inside out. We're too, too close, and as Chase watches me intently, I don't try to pull away. Not yet. He'll be nothing but a memory once I leave the Grave. What's another second before we break apart?

Just one more…

"Then let me come with you."

I expected that. "You can't."

"Why not?"

"Because the Grave needs you," I tell him honestly. It feels good not to lie to him for once, even if I'm talking to his chest because I can't bring myself to meet his eyes.

"Because you're one of the best trackers they have and you know how to destroy lurkers better than anyone else here. Thirty-eight kills since July? That's got to be some kind of record."

"Then let me go in your place," Chase says instead. He tightens his grip on my wrist and my eyes widen. "You stay here. We both know you've been on nearly as many missions as me. You protect the Grave and I'll go with the stranger to take out the nest."

I swallow the lump in my throat. "His name is Maverick."

Chase's fingers tighten, digging into my skin. "That's what he says his name is. He could be anyone. You can't trust him."

He's not really wrong. Some nobody breaks into the Grave—sneaking in or being caught by one of our patrols, it doesn't matter, he wasn't invited—and I'm willing to head out into the outside world with him? Why? Because he's as murderous as I am when it comes to the lurkers?

"Chase—"

"What if he takes advantage of you? What if he wants something from you... you're beautiful. Anyone with eyes can see that. I'm sure he'll be thrilled to have you all to himself."

Ignoring the way my heart jumps to hear Chase call me beautiful, I scowl at him. "Is that the problem? I fucked you so now you think I'll give it up to any guy who looks at me twice? Is that what you think of me? I'm going to kill lurkers, but in the downtime, I'll sleep with this guy?"

Chase's expression turns horrified. "What? No."

Could have fooled me. "See? This. This right here... this is why I have to go."

"I'm sorry—"

So am I. "Let go of me, Chase."

I don't think he even realized that he was still holding onto me so tightly. He glances where his fingers are circling my wrist, but rather than release me, he squeezes just a little more. "What about Jack?"

My stomach goes cold. "What about him?"

He shudders out a breath of his own. "Look. My family's dead. I lost them all in the Turning. Hallie..." He gulps, voice breaking on my twin's name before he tries again. "Hallie's gone. There's nothing left for me in the Grave—especially if you go. But, if you stay, I'll hunt those lurkers down for you. I need to know you'll be safe, and you'll be safe so long as you stay. There's nothing keeping me here anymore."

It's my own fault. Sometimes I can put the guilt behind me, but it's never gone for long. His subtle reminder that I'm the reason he's alone makes my stomach twist; his touch feels like it's blistering my skin. What the fuck was I thinking, letting him get so close?

I yank on my hand.

Chase tugs back, stronger than I was expecting. I'm not even sure how it happens, but suddenly I'm pressed against him. His free hand curls around my back, pushing me closer. My tits smash against his chest. I gasp, Denise's hoodie slipping from my hold, lips parting slightly as I tilt my head back up to glare at him.

Is it a glare? I'm not sure. Chase must've seen something in my expression—either that or, desperate as he is, he decided to say "fuck it" and go for it—because he dips his head, taking my mouth with his.

The touch of his lips against mine short-circuits my

brain. I stand there, letting him kiss me, letting him slip his tongue into my mouth, stroking his against mine as though his life depends on getting me to respond to its caress. He releases my hand, encircling me with both arms.

And I must've lost my goddamn mind because I slip my hands between us, clutching his t-shirt in my fingers, clinging to him for dear life as I kiss him back.

It doesn't last. As soon as I remember that this is *Chase Reynolds*, I yank my head away. I untangle my fingers from the fabric of his shirt, placing my palms against his pecs, shoving him away from me.

He stumbles two steps back before surging forward. His hands go to my elbows, clutching me as his hazel eyes darken in desperation.

"Can you tell me that you didn't feel anything? That you don't—"

I thrust down my arms, breaking his hold on me. "I'm not Hallie."

His expression is so pained, I feel like a heartless bitch for reminding him of the truth. Especially when the taste of his mouth is on my tongue and, damn it, it's taking everything I have not to dive in for another kiss.

"I know," he whispers. "But—"

There is no "but". "I have to do this. Okay? If you give two shits about me at all, can't you just understand that? Can't you let me go? Hallie would have."

We both know that if Hallie were still here, there wouldn't be any reason for me to leave. I don't give him a chance to point that out—or to try to figure out another way to stop me. Dancing around the frozen man before I give too much away—or say something I'll regret—I snag the sweatshirt, then stride purposefully down the stairs and away from the porch.

I thought I got through to him. I thought he understood.

And then Chase calls after me: "Do you really think this'll bring your sister back?"

That gets me to stop. Another lump rises in my throat, tears stinging my eyes. I won't let Chase see them. I refuse to turn around.

"Hallie is never coming back," I tell him. My voice is hollow, and every one of those words hurts deep in my chest. "You better get used to it."

When I start to walk away again, Chase doesn't follow me. Maybe my words stunned him or maybe he's finally figured out that it's pointless trying to argue with me, but I get all the way across the small parking lot out front before I glance back and see that he's resting on the balls of his feet, leaning forward on the porch as if he's about to take flight. He's hugging himself, and I can tell from the look on his face that he'd kill to have Hallie here again.

Him and me both.

"Goodbye, Chase."

"Wait—"

I should go. I should take my pack and run before Chase says something *he* will regret and there'll be no going back.

For either of us.

"I just..." His voice breaks again, and I feel my tough facade chip away a little like a crack in a windshield. If he doesn't stop, who knows how far it can spread before I shatter completely? "I can't lose my Hallie again."

And I know then that there's no way in any world that I can stay.

CHAPTER 9

Maverick is waiting for me at the corner of Ridgemond and Grove.

On the one hand, I'm kind of surprised he didn't put Madison behind him as quickly as he could. If he expected a solid troupe of hunters to join him, that sure as hell didn't happen, and I don't think he was all that eager to take me up on his offer to tag along. Sure, he sided against Jack, throwing out the 'vote' idea, but I wonder if that was only because he seemed convinced our community would lean toward safety, urging me to stay.

On the other hand, the fact that Eddie caught me heading to St. Matthew's and turned me around, telling me to head back the other way because that's where the newcomer had gone... I almost said 'fuck it' and went back to the condo.

I haven't been back to that part of the Grave since the accident. If I wasn't so determined to get away, I would've done anything to avoid the scorched asphalt where Hallie died. But if I stayed, it was inevitable that I'd have to face Chase again, and… no.

I hike my backpack high up on my shoulders, watching the stranger so I don't see anything else that might mess with my mind.

I approach him. "Thanks for waiting. I'm ready to go when you are."

Maverick doesn't move. There's a pack perched at his feet like a faithful dog showing loyalty to his master; it's about three times the size of mine, and he has a stained old bedroll stacked neatly on top. On top of *that* there's a Tupperware container full of pancakes, a plastic fork, and a bag full of fresh syrup. Looks like Mrs. Baker got to him, too.

A stack of papers are tucked neatly under his arm. He was studying one of the sheets as I moved toward him, but it's suddenly folded up and out of my sight.

A slight frown tugs on his lips. "This is a bad idea," he mutters. His voice is rough and quiet without the help of the microphone.

Not the sort of greeting any girl wants to get, though I'd be lying if I said I wasn't expecting this.

"You spoke to Jack."

"It's fair to say I spent a good chunk of my time in your town with him."

That didn't answer my question.

"And?" I cross my arms over my chest, a defiant tilt to my head as I look up at him. "We were both at the auditorium. It's no secret that he doesn't want me to leave the Grave."

"It's not that, Alexandra… it *is* Alexandra, right?"

"Xandra," I correct him.

"It's not that, Xandra. It's—when I asked for volunteers to join me, I thought I'd get someone like that Chase kid. Or a vet, like your dad or Eddie Collins. And, instead, I get—"

"A little blonde girl who looks like she doesn't know her ass from her elbows?" I suggest.

Maverick's lips quirk slightly, a hint of a smile on a hard, older man. "Something like that."

The whisper of a grin is a tiny improvement, but it doesn't make his expression any less guarded—or him any more eager to lead me out of the settlement.

I have to change his mind. If he doesn't want me to tag along, I'm not going anywhere, and that just doesn't work for me.

"He tell you about me?"

"You might have come up in the conversation."

"Did he tell you that, after Chase, I have the most kills in the Grave?"

A calculating look flashes across his features, so quickly that if I hadn't been watching for his reaction, I never would've noticed. He narrows his dark eyes, his lips pursed now.

"No," he says at last. "He didn't."

"Yeah? Well, I do. And after I help take out another nest, I'll have the most."

Maverick watches me for a moment, sizing me up. I know exactly what he sees. No one in the Grave ever thought me and Hallie could team up and kill so many lurkers until we proved it by just going out and doing it.

"It'll be a lot of roughing it. Walking through the daylight hours when the lurkers aren't out, sleeping in shifts if we don't find safe shelter when the sun goes down. You get that, don't you? Because if you don't—"

"I used to camp with my brother," I tell him. "You don't have to worry about me."

"A weekend on a camping ground is a lot different than going weeks at a time on the road. You sure about this?"

"I'm sure."

"You don't have to prove anything to me. You can back out now, stay here where it's safe. No one'll think any less of you if you do."

Safe? Where the fuck has he been the last nine months? Hallie is proof that not even living in the Grave can protect us for long.

I shake my head stubbornly. "You're right: I don't have to prove anything to you. To anyone. You know why? Because this isn't about any of *you*."

He starts to say something, but I cut him off before he can.

"And, hey, look… this isn't about me, either. Not really. This is about taking out as many lurkers as I—*we*—can. You're going out there to hunt. You asked for volunteers. I'm here. Maybe we can add on, gather a crew before we make it to the city. Either way, I'm ready to light 'em up."

Maverick looks me over again, though not in a pervy way. Not like how the boys used to check me out growing up up, or how the guys did after I had who were eager to get me into bed with them. Nope. It's an appraising-my-abilities way. His eyes linger on the backpack I'm wearing, the newer sleeping bag that Eddie dropped off last night looped around the top. The stranger can see that, for better or worse, I'm as ready as I can be.

The jut to my jaw warns him against even trying to call my bluff.

In the morning light, his expression darkens.

And I wonder: what's gonna be his next move?

He jerks his head at me before starting to gather his supplies. "Just make sure you keep up."

I'm at least fifteen years younger than this guy, and I want it *bad*. "Don't worry. I will."

He wasn't kidding when he told the Grave that this trip is going to take a whole lot longer than I would've thought. A walk that should've taken ten minutes in the before times—the journey to the end of the Grave, stepping over our self-proclaimed borders—takes half an hour despite my desire to get out of town as soon as possible.

Before we started off, Maverick pulled a battered compass from his pants pocket. He tapped it once, watched the way the needle spun, then nodded to himself before walking away from me without a word. Following his lead, I jogged at his heels, determined to keep up.

At first I was a touch nervous that he planned on taking us right through the trees in front of us; no matter how much I want to go, I don't think I could walk the path the lurkers took toward us the night Hallie died. But then Maverick turned left, heading down the middle of Ridgemond Avenue. It's the direction of the nearby train tracks, and I exhale softly as I match his pace.

Up ahead, there's an elementary school. It sits about two blocks past the rusted, unused train tracks. Martin Luther King Primary School marks the far reaches of the

Grave on this side, the outskirts of the boundary that our patrol teams watch over.

It's also the plot of land where we bury the few survivors who have died since the Turning.

Only our community-appointed gravediggers ever go this far. Even if a loved one is buried here, we're not allowed to visit. It's too dangerous.

At least, that's what Jack always said when I asked to visit Hallie's grave. But Jack's not here, is he?

"Wait," I call out. "Before we go... there's something I have to do."

Maverick pauses ahead of me. Interestingly, he's not staring straight in front of him. As I move past him, I notice that he's staring *at* MLK. I'm pretty sure that all he sees is the school. It's not like he has any idea about the cemetery behind it... and I believed that until he frowns, shaking his head, as he says, "I wouldn't do it if I were you," and I suspect that he might know more about the Grave than I would have expected.

Oh, well. He's not me, and I'm not about to let him stop me, either. So, giving him a tight-lipped smile, holding up one single finger to signal for him to hang on, I jog across the street before he can say another word to me.

I slow down to a brisk walk when I reach the front of the school. Something compels me to stop and check over my shoulder, and I do. I give a start when I realize that Maverick is right behind me. Though his boots look like they've gotta be heavy, he must have a gait like a damn cat because I never even heard him coming.

He raises his eyebrows at me. "You done already? Because I don't like stopping unless it's necessary. That includes bathroom breaks if you're wondering."

If he thinks he can convince me to give up while we're still in the Grave by mentioning I'll have to squat outside to go, he has another think coming. "Don't worry about me. I can piss outside without getting any on my socks. But that's not what I'm doing. And you don't have to come with me. I'll be finish in a few seconds."

He doesn't have to come with me, but Maverick doesn't quite get that. For a man who seems more than happy to go on without any volunteers after asking for them, when I inch my way around the back of the school, he's right there behind me as though afraid we'll be separated.

Oh, well. If he wants to come, he might as well. Maybe then he'll understand that this isn't a game to me.

Leading the way, I go around the perimeter of the school, more than a little nervous the closer I get to the cemetery. I've always wanted to see where Jack had Hallie buried. On the nights when my dreams were really bad—when I swore she was haunting me—I'd think of all the conversations I'd have at her graveside, of the apology I don't think I'll ever get quite right.

Now? Now I have my chance.

Except, the moment I turn the last corner, I stop short. Maverick does the same, pausing before he bumps into me. I don't even think I'd notice if he did.

Nope. I'm too busy heaving behind the hand I clamped over my mouth.

This might have been a cemetery once. For all I know, it might even be the place where they placed Hallie's remains. I don't know. The only markers for the actual graves for the Grave are these large rocks painted with the name of each survivor we've lost since banding together.

But the rocks… they're not set at the head of each grave anymore. All of them are strewn along the side of the field, tossed aside as if they weren't anything but a pointless obstacle.

The graves… they're not graves any longer, either. All they are are holes in the ground, big gaping holes where survivor corpses should've been allowed to rest at last.

At least, that's what we thought. The lurkers obviously didn't think so.

Instead, they feasted on our dead.

My worst fears have come true. The lurkers have eaten my twin.

Bile rises up in my throat, the acid burning my insides while also filling my mouth. I force it back. I'm all too aware that Maverick is watching me, watching for my reaction. I don't want to give him the satisfaction of proving him right. As much as I want to throw up, I tilt my head back, blinking away my sudden tears.

One deep breath, then another, and finally I can face him.

It's his turn to look at me with a pitying expression. "You can always turn back," he murmurs softly.

I rub the back of my hand against my mouth, allowing myself to shudder just the once before I push the sight of the rocks and the gaping graves where it belongs: far fucking behind me.

"No." My voice is just a touch shaky as I reply, "It's too late to turn back now."

And I mean that in more ways than one.

When I was about twelve, Hurricane Doreen tore through most of what used to be New Jersey. The shore was decimated, houses destroyed, cars floating away during the floods. I remember we were without power for over a week, and when the televisions and computers finally came back on, we were confronted with how truly devastating the damage was. It was one of the first real hurricanes to tear through the area where I grew up and, until the Turning, it was the worst disaster I'd ever seen.

That's what old Madison looks like now.

Whole side streets are gone. There's rubble and lumber and scraps of fabric strewn everywhere. I try to ignore the first pile of bones I find, knowing they'll only be more to come.

Broken toys, smashed glass, and destroyed electronics still litter the empty streets we attempt to walk across, each step an adventure. Potholes aren't just a few inches deep; whole patches of the asphalt are gone, ripped up, scattered on the sidewalks. After the first time I stupidly miss my step and my leg disappears up to mid-calf, I pay closer attention to the ground as I walk.

What can I say? It's much better than staring at the hell my old neighborhood's turned into.

Fires ran unchecked shortly after the Turning. We had about one week before the television was reduced to static and, in that time, the reporters who hadn't Turned into lurkers were telling everyone to attack the monsters with flames. I don't know who the first person was that figured it out—I mean, I killed my first lurker with a steak knife that first morning when they were still vulnerable—but it wasn't long before the world was full of black smoke and orange flames and the acrid stench of brimstone filling the air.

The further we move away from the Grave, the more that smell lingers, clinging to the shells of burnt houses and blackened trees. And that's not all. There's an air of abandonment down the main street we're currently walking on. There are no survivors left living on Montrose Street. Any houses that made it through the fires and the lurker's assault stand empty and forlorn, all black windows and scorched lawns.

This is the first time I've gone this far from the Grave. I'd kind of hoped we could raid some of the nearer houses, maybe gather some supplies that might come in handy later.

No dice.

Maverick refuses. At first, I think it's back to the whole "don't know my ass from my elbows" appearance... until my nose finally gets used to the burnt stink and picks up the sickly sweet odor of death and decay that permeates the air around us.

My stomach goes queasy, and all I can think is: lurkers.

Like Grove Avenue, Montrose is another thoroughfare that branches off of Ridgemond before cutting through this part of Madison. About an hour into our trek, we have to navigate around a four car pile-up that must have been sitting frozen mid-accident since it happened ages ago. I'm just picking my way around the mangled remains of a Honda when it finally hits me.

The second it does, I turn around, expecting to find one of the hungry monsters standing there. It doesn't matter that it's the middle of the day and the sun is high. It's purely instinctive.

But there's nothing there. Just Maverick off to my right, watching me curiously. From the set of his jaw and the way it's obvious he's breathing through parted lips, I guess he caught the rotten scent long before I had.

"Lurkers," he says, confirming my suspicions. "They lurk in the cellars, the attics, under beds, closets... wherever it's dark. They've infested this neighborhood already. Who knows how many are in each house, just waiting for the chance to get out and eat us."

I reach behind me, feeling for the front zipper of my backpack. "Shouldn't we be grabbing a match then?"

"No need," Maverick answers, checking his compass again and placing it back in his pocket. "They can't survive in the light. They won't leave their hiding places until the sun goes down."

Glancing up at the sky, I ask, "And when is that? How much longer?"

"Not long enough."

Great.

PART TWO
FIRE

PROTECT AND SERVE.

IT'S BEEN MORE THAN A DECADE SINCE I MADE MY PROMISE TO THE PEOPLE OF

DANBURY.

BUT DANBURY IS GONE.

MY BROTHERS ARE GONE.

LINDSAY... SHE'S GONE, TOO, AND I'LL NEVER FORGET HOW I COULDN'T PROTECT

THE ONE PERSON WHO MEANT EVERYTHING TO ME.

BECAUSE I SURVIVED. AND AS LONG AS I DO, I WILL PROTECT AND SERVE AND KICK

SOME LURKER ASS.

AND MAYBE THEN... FINALLY... I'LL BE FREE.

- JAMES "MAVERICK" BROOKS

CHAPTER 10

Again, I totally underestimated how long it would take to go from Madison to Manhattan.

I've been there before. Every Christmas, we'd take a train ride into the city to see the Radio City Hall Christmas Spectacular and gawk at the tree put up in Rockefeller Center. If you got on the express, you could be there in forty minutes.

By the time the sun starts setting, Maverick and I have only made it about four miles out of the Grave.

To be fair, we probably walked at least three times as many, but between backtracking and going out of the way to avoid holes in the road and decimated neighborhoods, we haven't really put that much distance behind us when Maverick announces that we'll be camping out on a grassy knoll along the edge of an old hiking trail.

Our plan is to sleep out in the open. With Denise's hoodie, Rory's jacket, and the sleeping bag, I'll be fine, though I'd be even more comfortable if he'd let me break into one of the empty houses so I could crash in one of their beds where the lurkers might not find me. Nope. He says it's because the risk of any of the houses being lurker nests is too high in an empty neighborhood and, well, he isn't wrong, is he?

It's a good thing that Eddie brought the sleeping bag over before I left. It never occurred to me that I'd need it—especially since I thought my camping days were behind me—and it's not like my new companion is about to offer to share his bedroll. In fact, apart from reminding me to watch where I step and telling me to hurry up whenever I duck out of sight to pee, he doesn't say much at all. He's a quiet guy, and since I don't have shit to say myself, that works for me.

Chase was so worried that Maverick might take advantage of me. If that's the case—if the stranger decided to let me come for the journey just because it's been too long since he's gotten laid—he misses a huge opportunity by laying out his bedroll as far away from me as he can get. He's a good fifteen feet from where I tossed my pack down on the ground, marking my spot.

He reaches into his own pack, pulling out a half sleeve of saltine crackers. "Hungry?"

I shake my head. About an hour ago, I ate two of the expired granola bars I stowed in the bottom of my pack. When I asked how he eats while traveling between settlements, he explained that he does scavenge in neighborhoods as long as they stink of fire and not lurkers. There are also abandoned grocery stores, like the one in the Grave, as well as convenience stores. There's food to be found if you're not picky, and water, too.

The last thing I grabbed from the Finches' condo was a steel tumbler that fit in the side pouch of my backpack. I filled it with water from the tap, and after I nursed it during the first couple of hours, Maverick waited until we reached our first lurker-free street before going inside to fill up my tumbler and his battered water bottle.

It was at that moment that I decided he at least knew a little bit of surviving on the outside. The taps still run in the empty houses, even if the water comes out brown at first. It's better than drinking from the few stray brooks we step across when taking shortcuts through the trees, and I know that—if I can hold out until we need a refill—I can always use a toilet during our infrequent pitstops.

We hit two houses before he picked out the clearing where we've stopped for the night. The saltines were in the pantry of the second one. Maverick grabbed them, plus a box of beef jerky; non-perishables that work well for a journey in case the next house he scavenges is empty. I found two foil-wrapped packs of breakfast pastries that I took for myself.

I did notice that there wasn't any electricity on that particular street, and I wondered if that's why it's abandoned since the lurkers hadn't moved into that neighborhood yet. Not like it matters. We scrounged through the cabinets, got our water, then left before we ran across any other rogues.

Because that's what we are. According to Maverick, survivors who bounce from settlement to settlement are known as rogues; the same thing we called them in the Grave. They can be even more dangerous than lurkers, and while the ravenous creatures aren't a threat until night falls, desperate outcasts can be a problem at any time.

Maverick doesn't seem interested in his female

companion. That doesn't mean that no one we run into will feel the same way.

So, yeah… when he says it'll be too risky to continue traveling tonight, I listen, rolling out my own sleeping bag as he munches on a stale cracker.

Once he's done, he washes it down with a swig of water from his bottle, then gets to work on building a fire. It's small at first, a spark and a flame that initially builds a fire the size of a baseball, but he feeds it with tinder and dry grass until it's a roaring campfire that reaches the top of his boots.

I watch him with undisguised interest. When he finishes and, brushing the slivers of dead grass from his hands, turns his back on me, I can't keep my mouth shut anymore.

"What's that for?" I ask. "I thought we didn't want to draw any attention to where we're bunking down for the night."

Despite how tired I am after a day of walking, I know it's not as simple as the both of us lying down and knocking out. Because of the dual threats—rogues *and* lurkers—that come with the darkness, we need to sleep in shifts. To prove myself I offered to take the first one. Though he hesitated, he agreed, and I can only imagine how long it's been since he's had a good couple of solid hours down considering he's been traveling alone for a while now.

If he didn't? I'm still prepared. I plan on using my pack as a pillow so that no one can get their grimy hands on it— or the precious antidote stored inside of one of the small pouches. In the pocket of Rory's leather jacket, I also have a four-inch pocket knife that I snagged this morning before I grabbed the steel tumbler.

I'm not *that* naive. I know that going off on an adventure with a man fifteen years my senior who talks of flaming lurkers is a big risk, but it's one I'm willing to take. And if Chase's fears are founded and Maverick turns out to be a liar or a perv—or both—I'm ready to use that blade.

A knife can't hurt a lurker. Only fire can. But a man… if Maverick gives me any reason to suspect him, I'll make him hurt.

I'll make him bleed.

My blonde hair and big green eyes and smaller build might make me look like an innocent little girl in over her head.

Tell that to all the lurkers I've killed.

While I watch the flames, transfixed by them, Maverick looks at me like I left my brain back at the Grave. "Is that what you think I'm doing? Sending a signal to another rogue traveler?"

Honestly, I don't know *what* he's doing. It's September, but even as the sun sets, it's not so chilly we need a fire to keep warm. When it comes to lurkers, they burn, but you need the element of surprise—or a molotov cocktail—to light 'em up. The flames will keep them away, and as I have that thought, I figure out that's the purpose behind Maverick's fire.

Hey. I'm tired. This is the most activity I've had since the accident, and I feel like I'm wading through the fog with how cloudy my brain is. In the Grave, we don't use fire to keep the lurkers away. We use it to eliminate them.

Especially now that we have tragic proof that fire can't be controlled, we use it as a last resort.

Not Maverick.

"It's important to keep those bastards from lurking too close when we're out in the open. The fire will keep them away, both because it's bright enough to hurt them and because they instinctively know the flames will destroy them. The light might catch the attention of another rogue, but it's worth the risk to keep the lurkers away from us. Besides," he adds, jerking his t-shirt up enough to show off something hanging by his hip, "I can handle a rogue or two."

In the gloomy dusk, I squint at what he's drawing my attention to. A moment later, my blood runs cold.

"A gun," I blurt out. "Why the hell do you have a gun?"

Fuck. Maybe I *am* that naive. How long as he had a weapon holstered at his hip, hidden by his faded t-shirt? I never noticed it, and now that I know he has it, I feel the urge to get away from him.

I have a knife. What can that do against a handgun?

"You don't have to be afraid, Xandra—"

"Who said anything about being afraid?" I ask, obviously bluffing. "It's just... I've never seen one in person before."

There's no crime in the Grave. We rely too heavily on each other, and that trust—while fragile—only lasts as long as we admit that we need each other to survive. When guns can't hurt a lurker, no one bothers to carry any kind of weapon. It's pointless. It would only make our neighbors wary of the one who holds it.

But Maverick isn't a neighbor. He's a stranger, and I'm

suddenly wondering if I made the biggest mistake of my life, agreeing to join an armed man on this suicide mission. I expected the lurkers to be the ones to finish me off, though. Not another survivor—

—and that's when Maverick flexes his jaw, then says, "I carry because it's habit… because I used to be a cop," and I'm not sure if that reassures me or not.

A cop. Shit. He's a *cop*.

I know the before times are over. But just like how Jack will always consider himself a firefighter, in or out of uniform, I'm betting Maverick—and I still want to know what kind of name is *Maverick*—is a cop whether he has a badge or not.

"Really? Wow. I wouldn't have pegged you as a cop."

And I'm still not sure how I feel about him being one.

He shrugs, though the gesture is nowhere near as casual as he probably wanted it to be. "Twelve years on the force before my chief turned into a beast and devoured half the squad on desk duty for New Year's." There's no emotion in Maverick's voice. He unholsters the gun, lifting it up, the burnished metal glinting in the firelight. "This was my service weapon. It's the last thing I have from my old life."

I tug on the sleeves of Rory's jacket. I know what he means.

Maverick re-holsters the gun. "I made a pledge to protect and serve," he says after a moment. "The world's gone to hell, and there's no such thing as law enforcement in a world with no laws, but that promise means something to me. It's why I won't stop until I take out as many lurkers as I can." He nods at me. "And it's why you can be sure you're safe with me."

If only I can believe that.

Still… "Did you tell Jack? About you being a cop, I mean."

He nods again.

Figures. No wonder Jack didn't fight against me leaving as hard as he could've. I don't trust the police. Even before, there was too much brutality, too much corruption. My dad… he wanted to believe that anyone in public service thought like him. He wanted to save lives, never lose them, and he'd feel a kinship with a former police officer if Maverick gave him the same kind of bullshit speech he just gave me.

Jack might believe it. Me? All I know is that, if necessary, I can unholster that gun and take it during my watch shift. He might look at me and think I'd never turn on him… and if he did? He'd be wrong.

The Turning changed us all, whether into lurkers or survivors. And Alexandra Holden will do whatever it takes to survive.

My phone is in my pocket. It's a habit of my own, I guess, one that I haven't been able to break even after all this time. Once it dies, I doubt I'll have the chance to charge it again. For now, though, I can use it to keep track of the time.

"How long should I take for watch?" I ask.

He seems a little surprised—or maybe suspicious—that I let the topic of his being an armed former cop drop so easily. Truth is, I'm exhausted, and the sooner he gets to sleep, the sooner it's my turn.

It's quarter after seven. Normally I wouldn't go to sleep until at least eleven, but we've had a long walk today, and tomorrow will start as soon as the sun's up. Might as well rest now.

He's thinking the same. "Wake me up around midnight," he says. "One if you can last. I'll take over for you then. Unless you'd rather three-hour increments."

"One will be fine," I tell him.

"But if you need me—"

Oh. Isn't he cute?

I have my lighter. My knife.

A gun in reach.

"Sure. If I need you, I'll wake you up."

I'm not waking him up.

"We're in this together, Xandra. Like I said before, it's not too late to turn back now."

Spend all day tomorrow walking back to the Grave? Or trudge forward, heading toward Manhattan?

"Get your rest, Mav. I'll wake you up to take next watch."

I wait to see if he'll correct me shortening his name the same way I corrected him for *not* shortening mine. When all he does is stretch up like a cat, arching his back and showing off his gun again, I slip my hand into my pocket, reaching for the familiar metal of Rory's pocket knife.

And then, after he settles down on his bedroll, I sit beside the fire, enjoying the warmth and watching the flames flicker while counting down until it's my turn.

My scream is muffled by a strong hand clamped over my nose and my mouth.

The skin is chilly and damp; it smells of pine and tastes

like ash. I have no fucking clue who this hand belongs to. As I'm ripped out of sleep, the night is heavy and still and dark enough that I shouldn't have to be up yet.

I feel like I only just got to lie down. Now, I have no idea where I am, what's going on, or why I'm being grabbed. Of course I scream, and even as I return to consciousness, I can't stop.

Someone shushes me.

It takes everything I have to try. Blinking rapidly, I attempt to swallow back my sudden panic. The moon hangs high overhead, the weak light strong enough for me to see that it's Maverick's hand pressed to my face. His dark hair shadows his eyes and the hollows of his cheeks as he bows over me. As soon as he sees that I'm awake and that I've stopped struggling, he puts his pointer finger to his lips and hushes me again.

I nod. My heart is racing, my every instinct tells me to get up, to get away, but I'll have a much better chance of doing that if he isn't clutching me to him.

Maverick finally lets me go, but not before he repeats the shushing noise one last time. I kick my way out of the sleeping bag, scrabble to my knees, falling forward and crawling away from him as soon as I can.

"What are you doing?" I hiss, keeping my voice low.

"Shh."

Fuck that. "Are you insane?" I squint, peering at him— and that's when I realize that the reason I'm having a hard time seeing him is because the fire… it's out.

It's *out.*

I reach for my pack. I must've knocked it away in my hurry to escape Maverick because it's not near my rumpled sleeping bag. Snatching it, I start searching for my matches while Maverick inches closer to me.

"Why is the fire out?" I demand. He had a point earlier. When fire's the only thing that can keep the lurkers away, it's a death wish to let the flames die out. "We have to get it started again."

"I put it out."

So I was right. He *is* insane. "Why?"

"Because I heard something out there. Listen. Okay? Just hold on for a second and *listen*."

"If it's lurkers, we need the fire."

"It sounded like a rogue. More than one. Did you hear that? Nine o'clock. Someone shouted."

Nine o'clock. My left. I strain my ears—and my stomach lurches.

"Lurkers," I breathe out. I'm suddenly nauseous. It reminds me of the time I ate a tuna sandwich that had been left out for two days, a gut-churning sensation that makes me want to hurl. "Lurkers. A shit ton of 'em. Four, maybe even five. If there's a rogue out there, they might be why they're screaming. The lurkers are coming right at us."

"How the hell do you know that?" His voice is an accusation disguised as surprise.

I don't blame him. "I don't know, but I'm sure of it." I don't even bother zipping up my pack. I just get up, shrug it on, then grab my sleeping bag. I crumple it up as best as I can, hugging it to my chest. "We've gotta get the fuck out of here. Now."

I don't like to run. When it comes to a lurker, I've always stood my ground, ready to fight; when it's me or them, the answer's forever a resounding *me*. But I'm not an idiot. For all my matches and Maverick's supplies, we haven't yet stumbled upon any secret caches of glass bottles amongst the trees. I'm fresh out of firebombs. And while a lit match and a pinch of luck might mean I could go after one lurker on my own, there's no way we can face so many with what we have.

Maverick hesitates. As though he doesn't quite believe me, he shields his eyes with his hand, searching for either the rogue or the lurkers.

Screw that.

"They're coming," I insist.

I finally get through to him. He nods at last. Stopping only to grab his own bedroll, plus his pack, Maverick turns around and gestures for me to follow him.

But I'm not there. I'm already twenty feet ahead of him.

CHAPTER 11

all me ridiculous and bitter if you want, but I refuse to speak to Maverick the whole next day. I don't even know if he realized, as quiet as he is as he constantly checks his compass, picking his way through the ruined streets and half-burnt trees. Probably not.

I don't care.

I'm so fucking furious that, after all his talk about surviving on the outside and gunning for a huge lurker nest, he screwed up my first night out of the Grave. He's the one who pointed out that a fire was essential to ward off the monsters. Keeping a fire going when avoiding threats is, like, Hunting 101. You only stay in the dark when you're trying to lure the creatures close enough to kill, not when one of you is asleep and defenseless.

And he *put it out*. It's not like he nodded off and it went out. He extinguished it purposely all because he thought he heard a rogue.

What happened to the gun, big shot?

Ugh.

So I keep quiet, stewing silently, and that actually works in my favor. The morning's march is rough. Maverick is relentless. Whether he's trying to make up for his mistake last night or he was just going easy on me yesterday, who knows, but he's like a machine. He doesn't stop at all for the first few hours, not even when he checks his compass, and he only pauses long enough to make sure I'm still behind him as we tromp through whatever woods he can find.

Maverick seems impressed that I'm there every time he checks. Of course I am. Anger has a way of keeping me motivated and I refuse to let him see me falter.

But no matter how pissed-off I was when we first abandoned our makeshift campsite, I'm not used to this; my anger can only take me so far, and don't forget that my sleep was cut short. My legs start to tire around midday, and the renewed thirst comes soon after.

It's not helping that I'm sweating so much.

Summer's returned with a vengeance. It might be mid-September, but it's got to be at least eighty degrees outside. I wear Denise's hooded sweatshirt at night when it dips down below sixty degrees, wrapping it around my waist during the day.

Rory's jacket, though? I'm stubborn enough that I wear that no matter what.

And then, by early afternoon, I stop sweating at all—and that's a problem. It's like someone stuck a pin in the back of my throat, that's how much it hurts each time I swallow. The last thing I need is to get dehydrated, but I don't ask Maverick if he has any water left in his bottle.

Mine was empty by lunch, and though we've exited the latest patch of trees we were in, cutting through a neighborhood with that same rotten stink that tells us it's infested, that means we're nowhere near a house where we can refill it. I still ignore how bad I need some water.

Shit. My pride is going to get me killed.

Maverick swears by his compass; turns out that one of the pieces of paper he keeps pulling out and looking at is an old, outdated map he took from the closed gas station back at the Grave. From his travels, he has some idea where we are and where we're going, but once he has a street sign to navigate by, he slows down. For the last two hours, he's begun to pause every now and then to consult them both. I don't mind. I start to recognize the signs and, after the third time he takes the map out to glance at it and make a turn down another side street, I know when to expect a small break.

And I need it desperately.

My boots fit well, but twenty miles in two days is enough to make any feet tender. Rory's jacket is weighing me down; so is my backpack and the sleeping bag. My gifted sweatshirt keeps untying, the sleeve dragging in the dirt. I yank it off, draping it over the edge of a cracked curb, then plop my ass down.

Looking as if he doesn't even feel the heat or the pace, Maverick crouches down next to me. He pulls out his crackers again, plus a half-empty jar of peanut butter from his pack.

Snacktime.

I'm not very hungry. The heat's doing funny things to my appetite, and the thirst is awful. Still, when he offers me a cracker with a dollop of peanut butter on it, I know better than to refuse; not when my own supplies need to last. Though it's thick and tough to swallow, I eat it because it has both protein and fats, and together it's more filling than just the crackers are.

I think of yesterday's meal of cookies and pancakes and wish that we had thought to save some for today. Of course, that means that I go on to think about what Mrs. B is baking today and... yeah. I stop that train of thought right there.

You left the Grave, I tell myself sternly. Leave it where it is: behind you.

After he finishes up his snack, Maverick decides we can wait a few more minutes before continuing. I don't argue. Right now, I'll take any respite he's willing to offer.

At first, I think he's feeling a little guilty that we've been moving since the fire went out early this morning, that he's giving me the chance to recover before we resume our trek. Then, after a few minutes of continued silence, he clears his throat, and it hits me that he has some sort of ulterior motive.

"So," the former cop begins, taking a lazy sip off of his bottle of water, oblivious to just how bad I want to snatch it from his hand, "last night. The lurkers."

Yup. I was wondering when he was going to say something about that. Smart move, I have to admit, that he waited until he fed me, then let me sit for a few minutes after half a day's walk. I'm not nearly as angry now as I was this morning.

Still super wary and suspicious, though.

"What about 'em?"

"Can you tell me what happened? Not the fire going out," he says without shame because we both know he did that on purpose when he thought he heard a rogue, "but the lurkers… how did you know?"

I shrug, playing dumb. "Know what?"

"How many there were. Telling they were out there… anyone can catch the lurker stink and know they're there. But counting them without seeing them? I didn't know it was possible."

Really? "You don't have sensors where you're from?"

He frowns, thick lines furrowing his brow. "Sensors?"

"Yeah. You know. Survivors who have this strange ability to, well, *sense* lurkers."

"You're fucking with me," he says flatly. "I know *that's* not possible."

"Sure it is. Not everyone can do it, but there's enough who can for it to be a thing."

And until last night, I didn't know I was one of them. So used to Hallie being the one to tell me when she could sense them coming, counting them for me while I busied myself with building a ring, I never paid attention if *I* had the same unique ability.

And why wouldn't I? We were identical twins. If she could do it, it only makes sense that—given the opportunity—I could, too. It just took until I was out of the Grave, woken from a deep sleep on the edge of the woods, the lurkers lurking ever closer for my sensing ability to kick in, I guess.

As if thinking the same thing as me, Maverick points out, "You can."

"I'm as surprised as you are. Back home, we had a handful, each one partnering up with a hunter whenever the lurkers got too close. Hallie's the best one we have. She's never wrong." A lump rises in my throat, and it takes me a second to realize why: I was talking about Hallie as if she's still alive. He might not have any clue who she is, and I'm not about to tell him, but it doesn't make it any easier. "Anyway, I relied on her so much that I had no idea I could do it, too. She always sensed the lurkers, then I killed them."

"What about now? Can you sense them now?"

That's a good question. It took a good twenty minutes into our race through the woods before my stomach settled enough that I was sure we'd outrun the lurkers. Since then, I've had a twinge here or there, but nothing like the absolute certainty we had at least four on our tail.

Was it a fluke? That's possible. At the very least, my stomach is calm, though the rest of me definitely isn't. "No."

"But you sensed them last night," he reminds me. As if I forgot.

There's nothing else I can do but admit it. "We're twins, okay? Hallie and me… we must've had the same ability or something and I just didn't know it since Hallie wasn't there to sense them for me last night."

Maverick caps his water bottle, slipping it back into his pack. Damn it. "Maybe we should've brought her along. Another little blonde girl who can sense lurkers might've worked in our favor."

Was he trying to lighten the mood with his comment? If so, he failed. Miserably.

A muscle tics in my cheek. "That would be impossible."

Maverick lifts his eyebrow. "Your sister have a better sense of self-preservation than you?"

If only. "She's dead."

"Oh." He lifts his hand, rubbing the back of it against his mouth. "I'm sorry to hear that." He pauses, and then, "Lurker attack?"

In the before days, people usually left it at "I'm sorry for your loss". Even if they were curious, it was bad form to basically be like, *hey, what did they die from* to someone who is still basically a stranger.

The Turning changed all that. If you died anytime after the new year, odds are the lurkers were the reason why. When Maverick asks if it was a lurker attack that stole my twin from me, what he really wants to know is if she Turned herself—what happens when the lurkers bite a survivor and they escape—or if she was devoured, one bite turning into another into another.

"Fire killed her," I admit. "A hunt gone wrong."

Maverick opens his mouth.

I push myself to my feet, snagging the sweatshirt so I don't leave it behind.

"I'm ready to go if you are," I announce, wiping my dusty hands on my even dustier jeans. "The rest helped, but if we can refill my water, that would be great."

And if we can never talk about Hallie's death again, that would be even better.

Maverick pulls out his water bottle, offering it to me. "Have some of mine."

I take it, hesitating before I uncap it.

He shares his food. He shares his water. He's given no inclination that he wants anything from me in return except for joining him on this hunt, but you never know. Just like I'm not too sure I buy his story that all he wants to do is take out a lurker nest for no other reason than it's a boon to humanity.

So it seems like I can sense lurkers now. Pity I can't figure out what Maverick Brooks' story is without digging into it. And since poking and prodding and asking questions of this stranger might make him think that I'm willing to be an open book, too, I just drink enough to quench my thirst before passing the water bottle back to him.

We make it another twenty minutes in silence until Maverick clears his throat. When I don't acknowledge it, he says my name.

Crap.

"Yeah?"

"You know, maybe you should take off the other jacket you've got on. Stow that and the hoodie in your sleeping bag, roll it up, and you won't have to lug them around separately. You might cool off a bit, too. You've got to be dying in that thing."

I am. And, honestly, shoving Denise's sweatshirt into my sleeping bag until night time is a pretty smart idea. But Rory's jacket?

"I'm fine."

His face calls me a liar. "You sure?"

"The jacket stays on," I say, firm enough that he has to know that's the end of the conversation.

He frowns. "Why?"

Because he doesn't need to see my burn. Because it's like a security blanket for me, and I need it. Because—

"Because it's Rory's."

Drop it, Mav. Drop it—

"Who's Rory?"

None of your business.

That's what I want to say. That's what I *should* say.

But I don't.

"My older brother." I grit my teeth. "He died, too."

That's all he's getting out of me.

I already feel like I made a mistake in telling him about Hallie. I won't repeat it with Rory.

In fact, I decide right then that I won't give anything else away until the stranger decides to open up himself. And maybe Maverick agrees. As we hike down another empty, broken street, he finally gets the hint and shuts up again.

Now if only I could stop my mind from screaming at me just as easily.

Who's Rory?

Rory Holden, Engine Company 33, Ladder 26. Five years older than Hallie and me, he turned twenty-eight last October. He had a long-term girlfriend. Nina Wright, a sweetheart who worked as a young lawyer for a non-profit. Like Rory, she got the Injection through her job.

Like Rory, she was one of the first lurkers to Turn.

I don't know what happened to Nina. With Rory working on New Year's, she went out with a few of her girlfriends and wasn't in Madison when the Turning began. Still, I figure it's the same thing that happened to Rory, and if there's one small mercy I cling to, it's that they didn't have to suffer the way that Chase suffers now. They died together, regardless of how they perished.

Sometimes, when I think about the accident, I wonder why the same thing couldn't have happened to me and my twin—and then I wonder if Chase would've been willing to take my place if it did.

He loved her as much as Rory loved Nina, but if there's something I've learned since January, it's that love… sometimes it's just not enough.

Give me a match and some gasoline any day.

CHAPTER 12

I might've managed to break free of the Grave, but I can never escape the nightmares.

Since the Turning, they've been bad, but they've gotten so much worse after what happened to my twin. There's not a single night when I don't have at least one. The only real question is just how bad it'll be.

Sometimes I dream of what the future could look like at the end of the world. Those are some of the scariest because there are fewer and fewer survivors these days. Supplies will run out. The danger only increases… but the lurkers keep on coming no matter what. They're endless, and that's why it's so important to find a way to take out a huge nest. Maybe I won't survive it, but if I can make a dent in those fuckers, it'll be worth it.

Some nights, I relive the past, thinking of what my life was like in the before times. I hate those nightmares the most. When I'm weeping, hot tears seeping through clamped together eyes, torn between then and now… I ache because of how much I miss the way the world used to be.

I miss Mom. Rory. Hallie. Our old neighbor Sam, and his sweet daughter, Genevieve. Jack's sisters died; no more aunts, uncles, and cousins. Neighborhood strays… the sweet orange cat I was working to convince to move in with me… they were easy pickings for the lurkers.

Raccoons who made their home in the trees behind my house. Deer. Skunks even… when the lurkers can't get human meat, anything will do.

Unbroken streets… our journey toward the city proves how damaged the world is now. Before the lurkers realized they could hide in abandoned houses to keep from burning up in the daylight, they used their inhuman strength to rip through asphalt and tear up the earth. Cars crumple on impact against their density. They destroyed more than just the way things were.

They destroy *everything*.

And that's why, most of all, I dream of the actual Turning and what it stole from me on January 1st.

It didn't happen all at once. It wasn't like there was a light switch that was flicked, engaging the Injection. The Turning happened slowly, with a report of a few hostiles going wild in one of the hospitals on the other side of town. They locked down the ER, the police and fire department—including Jack's engine—being sent to contain the situation.

Rory was on-duty that New Year's Day, but he wasn't on the truck. He was at the firehouse, holding down the fort with three of his colleagues. When four more reports came in about other offenders all over the county, he risked taking the five-minute ride from the station to the Holden house just to check in on the rest of us.

Hallie was at the Reynolds house. It was just Mom and me home… and we were the only ones there to witness it when my beloved older brother started to Turn.

His ruddy skin went pale. That was the first sign. Always an outdoorsman when he wasn't on-duty, he was darker than me, freckles dotting his arms, his face, his back. Not then. He went as white as a ghost, sweat pouring from his brow. His dark blond hair turned brown from the sweat, but when he shoved it out of his face, a whole hunk of it fell out with the motion.

I remember that so fucking vividly. All that hair stuck to his fingers, the way he stared at it with wide eyes.

Black eyes.

Rory had brown eyes, just like Jack. As the Injection took over, he doubled over, arms wrapped around his middle, a moan of pain erupting from him… I stared at his eyes. It looked like someone filled them with black ink. The irises were black. The sclera were black.

His eyes were black.

And that's when his teeth started to elongate—

"Xandra?"

Run, Mom, run! Rory, what are you… No—

"Xandra? Hey, Xandra!"

A sharp jerk of my shoulder and I thrash awake. The hungry drool dripping from what was once my brother's maw disappears in an instant as I blink away my latest nightmare, staring up at the moon overhead.

Maverick is crouched beside me. I'm hugging my backpack, face turned away from my fellow hunter, but his arm is still on the shoulder of Rory's jacket.

The nightmare is still too fresh. I have a flash of my brother in his firefighter uniform, the last thing he was wearing before I grabbed the steak knife and lost my fucking mind, burying it in him in a frenzy that I've blocked out so completely that all I remember now is walking into the kitchen to see him Turned and dead on the floor while Mom…

I shake my head, trying to dislodge the memories. At the same time, I knock Maverick's hand from my shoulder.

This jacket is the last thing I have of my brother's. He loved this damn thing. It had been a gift from Nina, given to him on their first Christmas together. He still lived at home; just like how Hallie and Chase were saving up to buy a place together, Rory and Nina were doing the same. When it finally hit us that he was gone, I asked my twin what we should do with it. We decided to keep it, and as long as I wear it, it's like he's still with me.

Same with Mom. When the lurkers began to infest our neighborhood and Jack realized we had to leave, we knew we couldn't take much of our old lives with us. Some pictures, some mementoes, as many clothes as we could carry… it was survival supplies that we prioritized, but my twin and I each took a piece of jewelry from Mom's jewelry box. She liked to collect simple necklaces, anklets, bracelets, and rings. Twins to the end, no matter how different we were, we both grabbed a silver anklet.

I'm wearing mine under my sock right now. I resist the urge to reach deep inside of the sleeping bag, patting it to see if it's still there. Instead, I pull myself up into a sitting position, searching for the fire.

It's still roaring within the pit that Maverick built before we settled down for the night.

That's a relief.

My heart rate slows. I didn't realize I could hear it pounding in my ears until the sound of the fire crackling against the kindling replaces it.

Shit.

What time is it?

I don't know. I don't feel like I slept enough, though that might be the aftereffect from my latest nightmare. After last night I hadn't wanted to fall so deeply asleep. Afraid that the fire might go out again, I planned on staying up as long as I could before getting enough rest that I'd be able to travel even further tomorrow.

Of course, that was before Maverick pushed me to my limits. As soon as the sun went down and Maverick swore he could be trusted to take first watch, I laid out my sleeping bag and passed out on the grass.

It's still impossibly dark out, with only the fire and the faint moonlight allowing me to see. Rolling on my back, releasing my iron-tight hold on my pack, I meet Maverick's curious gaze.

The fire silhouettes the man, throwing shadows over him. I sense his concern more than I can see it as he slowly draws his hand back.

The inside of my throat is coated in slime, like a snail has oozed its way down while I slept. I swallow a few times to make it go away, but when I talk, my voice is thick, the words slurred. "What is it? What do you want?" I sound like I'm half asleep.

I might still be.

"Here. While you slept, I made this for you."

At first, I don't see anything. He inches closer, blocking the light with his body, and because of the shadows that settle between us, I *really* don't see anything. I squint, waiting until my eyes get used to the dark. When they do, I see that what Maverick's holding between his two hands is—

"A piece of rope," I say flatly. This is what he woke me up for? "It's a piece of rope that's been tied into a circle with a knot."

"Yeah, but it's that knot that makes a world of difference. Here, watch." Maverick drops to his knees and lets the rope fall over his head. Tucking one arm out of the circle, he lets the other side sit on his shoulder so that it crosses his body. "You loop it around your body, then when you get too hot for your jacket, you take it off and rest it over the rope. It's obvious you don't want to let it get too far. This way you'll never have to worry about leaving it behind or keeping one hand full while we hike in the heat."

Smart guy. Not only did he catch on that I have an irrational attachment to the worn leather jacket, but he figured out a way to help me with it.

I'm actually kind of impressed, and just a bit touched that he's done this for me. It's a peace offering if I've ever seen one, but it's also more than that. This is Mav's way of showing me that he's accepted my company.

No more talk of "there's still time to turn back now". I'm here, and as long as I keep up, we'll be taking this trip together.

Okay. I make up my mind to forgive him for screwing up last night.

For now, at least.

"That's clever. I never would've come up with his," I say honestly, probably because I feel naked without my jacket, plus I don't like the idea of taking it off and showing the whole damn world my burn. Still, it's the thought that counts. "Thanks."

Not that I plan on using it. I'd rather sweat my balls off than part with Rory's jacket when I'm not in the sanctuary of Stacey Finch's bedroom. Taking my jacket off means severing that connection with my past—and letting my burn stand for my failures.

No, thanks.

Maverick slips the rope back over his head and holds it out to me, our hands brushing together as I take it. I don't mean to jolt in surprise, but his hand is cold. Like really cold. Even colder than it was when he pressed it over my mouth to stop my screams last night. His skin is clammy, too. A dead man's hand—

The fire.

The flammable haze.

The spark.

The explosion.

"Hallie! Get down!"

A gasp, and then, "Xandra…"

A nightmare without closing my eyes or falling asleep and, suddenly, I'm wide fucking awake.

I give my head another clearing shake before pushing off of the hard ground. "Hey. I didn't realize how much the temp's dropped. Why don't you warm up by the fire and get some sleep? I'll keep an eye out for trouble."

"Really?" He lifts his head slightly. I can't see his eyes, but the dark shadows from a sleepless night were there before the sun went down; he's got to be tired no matter how much he tries to hide it. "I'm still good for a couple more hours."

I think of the nightmares waiting for me should I fall back asleep.

"Really."

Maverick snores. Loudly. I almost want to take the spare sock that isn't hiding my antidote and stick it in his mouth to shut him up. Only the unexpected thoughtfulness he showed with the rope keeps me from taking my annoyance out on him.

Jesus Christ. Sounding like a freight train the way he does, I wouldn't be surprised if he summons either lurkers or rogues to the small park where we're hiding out tonight.

Instead of jamming his pie hole, I sit by the fire, throwing dry grass on the flames whenever it starts to dip too low. It's become a little bit of an obsession with me now that I'm on watch. I refuse to be the one to let it go out again. In my way, I guess I just want to prove to Maverick that I can do something that he failed at.

Maybe then he'll stop sneaking peeks my way, looking at me like he's made a huge mistake by continuing to let me follow him.

It's quiet in the park in the dead of night; with the exception of his thunderous snores, that is. I definitely was antsy at first that he would attract any dangers, but after an hour passes and my stomach is still calm, I actually start to appreciate the noise. If it were "drop a pin" quiet, the silence would drive me crazy. I would just be listening, convincing myself that I could hear a lurker's plodding step in the distance.

For now, I'm thinking.

The air is chilly and heavy with the promise of rain, but also undeniably fresh, and I breathe deeply, taking in the taste of September. There haven't been many lurkers traipsing through this park; their putrid stench has a tendency to linger. He picked a great spot to get some hours down, and I allow my thoughts to wander.

Watching the moon move slowly across the night's sky, I think about the Grave.

This is my second night away from home and it's harder than yesterday was. Last night, I was tired from walking, and the threat of the lurkers wasn't as real as it is today after four or five of them nearly found us. The nightmare about Rory and Mom—and that flash of panic surrounding the night of the accident—makes me feel like a coward for leaving the settlement behind. I couldn't help it, though.

There's a reason why I had to get out of the Grave— and it wasn't only because I believe in Maverick's mission to kill as many lurkers as I can.

I would've used any excuse to get out. I pretend to be brave because it's easy to kill a monster. But I haven't just killed monsters…

I think of Jack and what he would say if I could tell him how I sensed the lurkers' approach last night. I wonder what Chase is doing and, my traitorous imagination running away with me, I picture him lying in bed with Audrey, the nurse from St. Matthew's.

Shit. I'm jealous. There's no reason for me to be. I don't even know if there's anything between the two of them. I'm basing it all on the way she held onto his arm so proprietarily during the meet in the auditorium. I saw something there… but is it because he did move on, or because my guilt wants him to.

My guilt does. My jealousy does not.

Chase…

It hurts to think about him, just like it hurts to think about Jack, sitting there all alone in our kitchen with a cup of coffee he pretends to drink.

I'm just beginning to wonder if they're thinking about me, too, when my heavy heart turns into a sinking stomach and I immediately jump up. It's not as strong as it was yesterday, but I'm getting better at recognizing this feeling.

There's a lurker coming.

My pack is at my feet, already open. Following Maverick's example from earlier tonight, two lighters are waiting in my lap just in case something like this happened. For a moment, I ask myself if it's worth it to take this lurker out myself or if I should wake up Mav.

I pay attention to my gut. It doesn't seem like there's more than one. If I do this right, all it'll take is one match and a steady hand.

I can do this.

Standing behind the fire, I wait to see if the lurker really will approach our camp. As the feeling intensifies, I keep glancing down at our makeshift pit, checking that it hasn't gone out yet. There's no reason why a lurker would risk coming closer to a fire that's already raging—it's too much of a death sentence. At least with a match and the dark, there's the element of surprise on both our sides and it can be a struggle.

Right now, I have every advantage.

And then the lurker steps into the clearing about thirty feet from where I'm standing, and I suddenly understand.

It's a *youngling*.

I inhale sharply. I've never seen a youngling before, but I've heard the stories from some of the other hunters. They all agree that a youngling, despite its size, should never be underestimated.

Children who had been given the Injection and survived the Turning, children who were attacked by a lurker but not eaten... those are the younglings. Lurkers who are smaller and weaker than their adult counterparts, younglings are the desperate ones. They barely last more than a night because their bodies need even more food to sustain their metabolism.

Simply put, they're *starving*.

And that's why a youngling is desperate enough to walk toward a lapping fire if there's a chance of a meal. Maverick and I would be enough meat to sustain it for another week at least.

This youngling isn't strong enough to make my stomach any weaker than it is. There's a strange scent coming from it, almost like burnt caramel, but I breathe through my mouth and it's manageable. It's moving slower than any lurker I've met before, and I understand why when I see that it's tripping over the long hem of its over-sized robe.

No one knows where they get their cloaks from. Every one of those fuckers, big and small, seem to generate one after they Turn. Unlike the antidotes, they keep on coming —just like the monsters.

I give myself to the count of three before I'll surge forward and fling a lit match right at it. Though it's small, it's still a lurker, and that means it's far stronger than me. I need to be able to catch it off-guard—and that's when it lifts its head and I *freeze*. It's like a reverse-stare, and suddenly I understand why the other hunters insist that the younglings are so dangerous.

I can't tell if it used to be a girl or a boy, but there's definitely still something of a young child about its haunting face. It has the same black eyes, though they look more like ink than black marbles; its eyes are wet, silent tears streaming down its face, mingling with the drool escaping from its open maw, the same way Rory looked before I realized that he wasn't my brother anymore. Pale, alabaster skin is stretched so tight over its skull that it's almost like there's no skin there at all, just bone.

All it wants to do is eat.

All it wants to do is eat *me*.

Like last night, I'm fighting every urge I have to run—except running is not an option right now. I know I have to kill it, but the last thing I want to do is move toward it. In order to use a match, I have to come face to face with a lurker and trust that the stare will give me enough time to strike it.

Fuck me. How can I do that if I'm the one paralyzed?

There are only ten feet separating the two of us with the youngling still plodding forward. Maverick is lying behind me, unaware that there's any threat at all. I'm frozen in place, unsure what I'm supposed to do. It's like I've never killed a lurker before.

And then it hits me.

It's a good thing my pack is still open. I plunge my hand inside and, thank goodness, my hand closes on my can of hairspray with the first try. With one hand, I flip the cap off and place my finger on the nozzle. With the other, I snatch one of the lighters out of the dirt where it had fallen.

With shaking fingers, I quickly start to flick it.

My whole body is trembling which makes it nearly impossible. I almost drop the lighter once; my sweaty fingertip slips off the nozzle of the hairspray. When the lighter ignites at last, I let out a single satisfied cry before placing the flame in front of the hairspray and pressing down as hard as I can.

The stream of fire hits the youngling when there are only a few feet left; its hands were already outstretched, eager to wrap themselves around my throat, grabbing me and bringing me up to its terrifying teeth.

One short shot of the flammable aerosol spray combined with the lighter is all it takes. The robe and the unfortunate creature inside of it go up in the blast. Moments later, nothing but ashes are left.

All the same, I imagine the youngling's voiceless screams inside my head long after the queasy feeling in my stomach has passed.

The pile of ashes is still there when Maverick wakes up on his own at dawn. He takes one look at it, then nods with a thin-lipped frown before he starts to break up camp.

Huh.

It seems I've proven myself after all.

CHAPTER 13

t's only been five days and I've given up trying to figure out where we are.

It's not Manhattan, that's for sure.

It's a lot of outdoors. I was lucky enough to convince him to let us scavenge through a couple of houses yesterday so I could refill my water again, then wash up at the sink, but if I had grand visions of a cold shower, he shot that down real quick. He didn't want to linger, and I only hoped that he knew how to read that compass and the map he keeps poring over.

Maverick seems to think our safest course is staying close to the trees during daylight. There's enough light to guarantee that the lurkers won't come after us. Then, at night, the threat of the lurkers aren't anywhere near as bad as they would be if we marched through infested neighborhoods.

I'll tell you what. I never knew there were so many parks and woods, rivers, brooks, and streams within (technical) walking distance of old Madison. All I can remember of the before times are the roads and the power lines; I took all of the nature of the Garden State for granted until now, when shade represents safety and an open stretch of flat grass makes it easier to spot any lurkers on the hunt at night.

After what happened our first night, Maverick and I come to an arrangement that works for us: we continue to split the night watch, a strict four-hour shift so that there's always someone watching out for lurkers. I don't think he ever expected one to come so close with the fire burning bright, youngling or not, and I have this phobia that he'll let the fire die and we'll both end up lurker food. We still light it religiously, hoping to deter the adult creatures, but the nightly watches are more important than either of us initially imagined with younglings on the hunt.

The only problem is that, for me, getting only four hours of sleep a night isn't nearly enough after a good sixteen hours' of walking each day. After Hallie's accident and before I left the Grave, I used to get at least ten hours a night. I know this is making me move a lot slower than Maverick would like—especially five days in—but there's nothing I can do about it. His muttered comments and barely masked sighs aren't helping, either.

Thank you, Mr. Police Officer.

So far, I know three things about him: his name, that he was a former cop, and that he hates lurkers with a passion he doesn't show toward anything else. He's quiet and stoic, as mysterious as he was when we first met, and no matter how often I try to strike up a conversation so that we're at least on a more even footing, it doesn't work..

He knows way more about me than I would like. He's

super observant, too—a fact I figured out when he came up with the rope idea—and he's also smart enough to keep his mouth shut when he notices that I don't use it. He might not tell me anything about himself, but he's asked me a few pointed questions about Rory and Hallie and Jack that leave me uncomfortable enough that I close my own trap.

I do, however, ask him if we're getting any closer. He says we are, but as my blisters start to get blisters, I have my doubts.

The night before, we camped on the edge of a park, near a sign that is half-burned, half-gnawed, and dotted with the rust-colored spray of spilt blood. It says *anco Park*, leaving me to wonder what the rest of the name used to be. One thing for sure: we've left the Grave far behind us, and my habit of staying close to home in the before times is biting me in the ass. I wouldn't be surprised to learn that we're both traveling blind, with only an outdated map and a compass to guide us.

Wherever we are, Maverick wasn't happy with the park. Something about him had him anxious, and when we were settling down across from the fire he built, he didn't put his lighters in his lap.

Nope. He took out his gun, perching it on his thigh.

It's a revolver. Mav might not tell me about his life before the Turning, but when I asked him about the gun, he was at least willing to answer some questions about his weapon.

And that's how I know that there are only two rounds left in the revolver.

Was there six to begin with like most guns? Yup. One shot told him that a lurker was vulnerable in the first twenty-four hours after they Turn. Another told him that they *were*n't after that marker passed.

Do I know what happened to the other two rounds?

Rogues.

He's had to fire on two rogues.

I didn't get any further details on that. Just enough to know that Maverick spent the first four months since the Turning in a settlement a few miles away from his hometown before he went on the hunt, a rogue himself. It's only the last eight weeks that he's been focused on taking out the New York City nest, and after six other settlements turned him down, he found himself in the Grave.

I know there are rogues out there. He heard screaming our first night together, and, well, we're both rogues now, too. I want to say we're not dangerous, but then I think about how easily I made a flamethrower to take out that youngling. I ask myself: if someone came after us, am I a threat?

Yeah. I am. I'd kill to protect myself, and one look at Maverick when he doesn't think I can see his expression tells me that he's more than willing to do the same.

He fired on two rogues, and I'm damn sure he killed them.

This is the world now. It's us versus them, and sometimes the *them* aren't just lurkers.

The high-pitched cry of some bird pierces the early afternoon air.

Maverick freezes.

So do I.

Birds… I haven't heard birds in ages. The entire time we've been out in the woods, there's been no sign of any sort of wildlife. If there is any, they're hidden well enough that they can avoid lurkers, but that means they're as good as gone. So a bird? A small sliver of relief flashes through me as I think that there was at least one that the lurkers—or the flames—haven't found a way to destroy.

That relief is short-lived when it sounds again and, this time, it's not birdsong.

It's a whistle.

My stomach sinks to my boots.

It's not queasy. I don't sense any lurkers approaching us. Of course not. The sun is still shining brightly, another warm September day, though my whole body goes suddenly cold. They'd shrivel in the sunlight, like a vampire if a stray sunbeam hit any of the pale skin under their cloaks.

But it can't be a lurker.

Lurkers can't whistle.

"Rogue?" I breathe out.

Maverick sucks in his breath, his cheekbones jutting out of his face as he goes gaunt. "Worse."

Worse?

"What do you mean, worse?"

Rather than answer me, he slips his pack from his shoulders. It lands with a thump on the grass. There's a velcro section on the backside that he tears open with a crunching sound that makes my teeth ache. He yanks out a battered old baseball cap that's covered in a mixture of dirt and ashes that make the dark blue look like it's speckled with brown and grey.

He tosses it at me. "Put this on."

"Why—"

"No time for questions," he snaps. "Just do it."

I jam the hat on my head.

"Better," he mutters. "Too bad we don't have time to get the sweatshirt out. The hood would've covered you up more. Does that jacket have a zipper?"

"What? Yes. Yes, it does."

"Good. Zip it up. We gotta hide your tits."

I don't know what freaks me out more: that Maverick finally acknowledges that I'm a woman after all, or that there's some reason that he really wants to conceal that fact.

Well, duh. Isn't that what had Chase so worried about me? He thought that Maverick might make a move when it was just the two of us outside of the Grave. He never has. Up until this moment, I got the vibe that he was treating me like I was one of the guys.

He did. The rogue who's out there might not. And I'm wearing a dingy white tank top and a stretched-out bra. My cleavage has been on display for days now, a fact that I've gotten used to… until now.

Fuck. Fuck fuck fuck.

I grab the zipper. It catches. I mutter a curse out loud as I tug anxiously. Yes! The leather releases, allowing the zipper to go all the way up to my chin.

His eyes dart past me, over to where we might have heard the whistle coming from. I don't know what can be worse than a rogue survivor traveling through the outside, but this is the most worked-up I've ever seen Maverick and, for the first time since I left the Grave, I'm undeniably nervous.

"What's going on?"

His lips purse the way they always do when I ask a question he doesn't want to answer.

And then, before I can prod him to explain, he says, "I fucked up. Xandra… I'm sorry, but I fucked up."

My heart lodges in my throat. "How bad? Is this like a 'I put the fire out' kind of fuck-up or—"

"It's worse."

Damn it. Not "worse" again. "What do you mean?"

"I read the map wrong. I thought there was enough distance between us, but either I fucked up real bad or they've expanded their territory. I thought I could avoid them. I don't think we can now."

Panic. This is pure panic raging through me. I reach forward, clutching his sleeve. His shirt is dirt-stained and worn, and he traded it for a different one in his pack yesterday morning when we had a rare chilly morning. I dig my fingers in, almost ready to tear the fabric as I demand, "What are you talking about? Who? What?" I shake my head, squeezing him. "Where are we?"

"We're right on the edge of East Jersey," Maverick says quickly before adding, "Here, tuck your hair up under the cap. Don't let any of it hang out. And dirt— lots of dirt. Put some dirt on your cheeks, that should help."

There's no reason to refuse. I shove as much of my hair underneath the cap as I can before picking up a clump of dirt and rubbing it against my skin. "I've never heard of East Jersey before."

Maverick is still staring accusingly at the trees over my shoulder.

"You would know it as Rahway, I believe. More dirt, you're still too clean."

I smear another handful of dirt along the edge of my jaw and my cheek. "You mean, like the prison?"

He freezes, then turns his head slowly to look over his shoulder at me. "What makes you say that?"

"I don't know. I just remember that about Rahway. There used to be a prison there, right?"

"Oh, yeah. *Used* to be."

"You've heard of it?"

Maverick nods, glancing back at the trees before facing me again. "That's where the name comes from: East Jersey State Prison. All the cons got out when the warden Turned… I say all, the ones who *survived* got out and escaped. Most of them established their own place here. Made it a prison town."

What the hell is a prison town?

And why are we standing here talking about it instead of bolting in the opposite direction?

There's an easy answer to that last question. Before I can run, the high-pitched whistle sounds again. It's impossibly closer.

Maverick scoops up a handful of dirt and starts on my other side. "Hear that? That's their leader. Rex. He knows we're here."

"How do you know all this?" And why didn't he warn me before?

"Because I might've passed this way before in my travels. I'm so fucking sorry," he says again. "If I had any idea we were so close… shit. One of your curls is escaping. You've got to tuck it all under the cap. Keep your head down, and this part is real important: don't say a word. Leave all the talking to me. Got it?"

"I don't think we're in Rahway," I point out, yanking

down the back of the cap and shoving the rest of my hair up inside of it. His insistence isn't helping my sudden anxiety at all. "It shouldn't have taken so long to go… what, six miles from the Grave? And where's the dome? Rahway Prison had a big dome. Jack used to point it out when we passed it on Route 1."

Maverick looks at me in disbelief, almost like he can't believe we're having this conversation. I don't know why he's looking at me like that. He's the one who's standing here, having a chat instead of fleeing.

"We're not in Rahway, Xandra," he says gruffly, going slowly as if he's speaking to a five-year-old. "*This*," and he points at the ground, "is where the people who used to live in Rahway and the East Jersey Prison relocated to. Your Rahway is another town that doesn't exist anymore. Trust me when I say this"—Maverick leans in so close that I can smell campfire smoke on him, plus feel the chill from his skin. He lowers his voice—"if you don't do what I've just told you, *you* might not exist either. So, please, *do it!*"

The image of his gun flashes before my eyes again, plus all of the horror stories I used to hear of cops who snapped. Nine months after the Turning, maybe it's just Maverick's time to shine.

I don't have a choice. I have to listen.

And that's when I hear a loud shout split through the trees—

"Maverick Brooks! Well, I'll be damned! Never thought you'd come crawlin' back to East Jersey. Good to see ya, boy."

Because I'm staring down at the ground like he told me to, I can't see the face of the man approaching, but if the size of his shadow is any indication, he's a damn *giant*. My breath catches in my throat, my heart beating a mile a minute.

Okay. Maybe Maverick was right to freak out.

"Hey, Rex. It's good to see you, too." He claps me on the shoulder. I'm not expecting it and my knees almost buckle. "This is my buddy. Alex."

Alex?

Rex has a laugh that reminds me of Santa Claus, all "ho ho ho" and holly jolly. I already call bullshit. "So you finally found some sucker to take you up on your fool's errand? Good on ya, Brooks."

"That's right. We're on our way to New York, just like we talked about last time I was in town. So while it was great to see you again, you'll understand that we've got to be on our way."

I hold my breath, hoping like hell that'll work.

"What's the rush?" asks Rex, and my heart sinks. "You're not gonna deny me the chance to show ya a little hospitality? Come on. Head into town with me."

"I'll go. Alex, you stay here. I won't be gone long."

Looking down, I see it when Rex's big, scuffed boot kicks at the dirt. "Bring 'em with you."

"I don't think that's necessary—"

"Yeah? Well, I do."

At his side, Mav flexes his fingers. " Rex—"

"Formalities is formalities, Brooks. Rules is rules. I told you I'm offering my hospitality. If you want to make it through our territory, you're gonna follow our rules. You understand me?"

I think I understand. Just like how there's no refusing this guy, I get the idea that he's not saying we have to go back the way we came in order to avoid passing through his territory without permission.

Oh, no. He's not letting us off it in one piece, either.

And Maverick knows it.

"Yeah. I do."

An oak tree lying on its side marks the outer boundary to East Jersey. It's easy to tell because of the char marks on the other side, the piles upon piles of ashes that haven't blown away since the last flaming. One thing's for sure: this settlement can certainly take out its lurkers.

The moment we each climb over it, Rex stops, his shadow changing course as he swings around to face me. I jump back, startled, but that doesn't stop Rex from grabbing Maverick's cap right from my head. Disheveled blonde hair tumbles down and settles on my shoulders like a smoking gun.

I know I'm caught. From Maverick's barely stifled groan, he knows it, too.

Okay. I'm a woman. No hiding it now, and since the truth is out, I look up at him defiantly.

That… might've been a mistake.

Rex fits every image of an ex-con I've ever had. He's got at least a head on Maverick, and he's about twice as wide as me. His grey hair is long and unruly, flowing past his shoulders, ending in a tangle of knots. He's got tattoos covering every inch of skin I can see, except for his face, and I can only guess what the rest of his weathered skin holds; the only reason why his face is clear of the tattoos is because of his bushy, dingy beard. Stuffed inside his clothes like a sausage, his belly jiggles with each heavy breath. I'm pretty sure his overalls had been tailored out of an old prison jumpsuit.

Who else would own a pair that had **EJSP** imprinted on the side?

My first impression of his laugh sounding like Santa Claus isn't too far off, either. Take the Christmas icon, stuff him in a jail cell for a decade or two, and you'd end up with something like this Rex.

"Alex?" There's a twinkle in Rex's mud brown eyes.

I stick out my chin in a display of foolish disdain. "Xandra."

Rex raises his eyebrow. "Oh?"

Maverick grabs my arm and gives it a jerk, pulling me aside and taking my place in front of Rex. "Alexandra," he says, a compromise. "Sorry, Rex. I was trying to keep her to myself. She's mine."

I start to sputter in response to that claim, but stop when Maverick's grip on my arm tightens.

"She might've been, and I'm sorry for your loss, boy. But if you didn't think I could sniff a girlie out, you're fooling both of us. I was in the pen for twenty-five years. One whiff's all it takes and I knew exactly what your Alex was. And I'm sure ya know what *that* means. Seein' as how you agreed to come onto my territory."

"Yeah." It's an exhale, and an agreement, but it could've been a curse for how he says it. "I know."

I'm glad he does. I look over at Maverick, obviously confused. He might know what's going on. I have no clue.

And no one tells me.

CHAPTER 14

Rex takes us on a tour through East Jersey.

How kind of him. If only it was actually out of the kindness of his heart, and not because he wants to show off how impossible it'll be for us to leave without his blessing.

Despite being what Maverick called a prison town, it doesn't seem that different from the Grave. Most of the people live in a strip of houses that are connected together like the collection of townhouses on the far side of Grave; the idea that having your neighbors as close as possible is one that Jack believes in, too.

There are six interconnected apartment complexes that make up East Jersey. According to Rex, the next three streets beyond it belong to the settlement, too. Past that, there's a fully infested lurker nest. They keep the monsters at bay by a row of torches that one of the men in town lights every evening before the sun goes down.

The first apartment complex is built in a square. On the inside, there's a large patch of grass with a wooden platform erected in the middle. I don't know what that is, and —still listening to Mav's advice—I don't ask.

Rex doesn't explain. I guess he thinks it's obvious. That, or he and Maverick already know what the deal is with some kind of... I don't know. Stage? It reminds me of a stage.

There is more wood behind another one of the complexes. A stockpile, obviously. They have barrels of gasoline, too, and I'm envious of their supply. These ex-cons seem to know what they're doing.

After the quick tour—when I get the feeling that it's more about showing Maverick how guarded his territory is while also showing me off to the people who mill about, doing work and gawking at us—he brings up to his designated home. I'm not surprised that it's the nicest one on the block. A real McMansion, it's twice as big as the others surrounding it.

I can tell that Maverick would rather go anywhere than inside. I'm right there with him. Rex's friendly act is just that: an act. We're fucked, and I don't even need the warning Maverick gives me to know to keep my mouth shut. He's on his guard. His body is tensed, a small tic in his jaw as he attempts to hold up his end of the conversation with Rex.

I've never heard him talk this much at once. They're all meaningless little comments designed to keep the older man's attention on him instead of me, but no matter how many people think I'm innocent and naive, I'm not. I can see how closely Rex is paying attention to me even as he plays the role of host.

My zipper is still up as high as it can go. Pointless. Rory's jacket was tailored to his taller, broader frame, and it covers up my shape. Useless. The steely look in Rex's eyes makes it obvious that he's undressing me with his gaze.

What the fuck? I'm covered in dirt, my hair is ratty and tangled, and I smell of sweat, smoke, and the outside. He can't be so hard up for a little pussy that he's willing to ignore the fact that Maverick called me his, right? I mean, I'm *not*, and Mav's never given me any hint that he's interested, but if he's willing to stand between me and the men of East Jersey, I'm okay with it.

In fact, as I sidle closer to him, clutching his sleeve, I notice Rex picking up on the gesture.

He pushes in the door, holding out his hand so that we stay on the porch. Before I can yank on Maverick, hissing at him that we should find a way out of this, Rex sticks his head inside.

"Girls? Your husband's home. And I've brought guests so I hope we can squeeze two more in at the dinner table."

I don't know what stuns me more: the plural of "girls" or the way that he calls himself their husband.

Ten minutes later, when I'm sitting between Maverick and Rex at a large, oval table that seats ten, I decide: both. It's fucking *both*.

And how do I know that it seats ten? Because between me, Mav, Rex, and Rex's *six* wives, that's how many people are perched around it, eating the meal of spaghetti and some questionable meat sauce that Bernadette— Rex's first wife—had cooked with the help of Felicity—his most recent acquisition.

Dinner is quiet time. Thank God, and I don't mean that ironically. Rex makes a display of saying Grace before any of us are allowed to eat. Even then, his wives all wait like well-behaved robots for him to eat his fill before they pick up their own forks.

I've learned not to turn down food, but this is rough. With my nerves making my belly squirm, it takes every-thing I have to force mouthfuls down. It's obvious I'll offend our host if I refuse more of his hospitality. Maverick chows down, and so do I.

Because he started the meal first, Rex finishes before the rest of us. He disappears between the end of dinner and only returns about ten minutes later when one of the youngest wives—with a big belly that almost makes me lose my appetite when I realize why she's waddling—heads into the kitchen, returning with a cake.

I'm sure it's delicious. Since the Turning, so many survivors have altered recipes to suit whatever supplies are left, and this almost tastes like it could've been made from fresh milk and eggs in the before times.

Doesn't keep it from going down like concrete.

I don't know what to expect as dessert comes to a close. By now, it's gotta be getting close to sundown. Even if Rex sends us on our merry way, is there enough time to find a safe place to sleep for the night?

Or are we stuck here?

That's what I'm worried about, and I don't have to worry for long before I understand that Rex's "welcome" isn't over quite yet.

It's toward the end of the meal that this horrible clanging sound starts.

No one says a word. Rex stands up first, striding out of

the room as if he had been expecting the interruption; or, better yet, he *orchestrated* it. That would make sense. He was gone for a while, and as he invites Maverick to rise next, there's a smugness to him that has my hackles rising.

"Alexandra will join us," he announces, gesturing at me next.

Felicity, the newest wife, shoots a jealous look my way. "Why does she get to go?"

"Because I said so, darlin'. You're not questioning your husband, are ya?"

The poor girl pales. "No… Rex, honey, of course not. You know I would never. You know that, right?"

He makes a tsk-ing sound. "I thought I did. I thought you understood that us boys… we keep our women safe in the house. Unless you'd rather be the one the alarm bell's ringin' for?"

Her fingers jolt. Her fork falls to the tabletop. "No. I'm sorry, Rex."

"That's fine, Felicity. When I get back, you can join me in my room and show me just how sorry you are, my sweet thing."

A hint of fear, a touch of distaste… watching the slender brunette closely, I see that, followed by the same sort of determination that's stared back at me when I used to look in mirrors.

She'll do anything to survive—including this brute.

"Of course. I… I'll be waiting for you."

"That's my girl. And Kendra… you'll be next."

Another one of his wives nods. "Yes, sweetheart."

Rex shares a look with Maverick. "You got to show them who's boss. Eh, Brooks?"

Maverick says nothing.

I wonder if I can grab the knife that Felicity used to cut the cake and jab it in Rex's jugular.

Figuring that's pretty much a death wish, I rise from my seat, sidling over to Maverick's side again. I'm glad I get to go... wherever... even if the other women don't. Right now, Mav's the only ally I have. Rex is going to have to pry me away from him if the prison town leader wants to separate us.

Once he sees that we're ready, he leads us outside.

"This way. Follow the crowd. My boys know where they're going."

There's a sea of people, smaller than the Grave, but large enough to carry me along it like a current as we all flow in the same direction. Before I think better of it, I reach out and grab Maverick's chilly hand.

I glance up at him, and whether I want to assure him that the hand is mine or demand he tell me what we're doing now, I don't know, but I can't find my voice. There's such a strange yet curious expression on his face, one I don't think I was meant to see, because in a heartbeat, it's gone. He tugs on my hand, but doesn't let go. I follow his lead.

The crowd empties us out on the edge of that first apartment complex, the one with the open center.

The one with the wooden platform that is basically some sort of stage.

Most of the crowd ebbs their way closer to it and I'm suddenly reminded of the high school auditorium in the Grave. This is just like that last assembly we had, when Maverick arrived. This is East Jersey's way of coming together as a community.

But *why*?

It's no surprise to me when Rex is the one who mounts the stage.

The clanging had stopped. I didn't even notice until it starts up again as the big man moves toward the front.

"Tonight, I've gathered you all here to witness what happens when one of you don't follow the rules." He lifts his hand, raising his voice to be heard over the noise. "Clyde. Melvin. Bring him in."

Two men march from the other side of the courtyard. One is a couple of inches over six feet. Dark skin. Hair closely cropped to his skull. He's holding a handbell, ringing it out of rhythm. His partner is a little shorter, more squat, and with greasy black hair that's tucked behind his ears.

In between them, a younger man who can't be more than twenty-five. In the setting sun, his short hair is dark, his skin pale. He's not wearing coveralls like the two men surrounding him. I'm pretty sure that he was a survivor living in this neighborhood when it was overrun by the former inmates. Either that or a corrections officer, but the way he's dragging his boots as they carry him toward the stage, muscling him up the stairs, I go with survivor.

"You were caught trying to take one of my brother's wives from him. That's not allowed. You know that. I've told you this before."

"She was mine first. Olivia was my wife before the Turning. We've been married for two years—"

"And she chose Terry because he could protect her better than you could."

"But I love her—"

"There's no space for love now, boy. You've got to

know that. You could've had another wife. Someone would've accepted you."

The dark-haired man thrashes. "I just want Olivia."

Rex shakes his head. "And that's why Terry's asked to kick your sorry ass out of East Jersey. You won't leave his wife alone. He has to protect her, and I'm inclined to agree. Clyde. Melvin. Give him to the lurkers."

What?

No—

I surge forward. Maverick uses my hold on his hand to jerk me back against him.

"Don't," he whispers. "You can't save him."

"But it's going to be dark. If the lurkers get him, he's dead."

And all for the crime of wanting the love he had before the world went to shit.

"I know. We still can't save him."

Does that mean we can't *try*?

I guess not.

As I struggle to accept that—as the two men drag the kicking and screaming man out of the courtyard— Rex finds me. With me being the only woman present, it couldn't have been hard, but I get the idea that it's on purpose. That, of everyone in East Jersey, he wanted me to witness this and, now that I have, he wants to see my reaction.

That, or he wants me on display for all of the other men he's gathered together…

I know the shock and disgust at throwing away a survivor, of *sacrificing* him, is written plainly on my face. I don't even try to disguise it. I think my horror amuses him. His eyes seem to brighten and, despite his bushy mustache, I swear I see his lips twitch into a satisfied grin. He nods, proud of himself. At that moment, I'm absolutely positive it's no coincidence that this happened tonight, the same day we arrived here.

I don't know why, but Rex wanted me to watch this. He wanted me to see this, the power that he has, the way that things are done in this fucking terrible place.

And I hate him for it. I hate him almost as much as I hate lurkers, and that's saying something.

Oblivious to how I'd set him on fire with my mind if it was possible, he addresses the quiet crowd.

"Now, boys, go on. Go home to your wives, get to bed. Tomorrow's a big day, what with fresh meat and all. We'll start the bidding at noon."

I don't even get the chance to wonder what he means by "bidding" before he waves his hand and the crowd disperses. Fresh meat… maybe they have some kind of connection with the outside and get supplies that we don't have in the Grave. Bidding… I'd pay a lot for a good cheeseburger that I could be sure came from a cow.

I hope that the signal means that Mav and I can go, too. Not quite. Right as we try to sneak away, Rex calls out, "Maverick, hold on there. Your girl, too. Let me walk you both back to the house."

No. *No*. Go back to his house?

"Maverick," I hiss. "I thought we were leaving."

He glances down at me, expression apologetic. "I'm so sorry."

Not that shit again. "Mav—"

I'm on Maverick's left. Rex comes up beside me, sandwiching me between the two men, and I clamp my mouth shut as he brushes up against my side.

My skin crawls.

He nods at the empty stage. "Shame you had to see that," he says, and he's a damn liar. No way he didn't at least arrange for that to happen because we're outsiders. Message clear, Rex. If he'll do that to one of his people, he'll do it to us, too.

"He broke the rules," is all Maverick says.

"You understand. Good. That'll make this easier all around."

That'll make *what* easier?"

He waits until we're halfway back to his house before I have any idea.

"Alexandra here can spend the night with the wives I won't be needin'." Oh, barf. What does he do? Rotate them in and out of his bed, leaving the others in another room in the house until he requires their services? "They'll take care of her for her big day tomorrow."

Hang on—

"Tomorrow?" I ask softly. I want to get out of East Jersey *now*. I played their game. I took that tour, I ate dinner, I watched him sentence a man to die. I'm done. "What do you mean—"

Maverick speaks over me, raising his voice in an effort to drown out mine. "Does she really have to stay with the other women? I... come on, Rex. I wanted to be able to spend one more night with her." He lays his hand on my upper bicep, rubbing his thumb along the back. "Just in case."

It's like they're speaking another language. I don't understand any of it. Not why Maverick is agreeing to us staying over, not why he doesn't seem surprised by anything that's happened since he heard that whistle, and especially not why he's doing his best to let Rex think there's something going on between us.

Okay, so maybe I shouldn't have grabbed his hand, and maybe I've stuck to him like a shadow all day, but that's it.

And what does *just in case* mean? Just in case *what*?

I'm not sure I want to find out.

There's Rex's Santa laugh again. He rubs his belly and winks at Maverick, a secret between them. "All right. I got ya, Brooks. I think I can arrange for you to have one more night with your girl, and I hope—if you like her as much as I think you do—you've got something really good to offer up tomorrow."

I can't help it. I've been a good little girl, quiet and unassuming except for my earlier outburst, and that's so not me. "I don't get it," I blurt out, and I'm the only one who doesn't. "What *is* tomorrow?"

Rex gives Maverick a sly look out of the corner of his eye. "You mean he didn't tell you 'bout our rules before he brought you to us?" I guess the blank expression on my face is enough of an answer for him because he clucks his tongue. "No wonder he tried to pass you off as a guy. But rules is rules, as I always say, and tomorrow you'll take part of the most important one we got.

"Tomorrow, you go up on the block."

CHAPTER 15

"An auction?" I toss my pack on the lone bed in the small room with so much force that it hits the mattress and bounces right back onto the floor. I don't even care. So what if the antidote smashes? An antidote won't stop me from being made some ex-con's wife, will it? "I'm supposed to just stand there and *let* them auction me off like I'm a piece of fucking cattle. They're crazy! This is *crazy!*"

Maverick looks anxiously over his shoulder. One of Rex's too-many wives had shown us to our room, taking great care to close the door behind her when she left. From the way he's hovering near the doorway, he probably suspects that she's just on the other side—either she is, or someone else in this house. To be honest, I wouldn't put it past any of them to spy on us. I just don't give a fuck if they can hear me right now.

Let them hear me. I want them to know how angry I am.

Some cop. *Fuck.* Arrest these pricks. Tear down their prison town. Do something, Maverick.

All he does is bite down, the hollows of his cheeks on display as he sucks in a breath through his nose. He doesn't say a damn word, and after all the chit-chatting he did with Rex earlier, I get even more pissed.

Was this a set-up? *Oh, I'm so sorry, Xandra, I fucked up… I went the wrong way… I read the map wrong… I brought you to East Jersey to sell you to a man who already has six fucking "wives".*

I thought I could trust him. And maybe I'm as naive as I like to pretend I'm not because I wanted to believe his apologies. His whispered promise that this was an accident.

No, Mav. An accident is grabbing my pack instead of yours in the dark. Bringing me to this misogynistic hell-hole is way more than an accident.

It's a *disaster.*

There's a blanket spread across the bed, covering the pillows. A patchwork quilt is folded at the foot of the bed. Gathering it up in my arms, I throw it at Maverick with all the strength I can muster, satisfied when he catches it with a grunt.

"I get the bed," I snap. Because he looks so concerned, I drop my voice, but his paranoia that we have spies around us won't stop me from saying my piece. "You sleep on the floor."

"Xandra—"

I'm not done. Glaring at him, I say, "I don't know what you're thinking, telling Rex that you want to share a room with me. Let's get one thing clear. I'm not letting any of those creeps touch me. But you… if you've been biding your time and think that I'll fuck you now to get out this mess, you're wrong." I dip my hand into Rory's jacket, grateful I still have my pocketknife. I pull it out, flipping the switch that releases the blade. "Try touching me, cop. I'll cut your fucking fingers off."

A flash of pain dances across his weathered features, there and gone again as if my threat actually found a target. I trusted him, and he knew it, but now... he's just another rogue.

His eyes fasten on the blade, the way it shines in the lamplight. He takes a deep breath, then sighs. "You have a knife."

"And you're a regular Sherlock Holmes."

He ignores my flippant comment. "Good. Hold onto it as long as you can."

That's exactly what I plan on doing. *As long as you can...* he mustn't think that Rex will let me keep it. Probably not his gun, either, if the leader of East Jersey has any idea it exists.

And my antidote... I can't let him get his hands on my antidote.

Frustrated, I kick my pack under the bed for safe-keeping.

Maverick says nothing else as he lays the quilt on the floor, leaving his bedroll with his own pack.

I think about throwing him a pillow because the hard-wood floor probably isn't any more comfortable than sleeping on the ground outside. No. If he wants one, he can ask for it.

Once he's done, he exhales roughly. "You don't have anything to worry about from me." Him, maybe, but the rest of East Jersey... "But this was the only way I could think to keep you safe tonight from any unwanted guests. Rex gave us tonight. If we keep our voices down, we can figure out our next move."

"I know my next move," I retort. "I'm getting the hell out of here as soon as I can."

When he doesn't agree with me, my insides twist. I've gotten used to Maverick avoiding my gaze as if eye contact is some kind of crime with him, but he's usually more discreet about it. When he starts picking at his fingers before nibbling on the side of his thumb, even I can't pretend that he isn't purposely holding something back.

"I am… unless there's something you know that I don't." I pause and, grabbing one of the pillows, squeeze it between my shaking hands. "Which there might be, because you've been here before. Right?"

"It's not as easy as that—"

Yes. It is.

"You knew Rex. You knew him from his whistle, and then you tried to keep him from finding out I was a woman." His desperation should've been my first warning sign. "You knew about the men here practicing their warped form of polygamy." No denial there. He just looks away, and I take a shot in the dark. "You knew about the auction."

His head snaps toward me and I have to resist the urge to fling my knife at him.

My eyes blaze in outright fury. "You set me up."

"No.

"You did. Is that why you were alone when you came to the Grave? You'd sold the last idiot who agreed to come along with you to Rex and his boys, then you needed…"

What was it he called it? "... fresh meat? How much do they pay you for this?"

"Xandra—"

"Tell me. I'm young. Strong." I slap my side. "Got some birthing hips and a pussy they can use. I've got to be worth something."

There's that pained expression again. "You are. You're a fierce hunter, and I never lied about why I needed volunteers. I'm going to New York. I'm taking out that nest. I need all the help I can get, and I would never work with Rex." His voice turns dark. "*Never*. I don't agree with the shit he does here. I don't have to. I just need to survive it. That's what I am, Xandra. A survivor. That's what you are, too."

"Yeah? Say I believe you." Please let me be able to believe him... "How do you expect me to survive this auction?"

Because I'll kill myself before I be one of these men's "wife". With my knife or Maverick's gun, I'll take the easy way out.

No one owns me.

"I have a plan."

"I'm waiting."

"You're not going to like it," he warns me.

"Will I like it any better than being bid on by a bunch of men who only got out of prison because the world ended?"

"When you put it like that..." Maverick gives me a crooked grin that makes him look a little younger than usual. "I'm going to win you."

I'm gonna hurl.

"I hope that's not all." I close my eyes. "Please tell me there's more to your brilliant plan than that."

There has to be. While I don't want to be won by *anyone*, it's definitely better if Maverick can be my "husband"; at least I can hope that he won't suddenly decide he wants to climb into bed with me and fuck me. The other guys? I'm betting that's the first thing they'll try to do.

But this is Rex's town. Rex's rules. And he certainly does like having many wives... who is to say he won't decide *he*'s the winner?

Maverick seems certain that his plan will work. "I have something that Rex will want. I met him before, remember? I offer it up, he calls me the winner, and we'll be out of here before you know it. Trust me. The women in East Jersey do what their husbands tell them. If I say we have to go to New York..."

A frisson of hope fills me. " Rex's rules will say that I have to go with you."

I don't know what Maverick has that will be worth it for Rex to give up on fucking with me—or the idea of actually fucking me. I have to hope he's right because I'm pretty sure that's as much as I'm getting out of the tight-lipped cop about this brilliant plan of his.

Still, I have to ask, "But what if it doesn't work?"

"It *has* to work."

I highly doubt it will.

"Why go through all that? Why not just leave? You got out before, right?" Don't think I haven't noticed that you completely blew past the fact he didn't acknowledge *why* he's been in East Jersey before. "You have to know how. Fuck his rules. You can lead me out of here now."

"I do know the way. And I can leave whenever I want. It's just... *you* can't."

That's the wrong thing to say to me at the moment.

"Oh? I'd like to see them try to stop me," I seethe, crossing the room in five strides and tugging at the doorknob. It doesn't even turn a little bit. A rush of panic makes my hand slip off the knob, my heart racing a mile a minute. Grabbing it with both hands, I yank and I pull and I try to rip the handle right off the door, but it doesn't give at all.

Are you kidding me? We've been *locked* in!

"Xandra," and his voice is low yet urgent, "I need you to calm down. Think about it... do you really want Rex changing his mind and barging in here right now? Because, I tell you, it's only because he knows my face that he's giving us any semblance of privacy at all. Would you rather be with Rex? You saw him. You met his—"

I whirl around, pointing at him. "Don't even say it," I warn.

"—you've met the women he believes are his. He likes his collection. If you weren't in here with me, I have no doubt that you'd be up there with him."

My stomach flip-flops. I managed to control it when they sentenced that poor guy to the lurker, but it's definitely queasy now. Maverick's meaning isn't lost on me. I met Rex's wives. At least two of them were younger than me—and one was visibly pregnant which means he wasted no time after the Turning in knocking her up.

Oh, God.

I'm trembling as I march across the room, moving past Maverick so that I can drop down on the bed. "Fine. But you're still sleeping on the floor."

It isn't long before his muffled snores fill the room. Me? I'm still wide awake, and more than a little frustrated that Maverick was able to drift off so easily. Anxiety is a bitch, and despite the fact that I'm sleeping in an actual bed for the first time in days, all I do is stare up at the ceiling and hope like hell that this prison town has as good of a handle on their borders as they claim they do.

They'll need to. If they're in the habit of feeding their people to lurkers to keep the rest in line, they probably have more of the monsters nearby than we do in the Grave. It's like feeding stray cats. Once they know where food is, you can't shake them.

Is that dark-haired man already gone? His screams as two of the other ex-cons dragged him away will haunt me for the rest of my life. He could be lurker chow, or if he managed to get away with only one chunk taken out of him, he could be a lurker himself.

What are the odds he's another lone survivor, a rogue out in the world on his own?

That's wishful thinking, and I stopped with that sort of bullshit nine months ago. That man is dead, one way or another, and if I can't find a way out of this fucked-up mess, I could be next.

For now, I lie here, my ears open, my heart thumping, waiting for some sign, any sign that a lurker has invaded camp. My pack is half open and I'm holding onto a lighter, forever prepared because I know I can take out a lurker.

One of these East Jersey men? Not a chance. Not unless I have Maverick's gun, and since he snuffles and snorts and starts to wake up when I try to steal it, that's out of the question.

Hours tick by, but with my phone long dead, there's no way of knowing what time it is. These last few days with Maverick, I've grown used to making camp at dusk, then breaking it up at dawn. I know I should sleep. I'll need my wits tomorrow, and my strength.

But I can't. I don't move, lying there stiff and still, the night growing darker before it eventually begins to lighten. My body aches from all of the tension. I'm exhausted, but not sleepy. I tell myself it's the snoring and being in a stranger's bed, but I'm not fooling myself even a little.

The night seems to drag by and yet, I'm surprised by the knock at the door when it comes the next morning. The locks turns, and the door is thrown open.

It's time to get ready for the block.

CHAPTER 16

gaze down at the bed in abject disbelief. There's a two-piece bathing suit spread out on the quilt, a skimpy red and white-striped bikini that is little more than two bits of string and a couple of tiny triangles.

"I am *not* wearing that."

One of Rex's wives is helping me get ready for the auction; she meekly tells me she's the second one he ever picked out of the terrified women hiding in the neighborhood, shortly after the prison town was formed but months before the auctions were formalized. Chloe is probably about thirty, thirty-five, but there's something almost motherly about her. She's shorter than me by a couple of inches, and just a bit plump, which is more of a rarity these days when food is rationed so tightly.

Then again, that's how we did things in the Grave. All I need to do is look down at the bathing suit to be reminded that East Jersey isn't like anything I'm used to.

With auburn hair cut in a messy bob, plus a pair of dinged-up cat's eye glasses, Chloe looks like someone right out of the past. Like the other women I've seen here, she's dressed in a neat blouse and a skirt that's frayed at the edges. It's too long for her. I can see where, in the front, someone with a shaky hand had tried to hem it higher. She's friendly and soft-spoken yet, from the few minutes I spent with her in the kitchen before she brought me back to the bedroom, I can tell that in the seven months she's been with Rex, he's brainwashed her to believe this is the only way she can survive.

By catering to his every whim, fucking him when he wants, and setting up another woman for the same fate while her soft brown eyes scream for help behind her glasses...

"Oh, but you have to." Her voice is soft. Light. *Trained.* "It's Rex's rules. All the girls have to do it when they get their turn to find their husband." She smiles. It sends a shiver down my spine. How can she even pretend to agree with this? I'm convinced Rex has made her like this somehow; that, or she doesn't want to be lurker chow next. "I promise, it'll all be over before you know it, then you'll have nothing to worry about ever again. That'll be all on your new husband."

I don't want a husband. If I did, I could've had my pick of them back in the Grave. Hell, Chase would've been at the front of the line. That wasn't my style, though. I've always used a guy for a little pleasure, then dumped him and moved on when I was bored. Alexandra Holden wasn't the type of girl who was looking for a diamond ring and a white wedding, even before the Turning.

I sure as fuck don't want some jailhouse wedding to an ex-con.

Chloe is a lost cause, though. I could try to convince

her to help me get out of this, but when she seems to believe that this is the most a woman in East Jersey can hope for, I doubt that'll work. I've purposely been separated from Maverick so he's no help.

It's just me and a bathing suit that I'm not even sure will fit me.

She tries to cajole me into changing. I refuse. She pleads. I pace around the room, looking for something that could be a weapon. Unless Rex took it, Mav has my pack and Rory's jacket; I wasn't allowed to bring anything with me to breakfast or when she shoved me into a shower stall to rinse off all the dirt on me. It's good to know that my antidote, dwindling supplies, and the jacket might be safe even if I'm not.

Chloe's voice develops a more frantic edge. "If you don't hurry, we'll be late. Rex hates it when we're late."

I snort. "I couldn't care less what he thinks."

She gasps, and for a second, I think it's because I dared to defy her precious Rex—and then I glance behind me, realize that he's entered the bedroom, and I don't have any idea how long he's been standing there.

His expression is affable. The promise of pain in his eyes isn't.

"What's going on in here?" he asks. "Miss Alexandra. Why aren't you in your suit?"

I shake my head.

He huffs. "Time's wasting. Let's make it easy so ya understand what I mean. It's either the bathing suit or your birthday suit. Make your choice, girl. But make it quick. My boys are waiting for you."

Anger surges through me. Hot anger, sharp as a knife, making me both wild and reckless.

I glare up at Rex. "No."

He cocks his head. "What was that?"

"I won't do it. None of it. And you can't make me."

"Oh?" I hear the warning in his voice over the blood pumping in my veins. "I can't?"

I swallow roughly. "No."

Chloe flaps her hands, trying to get her husband's attention. "Don't listen to her, Rex. She's just nervous. You know that's all it is. Come on, sweetie. Let's get that suit on you."

That's when I make a mistake. Taking my eyes off the bigger threat, I turn to Chloe. "Weren't you listening to me? I wo—"

Fuck me, but his fist comes out of nowhere. One minute I'm standing there, the next I'm crumpled in a pile on the floor. It's that fast, and he hits that damn hard.

I see stars. My hand flies up to my face, the pain so sudden, so *intense* that I can't tell where exactly he hit me. In my face, yes, but the heat is overwhelming. I probe at the flesh with my fingertips, the softest of *oh*'s escaping me when I find the point where the blood pounds underneath my skin.

My cheekbone isn't broken—at least, I'm pretty sure it isn't—but I can already feel the area right under my eye swelling. Tears spring up involuntarily. No matter how much it hurts, I blink them back. I absolutely refuse to give him the satisfaction of seeing me cry.

Shit. If I don't have a black eye come tomorrow, I'll be super lucky.

Rex shakes his fist out, and I'm irrationally glad that my hard head at least caused him some pain.

"You'll do what you're told," he says hotly. The tears

are making it hard to see his sneer, but there's no way I can miss the venomous authority in his voice. "Wear the suit or head out onto the platform butt-ass-naked, I don't give a fuck. But you will give my boys an eyeful of what they're bidding on or else I might just keep you for myself. Your choice.

"Chloe," he says next, and I'm sure I don't imagine the woman's slight flinch, "you finish cleaning her up. Do her make-up all nice and pretty. And, while you're at it, do something about that." He gestures vaguely at the obvious burn scar on my left arm. "The boys don't like damaged goods."

I wait until he's marched back out of the room before I climb to my feet. Chloe starts fussing over me, murmuring how a little bit of ice will do the job in helping to keep the swelling on my face down, and I let her. Something tells me that she's been dealt a blow or two from those same fists. By the time she comes back with some ice, a nearly empty tube of foundation, and some powder, I've already changed into the bathing suit.

Chloe tells me I look beautiful.

I want to throw up.

The auction is like something out of my worst nightmares.

Chloe is the one who brings me to the block in the center of the first apartment complex. But it turns out that women in East Jersey aren't allowed to attend the auction, either, and she passes me off to a lanky man with hair like straw and a noticeable gap between his front teeth.

He cops a cheap feel as he helps me climb the wooden

stairs, and though my face immediately starts heating up while my fingers curl into fists, I know better than to retaliate—no matter how much I want to.

I can't even begin to guess how many men are gathered around the front of the stage. So it's not as many as last night when Rex sentenced one of his men to death-by-lurker. There's still at least a hundred guys of varying ages watching me in the barely-there bikini, and more than half of them are wearing the same sort of coveralls as Rex.

The prison town's leader has already taken his place center-stage, a wolfish grin poking out from beneath his bushy beard when he sees that I'm in that damn bathing suit like he ordered me to. There's a crate next to him, a bell and a hammer perched on top of it.

My eye is throbbing, the spot where he punched me pulsing as I purposely turn away from him.

Chloe did a wonderful job covering the blossoming bruise with as much foundation as she could get out of that tube. Even so, I'm sure Rex can make out his handiwork from across the stage. Out of the corner of my eye, I can see his grin widen.

I hold my head up as high as I dare, unwilling to give Rex the satisfaction of thinking he's broken me. So long as Maverick's plan goes off without a hitch, we can get the hell out of here, and I can start plotting how I'm going to make that bastard pay for humiliating me like this.

But where *is* Maverick?

My breath catches in my throat as I cast my gaze over the crowd, trying to pick him out. A soft exhale escapes me when, after a few seconds where the panic flooded my chest, I finally find him. He's stationed right at the front of the crowd. He catches me looking for him and quickly raises one finger to his forehead in salute.

Some of my nerves melt away now that I know for sure that he's here. A week ago he was a stranger. Now? All I can think is how good it is to have at least one familiar face out there.

Even if he's the reason I'm in this situation in the first place. If he hadn't veered too close to East Jersey…

Now that their guest of honor has arrived, Rex moves toward the front of the stage. He makes a speech that I'm barely listening to. It's mainly praise for his leadership, and a reminder of how important it is for the men of East Jersey to provide for their wives—and how grateful said wives have been in return since the lurkers took over.

The prick slips in some chauvinistic jokes that make the men laugh and my stomach churn. Every minute that passes, I'm more and more aware of the comments and catcalls being directed at me. I'm wearing the damn bikini, but as skimpy and tight as it is, I could be naked up here after all.

After introducing me as Alexandra, a twenty-three-year-old virgin—I do my best not to burst out laughing at *that* part—who likes killing lurkers as much as doing whatever she can to make her new husband happy, Rex opens the bidding. I don't know what I'm expecting, but it isn't this…

"I bid a jug of milk," says the first man.

Milk? Do they have cows here?

"Two dozen eggs over here. Fresh ones."

Chickens, too?

Maverick raises his hand. "Five lighters."

"A fresh-baked loaf of bread. Oh, and I'll get my Suzie to throw in a pot of honey for a sister-wife."

Rex nods. "I'm bid."

"Three rolls of toilet paper," offers another. He's standing up front next to Maverick, and he looks like he's about seventy years old. "Two-ply," he adds with a toothless grin.

"A bottle of mouthwash and half a roll of toothpaste."

Maverick raises his hand again. "I've got a bottle of whiskey, with all but a single mouthful still inside."

That gets a smattering of applause. I'm not surprised, though I'd like to know where he got a bottle of whiskey from—and why he hasn't shared any of that with me this week.

"High bid belongs to Maverick Brooks," announces Rex. "Anyone want to beat the outsider and his whiskey?"

The old man calls out hopefully: "Six rolls of toilet paper?"

"How about a trade, Rex?" That's a big, boisterous man standing in the back. He has his massive hands cupped around his mouth so that we can all hear him. "I'll give you three of my girls for the first night with this one."

Rex laughs while I have to fight from showing my outright hatred for these people. "No can do, Wyatt. You know the rules. High bid wins. So should we call it, boys? Alexandra, going once—"

I bite my bottom lip, thinking: *I fucking wish.*

"—Alexandra, going twice—"

Please let one thing go right for me… just one damn thing.

"Alexand—"

"A carton of cigarettes!" cries out a smug voice triumphantly.

I want to find whoever just shouted and kick them in the face. Looking at Maverick, I can tell he's thinking the same exact thing.

There's some groaning and a few curses bellowed after that list bid, and my stomach drops; they have to think nobody can beat that. Rex nods appreciatively before turning to Maverick with a sad shake of his head. He's still wearing that wolf's grin as he says, "A carton of cigs, Brooks, that's gonna be hard to beat. It's your bid. You got anything to add?" He glances over at me and there's no mistaking his leer. "Girl like this, she's worth a lot. To beat a whole carton... that gun tucked under your shirt, hanging on your hip might do it."

I can't read Maverick's expression. His lips thin, eyes unblinking as he stares at Rex first, glances my way, then back at Rex. I'm holding my breath. Maverick promised me that he would win me no matter what, he *promised*, but would he give up his gun? That piece of metal—that last relic from his old life—is like Rory's jacket. It's the one thing he seems to really care about.

And, somehow, Rex knows all about it.

Chloe had told me how to behave while on the stage. Just stand there, smile, and be pretty, she said, before warning me against doing anything that might piss Rex off while he was standing in front of his men.

Don't argue, don't cry, and don't show any emotion at what's going on—it'll be over in a few minutes and then, so long as I mind myself, I'll be won by a good man who'd be a decent husband.

Except that's not the way it was supposed to happen. Maverick had a *plan*.

I stare down at him, struggling to keep my expression

from revealing just how fucking scared I am all of a sudden.

He's not going to let me be sold for a carton of cigarettes… is he?

Mav's hand slides to his waistband, placed over the bulge that both Rex and I—and everyone in East Jersey—knows is his revolver. He looks away.

I want to *kill* him.

My rage returns, and I have to bite the inside of my cheek to keep from hurling angry curses at him. I actually bite down so hard that I clip it, the sharp pain making me even more furious as the rusty tang of blood fills my mouth.

I spit down at him and miss by a mile.

That *fucker*!

"Now, Alexandra," Rex says, and though he sounds like he's simply reproaching me like a genial old grandfather would, I'm not so lost that I don't hear the warning in his voice, "a carton of cigarettes is nothing to sneeze at. You'll be happy with Coney."

Rex points out in the crowd, and if I thought this nightmare couldn't get any worse, I was wrong. He's pointing at the same creep who grabbed me as he helped me up the steps. A crumpled carton of cigarettes is held over his head. When he catches me staring in open horror at him, he licks his lips, then blows me a kiss.

And I decide then and there that if Maverick doesn't offer up his gun to get me out of this mess, then I wouldn't rest until I used one of the two remaining bullets on him.

"High bid is Coney's cigs," announces Rex. His echoing laugh makes my skin crawl. "Going once—"

I can't keep quiet any longer. Through gritted teeth, I hiss Maverick's name.

"Going twice—"

Maverick lifts up his head. He opens his mouth, but something stops him.

It stops us all.

"Wait! I bid an antidote!"

A ferocious mutter ripples across the crowd. For a second, I'm stunned. I can't believe what I heard; from the rising volume of the men assembled, they can't either. An antidote? Even *I* don't think I'm worth *that* much.

Rex raises his hands up high. "Quiet everyone!" he roars, and the crowd falls silent.

He peers out into the sea of faces below him. They're all looking over their shoulders, searching for the owner of that voice. An antidote is a huge deal. We all know that.

Who is willing to use one to buy me?

Rex shields his eyes with his spade of a hand, looking for the bidder. "No one can beat an antidote… if you really have one, that is. Who bid it? Step forward, boy! Show us what you got, and if it's legit, you can come and claim your prize!"

It's like the parting of the Red Sea. Everyone in the crowd moves back and away, leaving an empty path that leads right up to the stage. A single figure stands at the back, his head bowed, a navy blue hood over his head, his hand cradled to his chest. It's folded into a fist and, as he approaches the front, he opens his hand.

Resting on his palm is a vial that's a twin to the one Jack gave me, down to the lilac ribbon tied around the bottle.

Rex picks up the hammer and rings the bell. "And

Alexandra is sold for one bottle of antidote to… to… show your face, man. I can't tell from here. Who the hell are you?"

He hesitates for a moment before he lowers his hood and lifts his head, and I'm finally able to see the face of the man who is willing to trade his antidote for me.

I nearly collapse to my knees when I do.

"Name's Chase, sir. Chase Reynolds."

CHAPTER 17

'm rushed off the stage before I have any time to process what the hell is going on.

Two goons have me by the arms, forcefully escorting me through the town. I don't recognize them but, then again, most of these prison brutes look the same to me: big and tattooed, super muscular, and in desperate need of a trip to the barber. The one on the right smells of body odor, the one on my left reeks of alcohol, and I can't help but feel incredibly exposed, sandwiched between them while in a bikini.

At least neither one of them is Coney.

Rex headed right for Chase. Maverick… he could've disappeared into the crowd for all I know. It's my turn to be carried off, and I'm not surprised when they march me to Rex's house. I'm hustled inside where three of Rex's six wives are together in the front room. Bernadette, Kendra, and the young pregnant girl with the wavy black hair.

The last thing I see before the two dickheads push me down the hallway is the pregnant girl getting up and waddling into the kitchen as quickly as her legs can carry her.

Down the hall, up the stairs—one flight, then another—until I'm standing in front of a closed door at the end of another hall. One of the guys shoves it in. The other pushes me after it.

"Wait here," B.O. says gruffly. Booze gives me a mock salute, then closes the door. I can hear their footsteps as they depart, leaving me alone.

Once they have, I race toward the window. Sure, I'm on the second floor, but I'm not above leaping out of it. To avoid Chase… to avoid Rex… to run after Maverick and kick his cop ass… I know that I'm willing to do anything to get out of this room.

I'm pretty sure the door is locked. A couple of rough tugs on the window and, yup, so is that.

Fuuuuuuck.

Okay. *Okay*. Let's just check the door—

Nope.

Also locked.

I go to the closet. At the very least, there's got to be something in there that I can put on. I'll even wear one of those dresses like Rex's wives if I have to, but after I throw the door open, I curse. It's empty. All that's in this room is a bed with a single sheet on it, plus a wooden chair propped in the corner.

I'm wondering if it's worth ripping the sheet off the bed and fashioning some kind of toga out of it when the doorknob turns.

I suck in a breath, hiding my hands behind my back so that whoever walks into the room doesn't see them shaking.

It's Chase.

Chase Reynolds walks into the room.

He has Rory's jacket in his hands. Since I'd left it with Maverick this morning at Chloe's suggestion, I have no idea how he's gotten it, but I'm glad to see it. It's the one thing in this fucked-up world that helps me make any sense.

He looks different than when I left him in the Grave. He's given up on styling his hair at all, letting the sandy strands stick up in every direction. Chase's eyes are no longer rimmed with red, but the dark circles underneath make him appear paler than he is. There's a long scratch from the height of his cheek down to his chin; clotted with blood and puffy around the edges, it looks fresh. So does the bruise on the side of his jaw.

"Xandra," he begins, and that's all he gets out before the door swings open again.

I expect it to be Rex or one of his boys. Nope. To my surprise, it's *Maverick*.

He eases the door shut behind him. If it wasn't for the fact that Chase is standing between us, solid as a statue and as quiet, I might've launched myself at him, throwing as many punches as I could.

He's oblivious to how pissed I am at him. He glances at the back of Chase's head, then moves his attention to me. The cop opens his mouth, but as his gaze roves over me, he pauses.

For a split second, I think he's checking me out. Seriously? I know I'm in a skimpy bikini, but this is the worst possible moment for him to... oh. *Oh*. He's not looking at my boobs or my figure.

He's staring at the burn that covers my entire upper left arm.

It hits me. Not counting when I was on the stage, this is the first time Maverick has seen me without my jacket on; the rope he gifted me was stowed in my pack and never mentioned again. But that was when he was far enough away that Chloe's handiwork kept my burn concealed. This close, he can't miss it.

I move my hand so that it's covering my arm.

Maverick gives his head a shake, like he's trying to erase the image of my burn. "Okay, okay... I've got to make this quick. Rex'll be here any minute, and I won't be able to stall him anymore than I already have."

I don't know what that means. Before I can ask, Maverick has stormed around Chase, his hands on my shoulders. "I didn't get to win you, but this is okay. Right? I remember this guy from your settlement. You know him."

Considering Maverick's possessive grab on my shoulders seems to have broken the spell on Chase, making my twin's fiancé growl under his breath as he surges forward as though he's about to rip Mav's hands off of me.... yeah. We know each other.

Me? I kind of just stand there. To be honest? I'm still in shock over what happened, but even as stunned and freaked-out as I am, I know Chase offering up a priceless vial of antidote to "win" me is anything *but* okay.

"Listen to me. Just follow the rules, do what you have to to make it until I can get us out of here, and you'll be fine. Rules are everything here. Do you understand?" When I don't answer him, he squeezes my bare shoulders enough for me to feel the pressure. "Understand?" he repeats in a voice that telegraphs "cop".

Bewildered, I nod.

"Good." Letting go of me, he turns to Chase. "Look, you own Xandra now—"

I find my voice for the first time since the auction. "Hey," I protest, "*no one* owns me!"

Maverick looks back at me with pity in his eyes and an imploring frown. "For as long as we're in East Jersey, he does. This isn't like your Grave. There's no democracy, no hands-up voting, and no shared goods. This is a prison town, and Rex runs it like a prison. He's the man in charge. You have to do what he says or he'll kill you, Xandra, do you understand me? He'll toss you to the lurkers. And not a single person here will say one word about it."

I think of Rex, of how grandfatherly and kind he appears until someone crosses him. Like when he first found out I was a girl or when I objected to being put up on auction like a piece of cattle and forced to wear this revealing bikini. He's the Dr. Jekyll and Mr. Hyde of ex-cons. I have no trouble believing a word Maverick said.

And then there's that man he purposely fed to the lurkers to prove a point…

Chase surges forward and wraps his arms around me. I'm so rattled, I don't push him away. For the moment, at least, I'm grateful for his protection. "I won't let anyone hurt her."

"Remember that. You're all that can save her now."

He nods. The bobbing of his head makes my whole body tremble—or maybe that's the reality slamming into me that this… the auction wasn't the end.

Oh, no. It was only the beginning of the trouble I'm in.

"I will do anything—"

Maverick puts his finger to his lips, hushing Chase. A second later, I understand why. Footsteps are thundering down the hall, growing louder and louder as they approach.

Someone's coming.

"Put that on," Maverick hisses at me, pointing at Rory's jacket hanging loosely from Chase's grip.

Shit. I don't know why I haven't already.

Rex bursts into the room as I pull my right arm through the sleeve, a satisfied grin splitting his face while Chloe yaps away at his heels.

"Yes, yes, yes, darlin'. You can have your turn with your husband tonight. First, I have to… mmm… take care of a little business, then I'll be searchin' for you." A low chuckle that sends a shiver down my spine. "When we're done here, I promise ya, I'll be needin' your special wifely attention. Wait for me." He glances at me, at Chase. "Look at 'em. Already touching each other… oh, yeah. This part won't be takin' long, sweetheart. Don't you worry about that."

Chloe clearly knows a dismissal from Rex when she hears one. Bobbing her head, bowing a little, she says, "Of course, Rex."

She hustles toward the door. However, before she leaves, she exchanges a glance with Maverick and, in a flash, I get it. She must've been the one stalling Rex. The only question I have is *why*.

I don't know, and in a second, she's gone.

Rex seems to notice Maverick at last. I guess he was too busy ogling my bikini-clad body beneath Rory's jacket, but it finally dawns on him that Mav has found his way to this empty room.

"Brooks. Bad luck at the auction. But you know how it goes. Rules is rules, eh? I can't let you have your girl back… not when this newcomer paid up with that antidote of his… but if you'd like to stick around and watch, I'm sure that can be arranged."

My stomach tightens.

Watch? Watch what?

Maverick sends me another one of those apologetic grimaces before he turns to Rex. "I think it would be best if I didn't."

"Yeah. I get that. Well, if ya decide to stick around, we've got another auction scheduled at the end of the month. Phil's wife has a girl hitting her sixteenth birthday. Soon as she does, she's going up on the block. She's a pretty young thing. You might like her."

She's *sixteen*.

Oh, God. When I noticed that one or two of Rex's wives were young, I figured they were at least eighteen. Now… I'm not so sure.

Maverick's expression darkens, though all he makes is a non-committal sound in the back of his throat. I've gotten to know him well enough to hazard a guess that the idea of "winning" a kid makes him angry—sick and angry —but he knows better than to voice them in a town where Rex is in control.

Rex's smile is smarmy. "Think about it. But since you're not interested in the show, why don't you go on downstairs? I'm sure one of my wives will entertain you if you tell 'em I sent you their way. Not Chloe, though. I have plans for that one tonight."

Poor Chloe. I have no idea what those plans are, but considering the way Rex is back to ogling me… I'm thinking poor Xandra right about now.

Especially when he waits for Maverick to reluctantly leave before he ducks his head out of the room, grabs something from the small side table in the hallway, then comes back in.

Rex holds up a box. It's wooden, about six inches long, four inches wide, and four inches deep.

"Congratulations on your nuptials, you two. Now come on over to ol' Rex. I've got a gift for you." He jerks his chin. "Hold out your hands."

"Why do you want—"

Rex lets out a sound that could've been a laugh, but that reminds me more of a wild animal's growl. "It's just your hand, boy," he interrupts Chase. "Don't worry, I'm not gonna bite it off or nothin'."

That thought hadn't crossed my mind before. You can be sure as hell it does now.

Remembering Maverick's warning, I start to do what Rex says, but Chase stops me. Releasing me, he brushes his fingers along the side of my hand, gesturing for me to put it back down.

"Here," he says, holding out his own once I do. "Whatever you have for us, you can give it to me. I'll take it for Alexandra."

"Ah, look at that. The outsider's a real gentleman. I like that. But your new wife had the right idea. Give me both of them."

Wife.

Wife.

Wiiiiiffe.

Oh, fuck no.

How did I not remember that? So preoccupied by the idea that he "won" me, I forgot how East Jersey regards a man and the woman he's responsible for. He's my husband, I'm his wife, and I'm surprised my knees don't buckle beneath me.

Marry Chase?

Marry my twin's longterm love?

Even if it's a jailhouse wedding... I can't.

I *can't*.

The steely look in Rex's mud brown eyes says: yes, you can.

I gulp, slowly lifting my hand up again. Maybe I want to get this over with so that I can get out of this room, find my clothes and my pack, and figure out a way to escape; maybe I just want to show Chase that he doesn't really own me, that I'm not about to let him tell me what to do; or maybe I don't want to give Rex a reason to punch me again... regardless, I put my right hand up.

"Good girl," Rex says approvingly. "Now, close your eyes. Don't peek. I get really pissed off when the newly-weds peek."

I swallow my moan at the word "newlyweds" even as I screw my eyes shut.

I hear Rex rustling in his box, followed by the sound of something metal clinking together; it reminds me of a fork and a knife scraping against each other. When the noise stops, Rex grabs my hand and places something cool and heavy around my wrist. A soft *oh!* escapes from Chase before a pair of creaks and clicks and Rex's satisfied chuckle.

"You can open your eyes again."

"What the—" I start, while Chase breathes out one word, "*Handcuffs.*"

He's right.

We've been handcuffed together.

I jerk my hand. It holds. The weight of it is enough that I'm sure they're real. These aren't a pair of chintzy handcuffs you get from a store. Oh, no. These are honest-to-God handcuffs that had to belong to one of the prison guards or something.

"What?" I breathe out. "Why?"

"Just a little precaution, Miss Alexandra. Here in East Jersey, our weddings are simple. He bought you at the auction and that makes you his wife. But it don't count until the wedding night. Once you consummate your union, we'll find you two a place to set up house. Until you do that, I'm keeping you together so that no one thinks you're up for grabs. You should thank me."

Thank him.

Thank him?

I open my mouth. Rex tilts his head. I remember the stars I saw, the pain that bloomed in my face this morning. It's numbed since then, though if I probe my cheek, it stings, and the last thing I want to do is let him hit me again.

I shut my trap.

Chase jingles his wrist. The metal clangs. His forehead furrows. "Consummate… you mean—"

"That you need to claim this woman as yours before you can keep her? That you won't get to protect her as your wife until I know you're able to fuck her and take care of her like a man? That's exactly what I mean."

He *can't* mean that. I can't *do* that.

Chase takes a step closer to me as though he can sense I'm seconds away from losing it.

"How will you know?" he asks. "We tell you after we're done, and then you take these cuffs off?"

And then we can leave?

We can fake it. I'm sure I can make that bed squeak, moan loud enough that the whole house thinks I'm being dicked down, then stomach being called Chase's wife until we can get the hell out of Dodge. Isn't that what Maverick said? Men can leave, and they get to control their wives' destiny.

I can—

Rex's bushy mustache dances as his lips quirk upward in the most perverted smile I've ever seen.

"Well, I can't just take your word for it, can I?"

That smile makes my queasy stomach drop down to the soles of my feet. Now that I have Rory's jacket back on, though, it's my suit of armor, and despite what Maverick has said, I haven't *completely* lost my backbone. "What does that mean?"

"That I'm going to have the pleasure of watching you, of course."

CHAPTER 18

Rex likes to think he's a gentleman himself. Instead of ordering us to strip and get to fucking, he tells us to take a few minutes to talk, to get to know each other, so that when he comes back, he can expect the show to get on the road.

If you believe that, I've got a bridge leading to Brooklyn to sell you.

I'm sure he can sense there's some hesitation on our part. As long as he doesn't get the idea that Chase and I already know each other, I think it'll be okay, but he probably didn't want to waste any time trying to cajole us—or threaten us—into having sex for his own enjoyment.

Not when he can get laid on his own.

How much do you want to bet that he went off in search of Chloe? For whatever reason—and I think I might have a guess—she basically threw herself at the grizzled leader. I wouldn't be surprised at all to know that he decided not to wait to see what she was willing to offer him.

Maybe I'm being catty, but the big guy looks like a one-minute man. In that case, I don't think we'll have that much time to ourselves.

The moment Rex is gone, I turn to Chase, taking him in again without anyone watching my actions with suspicion.

"You look like hell." The words just come out. I point at the scratch on his face. "Where did you get that?"

He brushes me off with a wave of his free hand before reaching for me. His actions are shy and gentle, and when his thumb nears my eye, it ghosts over the bruise I know is there. I'm suddenly aware that, while Chloe's make-up job was good enough to keep the men in the crowd from noticing the mark, Chase is only about a foot away from me.

He's so close that, when he takes in that sharp breath of air, it's like he's stolen it from me.

"Never mind about that. This looks painful... and fresh." His jaw clenches so tightly that I see lines in his neck as sharp as razors. "Who did this to you? Was it that Maverick prick?"

What? "Maverick? No... no, he didn't do that to me."

He exhales; I feel the heat on my skin. Chase wants it to have been Maverick, I can tell, but just because it wasn't, that doesn't mean he's any less furious. "Then who? Who did this to you?" His hazel eyes flash angrily. "Tell me. I want to hurt them back."

I could tell him. I could let him know that Rex punched me to get me up on the stage, but I know Chase. From our own friendship, and everything Halllie used to tell me about him. If I admit that it was Rex, the next time that man walks through the door, Chase will go after him—and probably end up lurker chow for his trouble.

"It's not worth it."

"Of course it is."

I shake my head. He doesn't get it. He wasn't there last night.

He doesn't know about the lurkers.

"It's okay. Chase, listen to me. It's okay. It's a bruise. It'll heal. But we need to talk about this." I shake the handcuffs. "There's only one way to get these off. You heard him. We have to have sex."

His entire expression shuts down. "I won't do it."

"If we have to—"

"They can't make me."

He's wrong about that.

"I know this isn't something we would ordinarily do." Unless we're drinking and reminiscing, that is. "I know I'm asking a lot of you. But, listen to me: this is a bad dude. Okay?" I swipe my hand over my cheek. "A bad fucking dude. I saw him sentence one of his men to the lurkers last night. If we don't listen to him, I don't even want to think about what he'll do to us."

Us.

His mouth parts, understanding written in his eyes. That's right, Chase. He won't only take out any defiance on you. If we don't do what we're told, it's my ass on the line, too.

That's all I have to say. After that, there is no argument. There's no more talking. It's just me, shivering in my bikini despite the weight of Rory's jacket, and Chase glaring at the door as though he could make it unlock with the might of his will.

But he can't, and as I expected, it isn't long before Rex walks back in, tugging the door shut behind him.

Chase stiffens. His gaze darts over to me, jaw flexing again as he glances at the bruise on my cheek.

I shake my head just enough to make it clear. Yes, this is the asshole who hit me. No, there's nothing Chase can do about it while we're handcuffed, trapped in this room, and expected to fuck on command.

In case I got it wrong, Rex makes a big display of adjusting his crotch as he swaggers into the room. Instead of the same EJSP coveralls he was in before, he traded them for a pair of sweatpants and a white t-shirt that stretches over his belly.

That should've been a warning sign. At first, I thought he changed because he'd been naked with one of his wives, and while that might very well be true, I learn the hard way that that's not the only reason why he changed when he plops himself down on the chair, reaches into his sweatpants, and pulls out his limp dick. He settles it on his thigh, crosses his arms over his broad chest, and grins beneath his mustache.

"Alright, kids. I've given you enough time. Let's get the evening started."

Chase blows air through his nose. He already hated the idea of doing this, but now that Rex plans on really turning this into his own porn show, complete with whacking off while he watches, I can sense the tension thrumming off of him.

He's going to refuse. I know it. He's going to—

His fingers go to my hair, slipping through the strands. Tugging lightly on his handful of curls, he tips my head back, leaning over so that he can slant his mouth over mine. His lips are soft. Sensual. His back might be tight, but his lips are gentle as he kisses me slowly, begging for entry.

I let him in, moving closer, throwing my hands up so that I can hold onto his chest.

To our left, Rex snorts. "What the hell is this shit? You're supposed to get her under you, boy. Stop messin' around and get to it."

Chase doesn't release his hold on my hair, though he does break the kiss. His profile is sharp and daring as he snaps, "What am I doing? I'm getting her to relax. She needs to want this."

Rex takes his cock in his hand, stroking it slowly, bringing it to life. "No she doesn't. She just needs to lie still and take what you give her."

Chase glares. "Is she my wife?"

"Once you're done in here, sure. That's how it goes in East Jersey."

"I don't tell you how to fuck your wives, *sir*. I'm going to be responsible for Alexandra. I'm claiming her as mine. I want her to trust me, not be afraid of me. So, if you don't mind, I'll take care of her the way I see fit, and you can wait as long as it takes."

My eyes go wide. My heart basically stops. Chase basically just told Rex to fuck off, and I don't know how the ex-con is going to react. What if he changes his mind? What if he kicks Chase out? What if—

He laughs. That holly jolly BS laugh. "Fair enough, Reynolds. You're right. She's your wife. I guess I can work on my patience." Another stroke, rougher this time. "So long as you make the show worth my while."

Chase doesn't answer him. Instead, he looks at me, making sure that I'm okay.

I am. So far.

And then, so Chase knows exactly who the boss in this room is, Rex says, "Take off her top."

It's not a suggestion. It's not a request. The laughter from his voice has hardened into something that not even Chase can fight against.

It's a *command*.

Will that stop him from trying to shield me? Of course not. And, this time, I have the feeling that Rex won't let him get away with more backtalking.

With my free hand, I take Chase by the chin, angling his head down so that he has to look at me.

"Do it," I whisper.

They're just tits. They're just tits, Chase. If it keeps Rex from deciding to retaliate, I don't care.

He hesitates.

I nod reassuringly at him.

Chase swallows roughly before reaching under Rory's jacket. His trembling fingers find one of the ties. He undoes it. He travels up my back, searching for the other. A quick tug and it's falling forward.

"All the way," says Rex. "Let me see what your antidote bought you."

Chase can't bring himself to do it. I jerk my hand, grabbing the material, ripping the bikini top off myself. The moment my tits are on display, the big bastard starts pumping his hand faster. He's fully hard now, and I want nothing more than to go over there and stomp my boot in his lap.

I'd pay for it. Oh, yeah, I'd pay for it.

But, damn it, it would feel so good.

It's Chase's turn to brush his fingers along my jaw, turning me back to face him.

"Focus on me," he murmurs. "Only on me."

It would be a lot easier if Rex wasn't grunting behind us.

I nod, and Rex calls out another other.

"Take him out, sweetheart. Let's see it." When I don't move, he clicks his tongue in impatience. "His cock. I want to see your pretty hands wrapped around his meat."

Can he be any more crude?

If Chase could undress me even when he didn't want to, I can do this. A quick peek up at his face, a stoic nod, and I have his permission to do just that.

My fingers shake so bad, the handcuffs jangle. I pretend not to notice as I undo his jeans, pull down the zipper, and reach inside of his boxer briefs for his dick.

The second I lay my fingers along his heated flesh, he jerks. By the time I release him, it's easy to see that he's also erect.

"I'm sorry."

For what? For his body reacting to being this close to me? I basically was in my underwear, the bikini was so revealing, and though he's trying not to stare at my boobs, I don't blame him for peeking. For all I know, Rex will call the whole thing off if he pretends not to notice they're there for him to see and touch.

To make it fair, I switch his cock to my cuffed hand. Using my free one, I snag his free wrist, lifting his hand, placing his palm on my tit.

An electric spark zips through me. Suddenly, I'm thrown back to the last time we were touching each other like this.

I'd been surprised to find Chase hard. I can tell myself I expected the booze to affect him, that he'd be suffering from whiskey dick, leaving him limp as a noodle. Of course, then I can excuse what happened by saying that I was drunk, too.

But I wasn't drunk. Neither was Chase. We were buzzed, sure, but when I kissed him… when he lifted my shirt over my head, his hands going right for my boobs… when I shoved him back on the couch and unzipped his jeans, tugging his erection out, knowing that I would die if I didn't shuck my own jeans and slip him inside of me, I was fully aware what I was doing.

I wanted to do it.

I wanted Chase.

I want him now.

True, fucking Chase with Rex as an audience isn't ideal. But it's not like I'm being forced to do something I wouldn't—or haven't.

"See? I knew she'd be into it once she got your hands on you."

Shut up, Rex. Just shut the fuck up.

He doesn't.

"Bring her over to the bed. A man takes his woman, boy. Get her beneath you and show her who owns her now."

Chase freezes. It's all happening so fast, and if he gets on top of me, it'll be easy for him to convince himself that I didn't want this. That he forced me.

There's no time to explain to Chase that, dubious as it is as we're under duress, I'm giving him my consent.

The closest thing I can do is offer, "I'll ride him."

If only.

Rex shakes his head. "That's not how it's done in East Jersey. If he wants to submit to a pussy when the two of you are in your own room, fine. But if I'm here to witness this union, he's gotta show me he can handle you. Not the other way around."

And I get it. I finally get it.

It's not that we're his very own sex video brought to life. With the death of television and the internet, there wasn't any porn left unless you were a freak with a hard drive full of the stuff.

It's control. He's getting off on forcing Chase to fuck me. He doesn't have any idea we have history, that Chase was my twin's true love, and that I *have* fucked him before. To the cruel ruler of this settlement, I'm a woman under his control, Chase is the stranger who brought an antidote to his people, and now I'm his reward. Whether I'm attracted to him or not… it doesn't matter. If Coney had won me, he'd already have me flat on my back, working his dick inside of me—or worse.

What if Rex doesn't just want to watch? What if he wants a turn? What if Chase hesitates and the bastard decides to go show him how it's done?

I press my mouth to his ear. "Please, Chase. Just do it. It's okay."

Chase gulps. "I don't want to hurt you," he mutters under his breath.

"You won't. You can't."

I believe that with everything I am.

To prove my point, I lead him to the bed. It takes a second to figure out how to get me on the bed under him without snagging the handcuffs, but once I do, I sprawl out on the bed and hold my breath.

Chase adjusts his position. He gets into the bed next, but instead of climbing on top of me, he shimmies down until the upper half of his body is wedged between my open legs. He throws my boot-covered feet over his shoulders, placing his face inches away from my pussy.

I lift up on my elbows. "What?"

"I will always make sure my wife is pleasured and relaxed. When she's ready for me to fuck her, then I'll fuck her."

It's another gamble. Will Rex think that Chase is submitting to pussy by going down on me or will that add to his perverse level of excitement?

For a moment, Rex thinks about it. But Chase... he doesn't ask for permission. He just dips his head, burying his face in my pussy, licking me so intently, I actually do forget about Rex for a moment.

Chase is no selfish lover. He meant what he said, and he works hard to get me to focus on him and his tongue instead of the creep watching us, giving him commentary.

"Yeah. That's right. Fuck her with your tongue. Get her nice and wet so she can take you."

I find Chase's head, gripping his hair in my hands. Grinding my pussy against his face, I pant softly, enjoying the way he does just that. He slips the tip of his tongue inside of me, gathering the moisture, swallowing it with a rumbled growl.

The penetration helps, and so do the vibrations, but when Chase sucks my clit into the heat of his mouth, nothing on Earth could stop me from coming all over his face.

Only once my legs stop shaking does he disentangle himself from the death grip I had on his head. A small satisfied smile crosses his shiny face as he moves up, kissing me while I'm still panting from the climax he gave me.

As he kisses me, he lines our bodies up. He slides the head of his dick up and down my slit. I know what he's doing. He's making sure that giving me oral was enough to prep my body to take him. Fucking me dry would only make this so much worse, but how the hell can he expect me to be aroused with Rex right there?

Because he's Chase. That's it. Because it's Chase, and there isn't anyone else I would trust in a life-or-death situation like this.

"It's okay," I whisper to him. "I promise."

He nods. His jaw goes tight, a muscle flexing in his cheek. He hates this. As much as I'm sure he would've jumped at the chance to sleep with me again, this isn't what Chase has in mind.

Same.

I never thought I'd have sex with an audience. But it's not like I haven't been with him before. He'll make it quick, I'll close my eyes and pretend it's just the two of us, and then we can work on getting the hell out of here.

I'll close my eyes…

I look up at Chase one last time. Our eyes meet—and then all hell breaks loose.

Chase was poised on top of me. Our bodies were nearly flush. He kept himself lifted up on his elbow so that we weren't quite touching yet, though his erection had brushed against my inner thigh a few times before he was lining us up. He hadn't put it in yet, though. He was stalling. Looking at my face, testing if I really was going to go along with this as though we had any choice, all he needed to do was position his dick at the entrance to my pussy and push.

He already made me come with his mouth. My pussy is slick, my body more relaxed than it was before he engaged in foreplay. I'd like to lie and say that I've forgotten the perv in the corner as Chase prepares to fuck me, but this is going to be a real "close your eyes and take it" moment. Once we're done, we can get the hell out of here, and never speak of this again.

At least, that's my plan.

Maverick, it turns out, had a completely different one.

I don't know if the door was locked. With Rex in the room with us, I wouldn't think so, but it doesn't matter. Maverick must've kicked it in because, over Chase's shoulder, I see the door fly in, smashing into the other side of the wall. His boot is still raised, though he lowers it immediately, stalking into the room.

His gun is in his hand. Finger already on the trigger, he turns toward Rex and fires.

With his pants down and his dick out, Rex drops to the floor.

It was a perfect shot. Maverick must've aimed for the forehead because the bullet shoots right through, spraying blood and brain matter all over the wall behind Rex before he falls to the floor, instantly dead.

There is no shock. There is no hesitation. There's no fucking time for it. Rex is dead, Mav killed him, and we need to *go*.

Chase climbs off of me, then stands in front of me. He throws out his free hand, shielding me from view. I scramble up, hiding my tits with one arm. Reaching down, viscerally aware of the handcuffs keeping us connected, I adjust my bottoms so that I'm covered there. I snag the bikini top off the floor, shoving it into my pocket.

Maverick marches toward us, his gun at his side. His eyes are fixed on a point over my shoulder, careful not to sneak a peak of what I have going on under my jacket. Tugging it closed, I hurriedly do up the zipper while Chase matches my motion, keeping me covered while respecting the tug of the cuffs.

There. I've got my boots on, tits covered, and while my ass might be hanging out, at least the bikini bottoms are hiding most of my bits.

Good.

Now I can kill Maverick—

No. Down, girl. He saved you. If it wasn't for Maverick, then Rex might have—

No.

Maverick's expression is a horrified one as he glances at Chase, then addresses me.

"I didn't know. Honestly, if I had any idea—" He throws a murderous look at the man he killed. "I found it. One of the wives told me after he worked her over… I had to do something."

"Don't even think about it." Chase answers for both of us, I guess. Hey, with the handcuffs, it's like we're a package deal. "If you hadn't shown up when you had, who knows what would have happened."

I know. Deep down in my gut, I know exactly what would have happened. Rex would've sat there, jerking his cock while he got off on Chase fucking me, and as soon as Chase was done, he would've come up with some bullshit story about giving away the bride or something. I have no doubt in my mind that he would've shoved Chase aside, taking his place.

He would've fucked me, and stuck in East Jersey, there wouldn't be a damn thing I could do about it.

But Maverick?

He shot the bastard.

He *killed* him.

And now we're in his house, with his dead body, and a prison town full of convicts who might not take too kindly to him being dead.

"Oh, no." It's not the hole in his forehead or the blood and brains everywhere that has me shaky. Nope. It's the promise that being raped by Rex might not have been the worst thing these bastards could do to me. "What do we do?" It's barely a whisper. "What do we *do*?"

Chase wraps his hand around my sleeve, tethering me to him even more effectively than the chain. "You're okay. I promise, baby... you're okay."

I want to believe him so badly, it hurts. But then I glance down at Rex again, and I moan in fear.

"Xandra?"

That's Maverick. Like his voice is a million miles away, I hear him call my name, but I can't answer him.

He snaps, "Xandra!"

I shake my head.

Maverick looks dead in my eyes. "We have to go."

Go. Yes. That's a good idea. Rex can't stop us, and as far as any of the other brutes in East Jersey know, I'm Chase's "wife" now. There's nothing keeping me in the prison town as long as I'm with him.

Chase tightens his hold on me. "Will they come after us? If we run, will we be safe?"

Good question.

"East Jersey respects strength. There's no loyalty here. Half these guys will want to take Rex's place. The other half will just think it's a shame that I took him out before they got the chance. Some of his cronies might want to retaliate, though, but we'll be long gone before they can."

Here's hoping that he's right.

CHAPTER 19

"Come on," I mutter, wiggling my wrist back and forth, trying to will the bone smaller so that I can slip it out of the cuff. I'm tugging on Chase's connected hand every time I yank mine, but he's standing beside me, silent as a grave. "Come on, almost out... Ugh! It's just too tight!"

"Don't worry, Xandra. We'll find a way to get those things off."

Maverick is marching ahead, peeking at his compass. He doesn't have to look behind him, though, to know that I'm desperately trying to remove the handcuffs.

Do you know how much of a bitch it is to run while attached to the one guy you'd avoid if you could? It's even worse that Chase is so much taller and faster than me. As hard as I try, I'm sure I'm only slowing him down since he has to match my pace to keep from overpowering me and sending us both to the ground.

We ran for almost an hour. The three of us made it out of East Jersey without any issues, but just because

Maverick believed that none of the members of the prison town would want to avenge Rex, that didn't mean someone wouldn't like the idea of eliminating Chase and Maverick to get their hands on another wife.

The threat of being snatched by someone like Booze or Coney... adrenaline got me through the first mad dash into the dense woods surrounding East Jersey. Add that to how thickly infested the neighborhood on the other side of the woods was and... yeah. I needed to get far enough away before I could worry about the handcuffs, Chase, and my lack of clothing.

I'm still wearing the bikini bottoms. I'm just grateful that I was given my jacket before Rex slapped these cuffs on me. I haven't been able to figure out how to pull a shirt on while connected to Chase, but as soon as we can get the cuffs off, putting my own clothes back on is the first thing I'm going to do.

Well, one of the first things...

"Good. And then *he*'s going back to the Grave."

Up until this point I've been civil to Chase because he was a safer bet than Rex, and I didn't want anyone to find out we already knew each other in case that made the auction null and void in the leader's eyes. I wouldn't have put it past that bastard. Hell, I would've rather stayed cuffed to Chase forever than spend another minute alone with Rex.

"Me?" Chase drops his hand, taking mine with him. "Why would I do that?"

He can't be serious.

"Because you weren't supposed to even be here in the first place!" We're far enough away from East Jersey that I don't bother lowering my voice. "What were you even doing in that hellhole, Chase? How did you find us? Tell me!"

Chase reacts like a cornered animal, backing up as far as the handcuffs allow, his eyes darting over my shoulder, searching for some sort of an escape. But there's only me, me and my fury, and my sister's fiancé has no choice but to answer to it.

Rex is dead. For the moment at least, the threat he posed isn't hanging over our head. Everything that happened in East Jersey... I had to do what I had to survive.

Now?

I want answers.

He hesitates before he confesses: "I tracked you."

I blink. "All the way here? From Madison to East Jersey?"

Chase gives me an impish smile. He lifts his hand, running his fingers through his hair, making the sandy brown strands stand on edge as he tugs. "Well, yes."

Alone. He left the Grave and camped out *alone*. He had no one to watch his back. No one to make sure he was safe whenever he got downtime to sleep. I only hope that he pushed through the night, following our path by the campsites we left in our wake, and it's only been a couple of days...

"I just... how long have you been following us?"

"Since the Grave."

Damn it.

Chase lowers his hand, rubbing the part of his wrist where the cuff is biting into his skin. I remember that every time I jerk my hand to make a point, it yanks on Chase's. There's already a red welt forming.

I try to calm down, even though his next words just make me all the more incensed: "I've never been that far behind you."

Maverick lets out a low whistle that has me glaring at him. He has put his compass away. Now, standing about four feet ahead of us, he has his hands in his pockets, looking impressed.

"You've kept out of sight all that time? I have to say, your skills weren't exaggerated by that pretty friend of yours." Pretty friend? *Audrey.* "You're a wicked hunter *and* tracker. I'm jealous."

Chase jumps at the chance to get out of my line of fire. He nods over at Maverick. "It wasn't easy. You two were tough to keep up with. I almost missed you heading into East Jersey. I had to backtrack and only just made it past the border patrol in time to be vetted and invited to the auction."

Yeah. I have a lot of questions about that. I guess, if he told Rex he was willing to play by his rules—and Chase has always done that—he could be invited to act as more muscle in East Jersey... especially after they threw that dark-haired man away the night before.

That was still a lot of dumb luck, and I'm kind of surprised he made it this far on his own with little more than the few injuries he has.

All the more reason for him to go back to the Grave before it gets even worse.

"Chase—"

"I was thinking," Maverick cuts in, like the idea had just popped into his head and it was so important, he needed to interrupt me to get it out, "since you've made it this far, maybe you should join us the rest of the way. You'd be a real help going after the nest."

Are you fucking kidding me?

The casual mention of Audrey hadn't helped my mood. Add that to the fact that Maverick has just invited Chase to New York and I'm so pissed, I want to spit nails.

"No."

"Xandra—"

I don't even know which one says my name. My blood is pounding in my ears so it could be either. "I said no. We get these cuffs off, then you head back."

"I can't."

Yes. He can. "The Grave needs you."

His jaw goes tight. "You need me."

What would have happened if Chase hadn't shown up in time to "win" me? Maverick would've been content to let that convict buy me with a carton of cigarettes to save his precious gun. Chase... he sacrificed that antidote. He was willing to do whatever it took to protect me, even going so far as to "consummate" our union with Rex rubbing one out in the same room.

I have no doubt that he'll have my back. I know that to the marrow of my bones. If for no reason other than the love he has for my twin, he'll protect me to his last breath.

"You should've stayed in the Grave," I mutter under my breath. "You never should've followed me to the outside."

"I had to."

I glare at him. "Maybe, but I didn't want you to. I don't want you here, Chase. Don't you understand that?"

His impish smile dies, replaced by that sad puppy-dog stare of his as his face falls.

Fuck me. I really am a heartless bitch, aren't I?

I broke his heart. No doubt about that. I hurt him, and that cools the fire of my fury as effectively as cold water dousing flames. It's nearly impossible to stay mad at a face like that. Though I know I'll regret it, I relent just a little.

"Sorry, but does Jack even know you're here?" I ask him, hiding my exasperation.

I can see his mind hard at work, trying to come up with the right answer to that question. But, if anything, Chase is honest to a fault, and I know I can trust that whatever he says is the truth. Even if I can hardly believe it—

"Yes."

"And he *let* you?"

Chase is the first one to look away.

"He actually encouraged me to come," he admits to me.

And suddenly I know how he got his hands on an antidote.

The sun is slowly peeking over the horizon as I wake up to find myself nose to nose with Chase. There are barely more than a couple of inches separating us; with each snuffle, I can feel the heat of his breath on my skin.

I must have rolled over during my fitful sleep. I know I passed out with my back to him once we finally found a small park that Maverick trusted enough to set up camp. He stayed on one side of the fire. Thanks to the handcuffs, I had no choice but to settle down with Chase.

We started the night flat on our backs. I unzipped the sleeping bag so that we both had something kind of soft to lie down on. Though it would've been more comfortable to scoot together and release the tension in the metal links on the handcuffs' chain, I refused. The alternative was staring into his face and having him stare back, not knowing if he's seeing me or Hallie. I couldn't do it.

And, yet, as I wake up, that's exactly what happened.

Damn it. Why does he have to be so attractive?

The pull toward Chase only gets worse when he wakes up, smiling as he realizes that I'm right there with him. As if I can go anywhere else. Handcuffs, remember? We're trapped, and it's another awful reminder when we both have to take care of business that privacy… yeah. We don't have any.

Having to squat on the grass after Chase helped me unzip my jeans is my last straw. I already had to do it once last night. The second time is even more awkward, especially when I have to turn back and not sneak a peek when he pulls out his dick so he can take a leak. Eventually one of us will have to take a shit and I'd rather gnaw off my wrist than deal with that while attached to Chase.

I wait until we make it to another neighborhood before I say, "I don't sense any lurkers here. Maybe it's time we do a little scavenging."

Chase's face screws up. "Sense? Since when can you sense the lurkers? That was—"

I cut him off before he has to say her name. "Once I left the Grave," I answer him. "It didn't start until we were on the outside."

"Really? Damn. That didn't happen to me. Do you know how much easier it would've made coming after you if I could tell where the lurkers were? Because, let me tell you, I had to guess and, uh, I didn't always guess right."

My heart stops. "You had run-ins with lurkers?"

"Well, yeah. They've pretty much taken over. Half the neighborhoods have those assholes lurking wherever they can find a dark spot."

Don't I know it. "But you're okay?"

A small shrug, and the return of his crooked grin. "I know how to take out a lurker."

"With your bare hands?" I arch my eyebrow. "I know you're good, Chase. I didn't think you were *that* good."

He laughs. "Nah. I had supplies. Handing them over to that goon in East Jersey is what bought my way in. Luckily, I smuggled my antidote in my underwear... and, not surprisingly, that Rex guy didn't think to check... but everything else, I gave it up."

I seize on that. Not the smuggling his antidote in his boxer briefs—and, yes, I know what kind of underwear Chase wears now even though I shouldn't—but that he needs some supplies of his own.

"And that's exactly why we need to do some scavenging. Mav, you saved our packs, but we need shit for Chase. What do you say? Let's start going through these houses."

Maverick sees through my concerns at once. "And maybe we can find some way to cut those cuffs off, too."

I widen my eyes as though the thought had never crossed my mind. "It couldn't hurt."

It takes four houses to find a pair of wire cutters.

They're not strong enough to cut through the thick

metal of the actual cuff easily, but with a lot of groaning and a few muttered curses, Maverick finally manages to snap the chain that keeps me connected to Chase.

As soon as I'm free, I take a few hurried steps away. I've never appreciated my personal space so much before, and if he frowns with disappointment to see how eager I am to put distance between us… I pretend not to notice.

Instead, I fiddle with the silver bracelet still locked around my wrist. "I guess this is good enough. Who knows? Maybe we'll start a fashion trend when we get back to the Grave."

My flippant comment—or maybe the idea that I'll be home again with him sooner or later—has Chase quirking his lips upward. He lifts his hand, twisting his matching bracelet. "We always were trendsetters back in high school."

Um. No. That would be Chase and *Hallie* who were the most popular kids when we were in Madison High. Football player and cheerleader. Both in honors classes. Prom king and queen. I was the third wheel until I found my own thing, making my own way.

I struggle to match his grin. "They won't have to know we got stuck in a prison town. We can blame Mav. He's a former cop."

"You were on the job?" Chase asks, surprise in the question.

Maverick matches it. "Yeah. You know about it?"

Chase shrugs. "My uncle was a DT in Madison. Had another one who drove around in a patrol car in Woodbridge. Grandpa, too. Made it to lieutenant before he retired."

"A family of cops," Mav marvels, nodding. "I knew

there was something about you I liked. Didn't enroll in the academy yourself?"

"Nah. My girlfriend pushed me to follow my own passions. Help people my own way." A wistful expression twists his handsome features and I know he's thinking of Hallie again. "I was getting my Master's in social work when the world ended."

And Hallie was taking nighttime classes in psychiatry while spending her mornings working at the local bagel shop to save up cash for her future with Chase...

Maverick nods in approval. "Would've made a fine officer, though. You ever handle a gun?"

"Yeah." A dark look flashes over his face. "Used plenty on New Year's."

After he dropped Hallie off, he went home to discover his family was just as lost. In the Reynolds home, there was a gun safe—and Chase used it until he ran out of ammo.

Like the rest of us, he doesn't like to dwell on the past. I don't want him here, but I don't want Mav to poke and prod and ask painful questions, either.

"Maybe we should start moving on again—"

"Wait. Your hands are free now. I don't have a gun... a spare gun," he corrects when he sees the glare I can't quite hide, "but this might help."

Maverick removes his backpack. Opening the front pouch, he digs around the inside of it. A few moments later, he pulls out a brown leather holster with something black stowed inside of it. It looks suspicious like a gun, only much thicker and fatter.

"Here. Put this on. If you ever need to disarm a rogue, it should help."

Chase accepts it from Maverick. "What is this?"

"A taser."

Whoa. "Really?"

Maverick nods. "I don't know if Rex had any handguns in East Jersey. Probably not." Which would explain his hard-on to get Mav's during the auction. "But they did have tasers. The COs at the prison carried these instead of firearms. Chloe knew where to find one. She snuck it to me."

From a distance, it would look like a gun. Up close, it's obvious it isn't. Still, if Chase can get off a shot, tasing a threat, he can take a rogue down if necessary without having to kill them.

I don't ask why he's giving it to Chase. It's easy to blame it on misogyny, but even I'd admit that putting a taser in my hand isn't the best idea. I have my pocketknife and my matches, and I'm happy with that.

Chase gets to work on putting the chest holster on while I think about what Maverick said.

Chloe…

"Why would she risk Rex's temper by sneaking you a taser?"

For a second, I'm sure Maverick isn't going to answer me. And then, with a sigh, he says, "Because she's family."

Excuse me?

Maverick thins his lips. "Cousin. That's how I found my way to East Jersey the first time. I was heading toward that part of New Jersey to check on Chloe and her family a month or two after the Turning. The prison had already overthrown her city, renaming it East Jersey under Rex's rule. Her husband was dead. Tim was dead. And she was married to Rex now."

Suddenly, it all makes a lot more sense. How Rex was pulled away, distracted by one of his wives, giving Chase and me and Maverick a few moments to talk before he came up to the room. How Maverick was able to sneak through the house to blow away the back of his head, and we fled, finding our packs and gear waiting for us in the living room.

Chloe did it.

She helped save us.

And how did Maverick repay her? By leaving her behind.

"What the hell is wrong with you?" I explode. "Why didn't you bring her with us?"

"Why would I?"

How can he act so stunned that I would ask that? "Her so-called husband is dead. Won't they realize she was in on it?"

"In on it?" Mav's eyes widen. "Oh. Shit. You don't know. Chloe… she wanted him to die. I could've disarmed Rex with the taser, but she knew that only way she could get out of her marriage was if he was dead. There's this other guy… Tony… she wants to marry him. Be his wife. She loves him, but if Rex knew about the affair, then—"

I understand. "Lurker food."

"Exactly."

My mouth flounders for a moment. "That sucks. Divorce used to be a thing. Now it really is 'til death do you part."

Chase's newly freed hand lands on my shoulder. "I hope you don't take the easy way out when we get married, baby."

Baby.

My chest heaves. I spin so fast, I knock his hand off of me.

"Go back, Chase."

"What?"

"You heard me. Take the taser. Protect yourself." Leave me alone. "But you're going back to the Grave tonight."

"Why? Besides, I'll just track you like I did before. I'm the best tracker you know, and you know I can do it, Ha—"

"That! That's why!" The words burst out of me, louder than I intended. "I'm not your 'baby'. I'm not your future wife. Damn it, Chase, I'm not Hallie!"

The same sad, sorry expression flitters over Chase's face. There and gone again just as fast, he gets his features under control as he fists his hand, pulling away from me.

"Xandra," he says, and I'm not sure who he is reassuring with that name: him or me. "I know…" His voice is soft, soothing. "I know. You're Xandra."

My chest is still heaving, but when I say, "Yeah," it's no longer a shout.

And I swear, if he calls me by my twin's name one more time, I don't give a shit if he goes back to the Grave or not.

But I sure as hell won't spend another minute around him.

PART THREE
BURN

Hallie and her twin were identical, but only if you didn't know them.

Besides their personalities being completely different, little things stood out.

The twinkle of amusement in her pretty green eyes. The way her yellow hair shines in the sun. The tiny birthmark that kisses the corner of her mouth the same way I'd wanted to do since I was a boy, and the body that fits perfectly against mine when she falls into my arms.

Her scent. Her taste. Her laugh. Her tears.

Her pain.

Her rage.

Her everything… *my* everything.

I can always tell which Holden is my Hallie, and I always will.

— Chase Reynolds

CHAPTER 20

'll never tell him so, but having Chase along makes things a little easier.

With three of us, that's three sets of ears to listen for any wrong sounds. Taking watch is easier with a three-man rotation, and the flamings go a lot smoother when there's an extra pair of eyes for the stare. Between us, we actually start looking for lurkers to hunt instead of hiding out peacefully most nights.

I mean, we *are* heading into New York to get rid of a nest. Why not do some hunting along the way?

Maverick, I notice, is in a much better mood, too. In the days following our escape from East Jersey, he's making an effort to be friendlier. I'm betting it has everything to do with the auction and the gun. It's almost like he thinks that I've gotten over it because we made it out in one piece.

Fat chance.

Alexandra Holden doesn't forget, and she rarely forgives. And it's not just what happened in the prison town. With Chase carrying the taser, me with my knife, and Mav holding onto his gun, we're armed enough that I've decided to hold off on stealing his gun. I'm still pissed that he invited Chase to join us without even asking me. Add that to how he betrayed me because of that gun, and I won't feel like we're even until I have it.

For now, I let it go. He had a point. With the three of us, we can hunt more effectively, travel faster, and if there's one thing I'm sure of, I can trust Chase in a way that I never could a rogue that I met less than two weeks ago. I know who's on my side, and no matter *why* he's there, it's enough to make me feel a little more hopeful about eliminating that huge nest in New York, and maybe even making it out again so that we can return to the Grave together.

Not that there's any reason to rush. I'm down with cutting a swath through the rest of New Jersey, killing lurkers as we go instead of doing our best to sneak past them. Hell, yeah, let's make a dent. It's not a race to New York, right?

Too bad that I'm hopelessly outnumbered.

I guess that makes sense. Chase came all this way, tracking me from Madison, so that he could bring me home once I was ready to go. Of course he'll want to finish the trip to Manhattan, do his best to make sure I survive, then herd my ass back to the Grave. And Mav... he agrees with him.

Actually, the plan to get to New York ASAP is about the only thing that Maverick and Chase see eye to eye on. Well, that and killing lurkers.

Oh, and how they both seem to think that I need to be coddled like a child. Seriously. I'm not allowed to wander off on my own or I get a lecture from Chase; with a satisfied gleam in his eyes, Maverick just sits back and lets Chase scold me. I take it because I hear the undercurrent of fear and concern lacing his voice when he talks about how dangerous it is out here. I still don't know what kind of shit he went through during the time when he was surviving on his own, keeping his distance so that I didn't know he was close. Considering the scrapes and bruises and the shadows in his eyes... it wasn't anything good.

And that was before he got worked over by Rex's boys before they released him, allowing him to attend the auction just in time to save me.

I understand why he's so afraid of something happening to me, even if I lie to myself and say he shouldn't care. He does, and it's not worth riling him up by shutting him down like I did after he called me by my sister's name.

That doesn't mean I let them get away with the coddling. Nope. I'm more determined than ever to prove myself—especially to Chase.

That's why, when I'm on watch, I refuse to wake the guys up when I sense any less than three lurkers on the edge of our campsites. Sure, Chase is terrified that I could've gotten hurt, but the way Maverick nods, impressed, when he sees another pile of ashes in the morning makes me feel like an important part of our little crew.

All in all, I'm slowly making a dent in Chase's thirty-eight recent kills and, one morning when I tell him so, Chase stops mid-lecture, almost like he's been thunder-struck. His mood shifts on a dime. From scared and worried to suddenly delighted, he laughs and gives me a quick side hug that has me freezing up before he just as quickly pulls away.

One good thing comes out of that awkward moment. From then on, he doesn't treat me like a porcelain doll that has to be handled with kid gloves. Our relationship is better for it, though I can't deny that the continued bickering between Maverick and Chase can probably be traced back to that hug. Their honeymoon didn't last very long.

I will admit that, every now and then, I do catch him looking at me wistfully, but as long as I'm not purposely avoiding him, we're both able to pretend that this is like the before times. When Hallie was still there, acting the part of the referee for any good-natured sniping between her boyfriend and her twin.

Since the time I exploded at him, he hasn't called me by my sister's name again, and as long as he remembers that I'm Xandra, everything is fine.

Well, not *everything*.

Though I never thought I would, I'm really suffering from homesickness. I was able to ignore it when it was just Mav and me, but with Chase here… fuck. I miss the Grave. Chase is an aching reminder of what life was like before I made the impulsive decision to go with Maverick on this quest. Most of all, I miss Jack, and I wonder how he's holding up, the last Holden left in Madison.

I can't wait to kill some lurkers and finally get back.

Chase takes first watch. Maverick usually goes second. I'm cranky if they forget to wake me up to take my turn, so I go third.

It's chilly out tonight; for the first time, Denise's hoodie and Rory's jacket aren't enough to keep me warm, especially when I'm drenched. The rain trickled on and off all morning making today's travel more difficult than it should've been. Though it's been four days since we left East Jersey, Maverick swore he heard a whistle mid-day and pushed us harder and harder until the slick rain made our muddy path treacherous and I slipped.

I fell flat on my ass, covered in mud, cursing as the rain stung my eyes. Chase hurriedly helped me back to my feet and demanded we find shelter until the rain—and the threat—had passed.

Maverick argued with him, but when I chimed in, voting for shelter as I tried to wipe off the mud, he gave up when he saw I was only smearing it all over my jeans. Letting me lead, using my better-tuned ability to sense when lurkers are near, we eventually entered a small cul-de-sac. Trusting my gut, we smashed a window and broke into a two-story house in the center.

It was a good find. Not many houses are locked-up tight after the Turning. If the house is abandoned, that means survivors either died where they stood or they fled. Maybe it's habit to lock up after yourself when you leave, but when a lurker is plodding after you, snapping its powerful jaws, locking the door is pointless when the lurker can just burst right through it.

This cul-de-sac is in nearly pristine condition. When the house we picked turned out to be locked, we fixed that easily with a large rock that Chase found in a nearby garden. It had never been claimed by a lurker before. My first lungful of air was dusty and stale. Instead of the lurker's rot, it reeked of helpless abandonment.

But there were non-perishables in the cabinet, some towels to dry off, and blankets for us to bring with us to wrap up against the rain. Even more amazingly, as I scavenge one of the upstairs bedrooms, I find a dresser and a closet with clothes that are near enough to my size that I can't help myself.

"I'm taking a shower," I announce to the two guys.

"No," Maverick answers, and it's nothing less than I was expecting. "We've already stayed here too long."

Too bad.

I pick up a hunk of wet hair. "I look like a poodle."

"You look beautiful."

I ignore Chase. "I'm wet. Soaked all the way down to my panties. My jeans are covered in mud. My toes are squelching in my boots. I'm changing—"

"There's time for that," begins Maverick.

No. "There's time for me to shower off the rain. I won't be long. Just enough to get clean. You guys can see if you can swap out your drenched t-shirts, too. When the rain stops, we can go."

Maverick marches over to the window. "It's stopping now. The sun's peeking through."

Of course it is. "Then we don't have to worry about lurkers again for a couple of hours."

"Xandra—"

I open my mouth to continue to argue. It's pointless. I should've just started to strip off my wet clothes. Rory's leather jacket is all but waterproof, but Denise's hoodie is soaked. I need a fresh shirt, fresh underwear, and new jeans before putting Rory's jacket back on. I'm not above stealing it from this house, just like I'm two seconds away from taking off all of my clothes in front of these two guys.

Tell me I can't shower then, Mav. Sure, I might give Chase an aneurysm, but it would be worth it to get out of these wet clothes.

And that's when Chase plants his boots on the carpet, crossing his arms over his chest. "You go if you want. I'll stay here with Xandra."

Great. I don't need a knight in shining armor to fight my battles for me, but the look on Chase's face says that he'll stay here all night if he has to to make sure I get that shower.

Maverick eyes him up and down.

For days now, there's been sniping. Little cheap shots back and forth that make me wonder why Maverick invited Chase along if he was just going to pick at him the way he did me the first couple of days. It's worse because Chase obviously has a chip on his shoulder when it comes to the older man.

It only becomes more noticeable when Maverick chews on the corner of his mouth before asking Chase, "How old are you?"

If Chase is as curious as I am why Maverick is finally asking a personal question like that, he doesn't show it. He just answers. "Twenty-three."

"If I make it to next February, I'll be forty."

"And?"

I'm with Chase. *And*?

"I'm your superior. In age. In rank. In experience. I say we move out now before someone catches up to us."

It can't be Rex. Maverick used his second-to-last bullet to spatter his brains all over that bedroom. But if any of the East Jersey inmates decided to come after us... if other rogues caught us coming into this cul-de-sac... if my sensing ability failed, the rainstorm tricked the lurkers into thinking it was night, and we get trapped by hungry monsters... yeah. Someone could catch up to us.

Damn it.

My shoulders slump.

Chase turns to me.

"Xandra?" he says, and there's a slight waver to his voice as he uses my name. "What do you want to do?"

What do I *want* to do? That's obvious.

I was lucky enough to scavenge a house that once belonged to a woman close enough to my size that I can borrow fresh clothes. The shower back at East Jersey was a tease. Chloe put me behind a frosted glass shower stall, keeping the chilled spray on long enough to rinse the tangles out of my hair and wash the dirt off of my face.

Four days later, and I still have some of that make-up on. That, plus I can't shake the fact that Chase's mouth was on my pussy, his body weighing me down right before he would've fucked me if Maverick hadn't shown up when he did... the rain on my skin has just made all the sensations worse.

I need a real shower.

"Five minutes," I promise. "In and out. Then I'll get dressed and we can go."

Without a word, Maverick turns toward the open bedroom door.

I take a step after him. "Where are you going?"

"You don't need an audience, and I'll feel better if I'm not closed-up in this house. I'm going outside."

"Are you going ahead without us?"

Maverick pauses, turning so that I can look at his face —but he's focusing on Chase.

"How many kills did you have in the Grave? Thirty-something since July, right? What about before that?"

"I don't know. They just needed to die so I could keep my… keep the Grave safe. It wasn't a competition."

For Chase maybe. For me?

"If they would've let me gone after those fuckers after" —*Hallie*—"that night, I'd have smashed his record."

For a moment, I think I fucked up. He laughed the other day, but reminding Chase of the flaming gone wrong that stole Hallie from him is probably the worst thing to do… and maybe it is, but though his eyes tighten at the corners, he lets out a short laugh.

"Yeah. She's an ass-kicker, this one."

I give him a small grin. "So are you."

"That's my point," cuts in Maverick. "I'm not as fast as I was. I don't recover as quickly as I used to. With three of us splitting the night watch, we can each rest a little more. Plus, nothing will stop me from taking care of business in New York. It might've been impossible on my own. With just Xandra, it still would be rough. Throw in another kid who understands why we need to stop the lurkers for once and for all if we can, and I'm not giving up the help. So, yeah. I'll be there."

"Five minutes," I repeat.

He nods, and then he's gone, leaving Chase and me alone in some forgotten woman's bedroom.

I clear my throat. "Thanks, Chase. For sticking up for me."

A small, sad smile tugs on his lips. "Anything for you."

No. Anything for *Hallie*.

But, like Rory's jacket, I'm all he has left of his love— and with that thought, I finally understand why he's so damn attached to me. It's like my obsession with my brother's jacket and my mother's anklet.

He's clinging to me because he can't have Hallie.

And I'll have to do what I can to keep my distance because I... I can't be what he wants.

Because, no matter how he obviously wishes otherwise, I'm *not* Hallie.

CHAPTER 21

'll say one good thing about Chase catching up to us, sneaking into East Jersey, sacrificing an antidote before tagging along on our escape: with Chase here, I haven't had a single nightmare.

My body has finally gotten used to the short hours. I wake up earlier than I have to because, if I don't, there's a chance one of the boys will leave me sleeping. It goes back to them treating me differently. It pisses me off to no end that I'm the one thing Maverick and Chase conspire on. If I don't insist on it, I'll completely miss my turn at the watch.

That's the first thought I have when I wake up tonight. It's so sudden, that hint of urgency making me go from sound asleep to wide awake in an instant. I wonder if my body can tell that I overslept, but as the hazy visions in my head slip away, I realize it's something else.

I didn't have a nightmare.

I had a *dream*.

And it was all about…

Chase.

I turn my head. Like usual, he's lying as close to me as he dares to. The first morning I woke up to find him there, I was pissed, but I'm used to it now. In a way, I kind of like having him so near. When he's asleep, he's unable to weigh me down with the weight of his expectations.

When he's asleep, *I* can watch *him*.

I must have slept through the first watch change. Shielding my eyes against the low light of our fire, I see Maverick hunched across the way, polishing his gun with his sleeve. Chase is curled up in a ball, turned my way, forever facing me as he sleeps. It's like he wants me to be the last thing he sees before he closes his eyes, and if that thought doesn't make me uneasy, I don't know what does.

Does that mean I don't take a few seconds to watch him myself? Not even a little.

I'm checking that he's actually fast asleep; at least, that's the lie I tell myself. His eyelashes flutter gently. A soft snort comes through his slightly parted lips. His hand is outstretched toward me, and I can see the lingering mark on his wrist from the handcuff bracelet we're still wearing.

I have one, too. I lift the cuff, rub my skin absently, then slowly shimmy out from the sleeping bag.

Careful not to wake him, I pick up the extra fleece blanket we snagged from one of the houses we scavenged. A quick shake before I let it settle over him. He deserves some warmth, and if this is the only way I can give it to him, I'll do it.

Chase's lips are pulled down in a way that makes my heart *hurt*. If his dreams are anything like mine, I bet I know why he's frowning. A lock of his sandy hair has fallen forward, resting over his shut eye.

The sudden and inexplicable urge to brush that stray stand away from his furrowed brow comes over me. It's all I can do to resist it. I like to think it's because of the dream that I haven't broken free of yet, but the fact that I had such a dream—laughing with Chase, smiling with Chase, talking about a future we'll never share with Chase—at all tells me more about my subconscious then I care to admit.

"You like him."

I give a small start. Maverick's deep voice is a sorrow-filled lilt that drifts over to me on the muggy night air. For a moment there, I think I forgot he was so close.

How long was Maverick watching me watch Chase?

I don't think I want to know.

My cheeks heat up. I hope that he can't tell from this far away.

"I don't," I argue pointlessly. It's just a reflex at this point. I have to say it even if we both know I'm lying. And maybe that's why I feel compelled to blurt out: "He was going to marry my sister, you know."

"Hallie?"

"Yes."

Maverick pauses and, by the light of the flickering flames, his eyes seem like they're sparkling all of a sudden. "You remember?"

I glance down at Chase. "How can I forget?" I mutter.

He's breathing softly, in and out, and I can't remember the last time he was so content. So at peace. It had to be when Hallie was still around.

I close my eyes and give my head a little shake. "Every time I look at him, I remember."

When I open my eyes again, it's to find that I've shifted away from Chase, turning toward the fire. Maverick is watching me curiously, his gun settled nicely in his lap. My fingers itch to grab it. Unaware that I'm coveting his weapon, the cop nods at the place opposite him, right across the fire.

He doesn't have to say it out loud. The invitation is clear.

I take the seat, grateful to have an excuse to move just a little further away from Chase. Ever since that forced moment of intimacy in East Jersey, the temptations are starting to edge up on me. I'm not sure how much longer I'll be able to fight them down.

Worse, I don't know how Chase would react. I still don't know for sure what he thinks about that night back in the Grave, and just like then, I've been careful to avoid discussing what happened in East Jersey. We were both Rex's victims, and he's following my lead. I don't want to talk about it so we don't, and that's that.

Maverick's the same. He walked in on the worst of it, shooting Rex before it could go beyond the point of no return... again. Like me and Chase, he's refrained from discussing anything but hunting, lurkers, and our path to New York.

Something is different about tonight. I should probably stand up, walk over to my sleeping bag, lie back down, get some more sleep... but I don't.

Instead, I say, "Thanks," and get comfortable on the fallen log I'm sitting on. There's a thin stick lying right next to where I plopped down. I pick it up and start aimlessly poking at the heart of the fire.

"You really care about your sister, don't you?" he asks after a few tense moments.

That's an understatement. "I guess."

Maverick rests back on the heels of his hands, head tilted skywards. "We all deal with grief differently," he says quietly. The flames crackle and spit, sparks flying high, but Maverick's rumble is clear. "I'd say you care about your sister a great deal. I've been around you long enough to have seen there's an ounce of her in everything you do. You've put her on a pedestal." He pauses. "Chase has, too."

I don't know what he means by that. I don't ask, either.

The end of the stick has caught on fire. For a few seconds, I watch it burn before dragging it through the dirt and putting it out. Once every ember has been reduced to ash, I start to trace six letters in the dust—

H-A-L-L-I-E

—before scratching it out, erasing every one of the sharp lines.

"She's gone now." I remember that long ago morning in the kitchen with Jack, the heartfelt words I still can't get out of my head. "Hallie's gone and she's never coming back. I know that."

Maverick keeps his face turned away from me so I can't see his reaction. On the plus side, that means he can't see mine.

Then, even softer, I hear him say, "Why don't you tell me about your jacket, Xandra."

He struck a nerve.

"You tell me about your gun first," I shoot back. "Why it's so important you would've rather kept it than save me from the auction block? Your precious bullets… you had to throw one away anyway."

Maverick's head snaps my way, looking at me.

I don't back down.

He should've expected this. He had to have known that, eventually, I'd call him out on what happened in East Jersey. I'm prepared to have to discuss what Rex put Chase and me through in that room, but not before I get this part out.

Maverick frowns.

We're at a stalemate. It's like our first night in the trees, back before I knew Maverick at all. Even now, after all these weeks together, I'm not sure I know anything more than the few things he's told me and all I've seen.

And then I think about myself. What exactly does he know about *me*?

Oh, sure, I'm Jack's daughter, and Hallie's twin. I'm a survivor, too. I once had a brother named Rory. But what else? I never even told him a damn thing about Chase, though I suspect he's figured it out since then.

You've put her on a pedestal. Chase has, too…

There's a sudden lump in my throat. I swallow it, watching as the flames reflect in Mav's dark eyes.

Okay. Look, there has to be some sort of give and take. Maybe, for once, I should do some giving.

I toss my stick into the fire before climbing to my feet. From Maverick's hooded expression, I'm willing to bet he's expecting me to storm off and, ordinarily, that would be my initial response.

Not tonight.

Taking care to move around the fire without getting burned, I ease down and take a seat beside him.

"This jacket belonged to Rory," I tell him, plucking at the sleeve.

"Your brother."

He remembers.

"Yeah." Hugging myself, I pull Rory's jacket close. If I breathe in deep enough, I swear I can still smell him. "It was his favorite. A gift from his girlfriend, he wore it all the time when he wasn't in uniform. It's the last thing I have of his."

Maverick turns to his right, grabbing some of the dry grass he's stockpiled. He tosses it on the fire and, for a few seconds, we watch as the flames leap up for a taste before settling back down, burning a little brighter than before. The fierce snaps die down to a soft crackle that is strangely calming.

"Your brother," Maverick murmurs, "was he a victim or…"

Technically, anybody who died during the Turning is considered a victim, whether they were a victim of the Injection or a victim of someone who Turned.

But that's not what Maverick is asking me.

"Rory was a firefighter, just like Jack. Except he took the Injection when they offered it to him. Not everyone did." Maverick obviously didn't, and cops were some of the first groups offered the Injection. "He was always so sporty and outdoorsy, taught me everything I know about camping," I add wistfully, "and he liked the idea of never getting sick, I guess. He never wanted to feel weak… he liked saving people. He was a good guy. He didn't deserve what he got."

With a soft nod of agreement, Maverick silently encourages me to continue.

And I think with a wry smile, *it's too late to turn back now.*

I shudder and close my eyes. It's like a movie playing in my head, the memory of Rory as he Turned, and the look of hunger twisting his unfamiliar features as he fought becoming a monster. My screams for help, and the way Mom came up from the basement, carrying the laundry, both of us unprepared for a fucking *lurker* in the house—

"I was home on New Year's," I begin, my voice shaky and quiet. I've never told anyone except for Jack and Hallie what happened that day—and Hallie, of course, told Chase—but that's it. It's my biggest secret, one I've tried so hard to forget… that I've done too many questionable things to protect… and here I am, spilling it all out to someone I've only known for a few short weeks.

"I was home the first day of the Turning," I start again, "just me and my mom. Rory was at the firehouse. Jack was on the truck, like always. Hallie spent the night at Chase's house. She missed the worst of it. She wasn't there to see—"

My voice cracks, raw emotion already bubbling up inside of me. This isn't a good idea. It hasn't been long enough, and thinking about Hallie just makes it worse.

And then Maverick reaches over and places his hand securely on top of mine—and the words start flowing out of me. About how I was just sitting there when Rory popped in, telling us about the reports of people going crazy. Hostiles. Cannibals. Reports of humans eating other humans… he came to make sure Mom and I were alright.

Only we weren't because that's when Rory Turned.

It was me or Mom. I don't know why he grabbed her first. I screamed for her to run when I realized something was wrong, I told Rory "no", but he was too far gone.

He had her, and he… he started to *eat* her.

"I had to do it," I blurt out suddenly. It's like I'm trying to convince myself more than Maverick. "I grabbed a steak knife from the sink and I stabbed him. I didn't mean to kill him, I just wanted him to stop biting Mom... but he wouldn't and I kept stabbing and stabbing and stabbing until they were both dead."

Maverick pulls away from me, stunned. At first I think it's because of what I said and, horrified that the truth made him react that way, I push on the ground to get to my feet.

But Maverick grabs my hand again, yanking on it. I'm not prepared for the sudden tug and my legs fold beneath me so quickly that I nearly land in his lap.

"Maverick, I—"

"Don't go," he says firmly. "I'm so sorry, Xandra. I shouldn't have asked—"

"No," I reply, cutting him off. In a way, I feel a tiny bit better. I've carried the truth around with me for more than nine months, and to tell someone who isn't judging me, who knows what the world is really like now, it's as though someone managed to pull the venom from a festering wound.

It hurts, sure, but nowhere near as much as if it was left behind.

And, suddenly, I know I have to finish the story.

"You asked me, and it's all true: I killed my own brother. I held the mangled remains of my mother as she died. It was like I was in a trance," I confess. "I left the bodies in the kitchen, then locked the doors because I didn't know then that that wouldn't do shit to stop a lurker. I sat in the living room and waited for someone... Jack or Hallie... to come home. I kept that bloody knife by my side until we learned what fire can do. When Hallie finally let herself into the house, she found me sitting by myself on the couch."

I realize how cold that sounds, but it's the truth. I wish it wasn't, and I don't know why I'm telling him all this.

But I can't stop.

"I was shaking," I add, shaking now like I did then. "In shock, I guess, but Hallie thought I was cold. Rory had his jacket hanging on the back of the chair, and my twin wrapped me up in it. I remember her asking if I was okay, she said the news said to stay home, to stay safe, so Chase dropped her off. She asked me about Mom and Rory... I couldn't tell her what happened. Fuck, I couldn't talk at all. I only pointed toward the kitchen. Hallie found the bodies. She covered them up. Together, we waited for Jack to come home to figure out what to do with them."

We needed our dad. While he was on the fire truck, saving Madison, Hallie and I clung together and cried for our brother and our mom.

I exhale roughly.

There. That's all of it. I wait for him to say something else, and then he does.

"I was married."

Okay. Not what I was expecting.

But it's a bombshell all the same.

My eyes immediately dart to his left hand, to the bare ring finger I know is there. It's one of the first things I've always noticed about a stranger. I would've noticed a wedding band by now.

But there isn't one. In the nine months since my mom died, Jack has refused to remove his band. Most of the survivors in the Grave responded to the Turning and the loss of their loved ones the same way. Why hasn't Maverick?

Where is his ring?

Where is his wife?

There's something else, too. I turn and gaze at his profile, silhouetted by shadows in the firelight. His head is bowed, lost in thought. Though I never asked and didn't know until he and Chase had the discussion about their ages, it was always clear that he's older than I am. He was a cop in the before times, and for a while, too.

Why didn't I think that there were other things he experienced before the Turning?

I don't know what to say. I make a non-committal noise in the back of my throat, one of interest and surprise. It's the best I can do.

"Her name was Lindsay. We were married almost fifteen years." Maverick pauses. His words are short. Clipped. I can tell that he's unsure how to say any of this —but he feels he owes me. "Would've been fifteen in April."

Though I know better to ask, I can't help myself. "What happened to her?"

"I did."

Like usual, Maverick's gun is resting in his lap. He picks it up, trying to hand it to me, but I don't take it. In the back of my mind, I remember how he said it's been his only constant since the Turning.

Suddenly, I know exactly what happened.

"I shot my wife with this gun." As if the metal is sizzling hot, he takes it gingerly by the tips of his fingers and lays it by his feet. "I came home right after she Turned. Can you even imagine walking in on that?"

I don't respond to his whispered question. After my tale, we both know the answer to that.

"Did she... did she try to bite you?"

Did she try to *eat* you?

Maverick's voice is hollow. Like I did, he's reliving his past. Remembering.

Hating himself.

"No time. I came home, searching for Lindsay. She hadn't answered her phone. I tore into the house... I found her in the kitchen. She was already covered in blood, her eyes black, her teeth... she ate our dog. All that was left was the collar... and I knew that my wife was gone. She was one of them. She came at me and I... I emptied my entire revolver into her chest."

I close my eyes, but that doesn't stop me from seeing Maverick pulling the trigger, blowing away a faceless woman while wearing the same stoic expression he's had on since I first left the Grave with him.

"I insisted she get the Injection," he whispers harshly. I peek open my eyes. He's glaring at his gun. "She was a scientist, but she was afraid of needles. I told her it was just a little prick and then she'd be set... and she listened to me. It's my fault. Because of what I asked her to do, I had to empty my revolver into the only woman I've ever loved. I watched my wife Turn, then die right before my eyes."

Suddenly, I understand his fixation with that gun, and why he hesitated when Rex demanded it. He doesn't need to wear a wedding band to remember his wife—as I once thought, just like what Rory's jacket is to me, Maverick's gun is a reminder.

The burnished piece of metal won't ever let him forget

what he's lost. He must've reloaded it after, but then the world went to shit and maybe that was the last of the ammo he got his hands on.

But he remembers. The horrors of those days… none of us will ever forget.

You don't say I'm sorry. The best we can do is share our stories and let each other know we're not alone.

Which is why, before I can stop myself, I lean up against Maverick. He stiffens for a heartbeat before relaxing and wrapping his arm around my shoulder.

I smile sadly to myself. Tonight, at least, we don't have to be alone.

You like him, Maverick accused me earlier.

And I do. I do like Chase. But, with a little flutter of my heavy heart, I realize that doesn't mean anything at the end of the world.

It's too dangerous.

Maverick and his lost wife are proof of that.

Rory.

Nina.

Hallie…

So, yeah. I like Chase.

But that's not enough.

CHAPTER 22

I wake up to find Chase hovering over us.

I don't know how long he's been standing there. It's bright out, dawn, but the fire is still burning. With a start, I realize that I fell asleep leaning up against Maverick, his arm wrapped around the small of my back, keeping me there instead of my head dropping down in his lap to use his thigh as a pillow.

You'd think Chase would be glad that I didn't wake up with my face inches away from another man's crotch—and if you think that, you haven't been paying attention. Jealousy has his features going tight as he peers down at me with a pained look in his hazel eyes.

"Chase?"

His Adam's apple bobs as he swallows roughly. "It's morning. I'll be ready to head out when you are. Just thought you should know."

Before I can respond, he turns on his heel, striding back to where he left the rumpled blanket and my abandoned sleeping bag.

Honestly? What could I really say? I know what it looks like, but if he's been traveling with us for this long already and still thinks there's something brewing between me and Mav, then nothing I can say will convince Chase to give up on his jealousy.

Especially when he has no reason to be jealous at all.

Still, I glance over at Maverick, wordlessly asking for an explanation. If it's morning—and the sun overhead tells me that it is—then we should've already been up and breaking down the campsite.

He shrugs. "You seemed so peaceful. Chase was snoring up until a few minutes ago. I figured I could let you two rest a little longer. The sun's only just coming up."

It was a kindness that would've been a whole lot kinder if Maverick had poked me in the side, waking me up before Chase figured out that I spent the night as far away from him as I could.

That pained look is branded in my brain. I can't let him walk away like that.

I get up, leaving Maverick to tend to the fire while I tentatively approach Chase. He's bending over, grabbing my sleeping bag, ready to roll it up. The blanket I placed on top of him is already folded neatly and placed by my abandoned pack.

At first, I think he's just busying himself with getting ready to head out… and that's when I see him struggling to roll up the sleeping bag. Of course he's having trouble. I mean, it can't be easy with the way his hands are trembling so viciously, the handcuff bracelet is knocking against his wrist bone.

Ah, fuck. If those were angry shakes, I could deal. It

would be easy to remind Chase that he's being ridiculous, that he has no reason to be angry.

But they're not angry shakes, are they?

Oh, no. I'm way too familiar with how a body responds to being emotionally beaten not to recognize how Chase is reacting right now.

Damn it. I don't know what I'm supposed to say. I warned him when we left East Jersey that he needed to keep his distance; as difficult as it would be while we were travelling, we needed our space from each other. That's the only way this would work. And, except for the last time he called me by my twin's name, I thought we were doing all right. Sure, I falter from time to time—like last night, when I had the urge to stroke his hair while he was sleeping— but never when he could tell.

That's when it hits me that Chase… he's trying. That's why he turned his back on me, that's why he's busying himself with folding our borrowed bedding. He doesn't want me to see how much he's struggling.

I do us both a favor and walk away.

Maverick is careful not to look back at us. He starts rolling up the bedroll he never returned to last night, going as slow as he possibly can. With Chase tending to my sleeping bag, I use the rest of our water to put out the fire. It sizzles and fights against the flood, but the water wins in the end. Pale grey smoke floats up in the pinkish light of dawn.

I don't realize that I'm standing there, staring at the wisps of smoke as they fade away until I hear—

"Xandra?"

It's Chase who calls my name. He's standing about five feet away from me, the point in the triangle we've unconsciously constructed: Maverick to my right, Chase across the smoldering remains of the fire.

He's holding his blanket close to his chest, kneading the fleece so tightly with his fingers that his knuckles have gone white with the force. When he speaks, though, he sounds calm and collected, as if he's made up his mind about something. "Do you… can I talk to you?"

I freeze, unsure how I want to respond.

No. That's not true. One part of me wants to pretend I didn't hear him and continue to get ready to leave. The other part? It's almost willing to do anything to bring the light back to his eyes.

Maverick clears his throat.

"I'm going to go scout ahead a bit, see if I can find some water. I think I'll feel a bit more awake after a quick splash in a lake or a stream. If not that, I'll check for signs of lurkers in the next neighborhood." He pauses as if he's going to say one thing before deciding against it and going with another. "Wait for me here. I'll be right back."

I want to go after him. I certainly don't want to be left alone with Chase, not when he looks like I've clawed open his chest, used my dirty fingernails to rip out his heart, then stomped on it with my boots. But, hey, what else can I do?

Tucking my messy hair behind my ears, I nod, then take the blanket from him before his worried fingers rip a hole right through the material. I set it on the ground before waiting for him to talk.

Chase's fingers are still nervous. Without the blanket, he starts playing with a dime-sized hole on the hem of his t-shirt. I frown. How much do you want to bet that that hole wasn't there last night?

He exhales, careful not to meet my eyes. "So, I was thinking… you're right. Maybe it's time I go back to the Grave. Let Jack know everything's under control."

Glancing down now, he stares at the grass, flattened from where we were both sleeping last night before I woke up and joined Maverick for his part of the watch, completely sleeping through mine. I follow the direction of his stare. I can see the curved shape where Chase had slept, and there, not more than a foot away, a pressed square, the size of my sleeping bag.

Should he go? Right after we broke out of East Jersey, I would've been delighted to see the back of him. Something's different now… something's changed. I could say it's as simple as I got used to him, and I like the idea of having another set of eyes to keep watch for lurkers, but it's more than that.

I just wish I could admit to myself what it is…

Shoving my hands in the pockets of Rory's jacket, I fiddle with my folded knife. "If you feel that," I begin before stopping abruptly. I clench my left hand into a fist inside the pocket. "You know what. No." I relax my fingers, pull my hand out, and reach for Chase. I think he's almost as shocked as I am that I boldly grab his arm. This is the first time I've made contact with him instead of pointedly ignoring how often he finds excuses to touch me, and we both know it.

His head picks up, surprise written in his eyes. Good. I'll take that over the pain any day.

That gives me the boost I need to be honest with him.

"No, Chase," I tell him before I lose the nerve. "You have to stay."

"Why?" He bites down on his bottom lip before a

short, bitter laugh escapes him. He throws his free hand up in the air. "C'mon, Xandra. You know the old saying: two's company, three's a crowd."

"It's not like that," I argue.

"Really? Then what is it?"

It's his tone. So different than anything I'm used to when it comes to Chase Reynolds, it puts my back right up.

"Does it matter? It's not like *I'm* the one you were engaged to."

Holy hell. I regret the words the instant they're out of my mouth, but it's too late to take them back. A dark shadow flashes across his face in the morning light, quickly replaced by one of resignation.

Somehow, that's almost worse than the hurt.

I'm suddenly reminded of the last argument we had before I left with Maverick. Chase and I standing on the front porch of the Grave, me secretly jealous of Audrey, Chase kissing me, afraid of letting me go... it's all happening again, but we're playing opposite roles this time.

What would he do if I gave in to my need for him, grabbed his face, and kissed him? Would it erase what I just said—or would it only make things worse?

I huff out a breath. "Shit, Chase. I'm sorry. That was fucked up of me. I... I shouldn't have said that."

"But did you mean it?"

I don't answer.

I don't think he expected me to.

"Forget it. I pushed you too hard. If I have anyone to blame, it's me."

Forget it? I don't think I can, but for his sake, I'll try.

"Okay. I will, but you have to stay. Please? We're so close. Maverick says—"

Chase snorts under his breath, "*Maverick.*"

Oh, yeah. There's still bad blood there, isn't it? "He just wants to kill the lurkers. Isn't that what you want to do? Isn't that why you came after us?"

The look Chase gives me says that he knows as well as I do that I'm full of shit. He doesn't have to use his words, but we both know exactly why he's come this far out of the Grave—and it has nothing to do with lurkers for Chase Reynolds.

He's here for me. And if I say I need him here with me, there isn't anywhere else he'll go.

But can I say that?

"Chase—"

He takes a step toward me. It takes everything I have not to match it, moving away from him so that I don't say "fuck it" and throw myself at him.

He can tell. From the way I'm all but hugging myself inside of Rory's jacket to how I'm watching him on bated breath… he doesn't know me as well as he did Hallie, but we've been friends since elementary school. He knows me *enough*.

"Do you mean it? You really want me to stay with you? Do you need me?"

There's no use in lying. Not now.

Not to Chase.

"It's hard… I don't want to tell you how hard 'cause I know you know, but it's hard, Chase. I don't know *what* I'm feeling these days. Ever since Hallie…" I shake my head. "I'm angry all the time. I'm so fucking confused, and it's like my head's been stuffed with cotton. It's fuzzy.

Sometimes I can't remember the simplest of things... I thought getting out of the Grave would help me clear my head."

He purses his lips. "Did it?"

I shrug. "A little bit. But I missed you. Not just you," I add hurriedly because I don't want him to think things I can't let him think just now. "I miss everyone in the Grave. And... I don't know... when you showed up in East Jersey, it's like you brought the Grave with you. You saved me, and I know I never said thank you—"

He surges forward, fingers ghosting over the leather of my jacket. "Don't. You never have to. If anything, it should be me saying I'm sorry—"

"No," I say firmly, cutting him off. "We're not going down that road, either. You did what you had to. Fuck, you did what I asked you to. You have nothing to be sorry about."

"And you have nothing to thank me for."

We'll have to agree to disagree on that. He saved my ass, and I'll never forget that.

He moves away. "You still didn't answer me, you know."

I arch my eyebrow.

"When I asked if you needed me. I can stay if you want me to. You know it'll take a lot to get me to go... so, tell me: you need me?"

Isn't that what I've been saying?

"Aren't you listening to me? It has to be you. When..." I swallow roughly, biting back the irrational dislike that rises up at the thought of the nurse. "When Audrey said you were the best hunter in the Grave, she was right. So, yeah, I need you to help us take down that lurker nest."

Chase gets this strange look on his face. "Why do you say it like that?"

Huh? "Like what?"

"Audrey's name. You say it like you have a problem with her." He cocks his head slightly. "You say it like you're jealous."

I want to deny it. I could lie. I could pretend that I like the pretty nurse back in the Grave because she helped me after the accident, instead of secretly seething over whatever relationship she has with Chase now.

I could, but he's been picking up on my cues, reading me left and right. I could lie, but he'll know, and somehow that'll make this whole thing even worse.

"I don't know. You two just seemed really close before I left."

There. No need to tell him that I have visions of him fucking her that make me want to scream. That's a girlfriend's right. A fiancé's right.

I'm neither. I'm just her twin.

Hallie's gone. You can't cheat on a dead woman—

"Audrey," murmurs Chase, and I hate the way my fists involuntarily clench to hear his voice caress the two syllables in her name. Then, to my surprise, he actually lets out an amused laugh. "You still haven't figured it out yet, have you?"

"I don't know what you mean."

"Audrey—"

This time I grit my teeth, and I won't deny that the thought of the nurse going nose to nose with a lurker makes me the tiniest bit happier.

"—I owe her everything. She was your nurse. She's the one who did everything she could to make you better after the… after what happened. Jack was there every day, and so was I. Audrey is the one who kept us sane. She wants you to be okay. All she cares about are her patients and their happiness."

As if the guilt isn't bad enough. Now I have to feel bad for my imagination.

"I know," I tell him. He hasn't said anything I didn't already know. "But at the meeting—"

"I spent weeks inside of the church. You slept most of the time," he says, and I decide then and there that he'll never find out that I faked those naps if only to keep from having to face Chase so soon after Hallie's death, "and she kept me company when she could. She's like the sister I never had." Chase's hand is hesitant, still shaking as he reaches out and plucks one stray curl away from my cheek. "Let's just say that I have a thing for blondes."

"So, you two, you're not… oh God, forget I ever said anything." I'm too embarrassed to add anything else but a simple, "please."

But no amount of embarrassment can hide the fact that that's the best thing I've heard since leaving the Grave. And then I remember that I shouldn't be so pleased that my twin's fiancé has just blatantly admitted that he's attracted to me.

It's official. I've spent the last few days with him, from the moment I wake up until I close my eyes at night. I can't pretend that he thinks of me as Hallie anymore.

Just Hallie's replacement.

Still, if I'm being honest, I don't want him to leave me. And not only because he'll be an asset when we make it to New York.

"Chase. Just…" I can't think of the right words. "I—"

"I'll stay." His expression softens. I let out the breath I didn't even realize I'd been holding. "Not for him, though. Not because of his insane desire to kill this nest. But because I think we all know what this really is. It's suicide. But I'm not going to let you die alone."

And then, under his breath: "Not again."

CHAPTER 23

Ever since we left the Grave, I've been on my guard for two things: lurkers and rogues.

We've met our fair share of lurkers. There's ash all over New Jersey thanks to us. But, despite Maverick's insistence that there are plenty of rogues on the outside, we haven't met one yet.

Until Mav returns from scouting ahead with a woman wearing a backpack of her own—and a pair of sunglasses.

She has basic survivor gear on: a pair of muddy jeans, a faded grey t-shirt, and tennis shoes that have seen better days. Her curly black hair falls around her shoulders. She has a mid-size build, but curves that are enviable.

After the Turning, a frame like that says you not only survive, but you have plenty to eat.

I'd put her around thirty-five, maybe a year or two older. Definitely closer to Mav's age, though I wouldn't describe her as motherly the same way I did Chloe.

Something about her is attractive. I see it. I hope Chase doesn't.

I know from one look that Maverick does.

"Veronica McLean," she says after Mav introduces Chase and me to the rogue. "Aren't you two adorable? They make a cute couple." She nudges Maverick in the arm. "Don't you think?"

I pretend not to hear her. Instead, I focus on the shades.

It's sunny out. I'm beginning to think all the non-stop fire all over the country has really put global warming into overdrive because we're knocking on October's door and it's still way too damn hot outside. In the before times, I wouldn't be surprised to see a woman like this Veronica wearing sunglasses.

But now?

"Sunglasses?" I ask her.

She knocks the ear hooks on each side, making the frames dance. "Of course. They make me look good."

I watched her do it. I'm pretty sure her eyes are blue. Not black.

Not a lurker.

Okay, then.

It's weird, having a fourth travel companion.

On the one hand, it works out. Veronica and Maverick hit it off almost at once. I'm not sure if it's because they're closer in age or they've both spent a lot more time on the outside so they have that in common, but almost immediately after he introduces her to us, they partner off, Maverick leading the way while Veronica keeps up easily.

And that's the problem. Those two are getting along like flies on honey, but that leaves me with Chase. I got so used to refereeing between him and Maverick, without the two squabbling over stupid shit, it's just me and Chase and a whole lot of baggage between us.

I'm not talking about our backpacks and bedding, either.

It doesn't take long before Maverick invites Veronica to New York. At first, I thought she was just enjoying the company, but when he tells her about the lurker nest we're targeting, she shrugs her shoulders and says it sounds like fun.

Fun.

Man, rogues are weird.

I'll take the help, though. And, well, it's nice having another woman around. Maybe with Veronica here to distract Maverick, Chase won't shoot daggers at him with his gaze for the sole crime of being friendly with me.

He's jealous. Chase, that is. He's so jealous, he's almost green with it. I try to act as if I don't notice it. Maverick, realizing that a younger man's issues aren't his problem, totally disregards it.

If anything, I'm basically like a daughter to him, not a prospective lover. Veronica, on the other hand…

I'll give the two of them credit. At the end of the world, it's nice to see two people who aren't screwing around, dancing around the subject of attraction and having sex just to have it. All through today's travel, Veronica's laid it on pretty thick. I guess I should be glad she didn't target Chase with her flirtatiousness, but Mav… he's no match for Veronica.

They don't even wait until they've known each other a couple nights. Almost immediately after we made camp for the night, setting up a fire and eating whatever we have in our packs, Veronica buddies up with Mav, the two of them bowing their heads together, murmuring about something I can't hear over the roar and crackle of the fire.

Chase noticed their instant spark, too. He noticed it, and I don't think he's a fan. Jealous, remember? When he looks at the two of them cozy and intimate, almost like it was love at first sight for them, I know he's wondering why I'm purposely keeping my distance.

To be fair, I'm thinking the same thing.

It's dark out now, but not that late. I'm on lurker duty for the moment due to my strange sensing ability; when she heard I can do that, Veronica pronounced it "cool", then went back to flirting with Mav.

I'm surprised they managed to hold off on jumping each others' bones as long as they did. About an hour after sunset, Chase couldn't take it any longer. He got up, making that hemming-and-hawing announcement about slipping into the woods that usually means he has to take a shit—because after the last time I wrinkled my nose when he said that plainly in front of Mav and me, he's tried to give me some reasonable doubt to what he's doing —and disappeared.

Maverick makes sure I'm okay with watching the campsite. In my experience, if a lurker finds us out in the woods, it's closer to the middle of the night or later. That's why I usually take the last watch, but with the promise of a pretty woman dragging him into the woods, it looks like Mav is okay with switching the order around.

So there the two of them go, and I sit by myself, wondering what's taking Chase so damn long.

Dudes can sit on the toilet forever when they're taking a dump. I know Rory used to. Jack, too. But we're outside.

Dig a hole, do your business, and hope you can find something to act as toilet paper before splashing some water on your hands to clean up as best you can.

He should've been back by now.

I give him a couple of minutes more. The last thing I want is to interrupt him if he's busy, but I start to get antsy. I don't like Chase being out there where he won't be able to tell if a lurker is coming, and it bothers me that he tends to do that a lot. And, sure, he proved himself by tracking me, but still.

I need to go find him.

The fire should be okay. If not, I'll re-light after I drag Chase back to the campsite.

That's my plan. I'm hoping that I'll come across him after he finished his business or, if I can't find him, stumble around for a few minutes just so that I don't have to sit alone at the campsite, praying that whatever Veronica and Maverick are doing together doesn't drift back to me on the too-muggy autumn wind.

I don't call his name. Just in case there's another rogue around—and not just Veronica—I listen for the sound of something that could be a built twenty-three-year-old former athlete making his way back to the camp.

I hear something alright. And, considering Maverick and Veronica went off in a totally different direction than Chase and I did, it can't be them.

It kind of sounds like it *could* be.

Panting. Grunting. Flesh on flesh, and something just enough *squelch*-y.

My eyes fly wide open. I know this sound. I shouldn't be proud to be able to recognize it as easily as I do, but I know it… and before I can think better about what I'm going to do, I follow it.

Beneath the moonlight, I see a man bracing his hand against a tree. His other hand? As he's bowed a bit, reaching down, there's no missing the way his right hand is going back and forth, back and forth, pumping wildly as the silver handcuff on his wrist catches the moonlight with every stroke.

It's Chase. It has to be.

And when I murmur his name, causing him to whip around, his hand wrapped around his cock… I know exactly what he was doing.

Seeing me standing there, Chase lets go of his cock as if the skin burns. He doesn't do anything else. He just gapes at me, waiting for me to say something.

I don't think he expects it to be what comes out of my mouth, though.

"If you were coming out here for a little playtime, you should've told me. I would've come with you."

He blinks. Once. Twice.

"Xandra?"

I nod. "Who else would it be?"

If he says Hallie, I might bolt in the other direction before giving in to the sudden insane idea that just popped in my head.

"I don't… fuck. I'm sorry." He reaches for his dick, about to put it away.

I stop him. "Don't. I… I don't mind. I mean, if you want to finish what you were doing…" I inch closer, eyes locked on his straining erection. He was nowhere near finished when I found him, and I can only imagine how much he wants to return to it. I nod at him. "Is that what you've been doing every time you find a reason to slip out of camp?"

I'm being bold. I guess Chase decides it's a good idea to follow my lead.

"The lurkers don't like it. They're basically the living dead, and this is something only a real alive guy can produce."

"I sure as hell hope so. Can you imagine if lurkers could fuck? Could breed?"

The idea gives me nightmares. Younglings are bad enough. But a lurker baby? No, thanks.

Chase nods in agreement, almost relieved I bought his excuse. "So, yeah… sometimes I mark our border like this. It's added protection to keep the lurkers away."

I move even closer. "Is that true?"

He opens his mouth. Pauses. Laughs under his breath. "Honest? I think it's something Luke made up when me and Kev caught him on patrol one night with his pants down. He didn't want Jack to hear he was whacking off when he was supposed to be looking for lurkers. But, well… you never know."

I tilt my head. "Are you sure there's not another reason why you need a little relief?"

Come on, Chase. Throw me a bone. Give me a reason to do this tonight…

Chase swallows roughly. "Honest?" he says again. "Yeah. You want honesty. Okay. Yeah." He gestures at his erection. "Being around you, I'm always like this. There isn't anything else I can do about it, and when it gets bad… someone else can do the watch. I can finish in five minutes or less and then…"

And then.

"No one's watching the camp right now. But, you know what, I think that's okay. I think I want to take you up on that challenge anyway."

His face screws up, confused. "What challenge?"

I shrug. "I want to see if I can make you last for longer than five minutes."

Poor Chase. He looks like he's torn between running toward me or running away.

I wait.

"What about Maverick?"

His tone is deceptive. Part of him doesn't give a shit where the other man is. The other part? He just wants to see how much *I* care.

I gesture vaguely behind me. "He went off into the woods with Veronica. They said they're going to scout for lurkers, but..."

I saw the way that Maverick was looking at Veronica. When he thought no one was paying attention, there was something there. I'd call it desperation, but that doesn't make sense—still, it was pretty similar to the way that I catch Chase looking at me.

He's frowning now, nowhere near as fascinated by me as he usually is. "So I'm your second choice."

What?

"There is no choice."

He looks away.

I don't like that. "I mean it, Chase. It's just you." I pause, then take a step closer to him so that the back of my fingers brush against the erection that he still hasn't tucked out of sight. "And that."

I can't tell if he wants to flee or lean into my caress. It was a simple touch, a fleeting touch, but all Chase does is blurt out, "I haven't even looked at another woman except for Hallie."

I don't doubt it.

I move again so that I'm standing directly in front of him. Then, in a throaty voice I can hardly believe is mine, I murmur, "Look at me, Chase."

For a moment, he refuses. My heart thuds, and I think that I... I read this... him and me... *us* all wrong.

I take another step, turning slightly, prepared to disappear into the woods and pretend this never happened—right as he meets my gaze, and all I see is lust warring with need and a hint of trepidation as he whispers back, "I thought..."

"What? That I hated you?"

He swallows roughly before nodding once.

"No. Chase... I could never hate you." That's true. I don't know how to get him to believe me, but that much is at least true. I move into him, letting him see the honesty written on my face.

The honesty, and the offer.

CHAPTER 24

"You didn't have to come after me," I tell Chase.

"You did. For whatever reason you left the Grave… you're here. You've got my back. Let me repay you."

His expression turns puzzled. "Repay me? What do you—"

Another brush of my fingers against his dick. It all but jumps into my hand.

"Oh."

Yeah. Oh.

This time, he gulps. "I don't know—"

Maybe not. Or maybe he needs me to be a little more obvious with what I've wanted to do since I accidentally found him leaning up against a tree, jerking of where no one was meant to see.

I saw—and now I *want*.

I gather my hair together, tossing it over my shoulders. "Ask yourself this: would you rather party with your hand tonight or get your dick sucked? Because I'm offering."

"Xandra, I—"

"Hey. No pressure. But if this is about cheating on your memory of my twin, I get it. It was just an offer."

"Yeah, but if this is because of what happened back at East Jersey…"

He looks so spooked, so afraid, that I feel like I need to do something, *anything*, to lighten the mood a little.

"Technically you're my husband." It's a tease, but the words are too heavy for it to really be one. "Or you would've been if Maverick didn't stop you before you put it in."

Jesus Christ. What the fuck is wrong with me?

Even worse, he doesn't seem to understand that it *is* a tease.

He shrugs, though it's nowhere near as casual as he probably wishes it could be. "If you're willing, I'll make you my wife."

My smile slides off of my face.

If I was smart, I'd laugh it off, then hightail it back to the campsite. I could pretend I had to take a piss, then go back to watching over the fire until either Chase or Maverick and Veronica return.

If I was smart…

"I'm not going to fuck you tonight, Chase. But I'm going to take care of you." His momentary disappointment turns to confusion… until I add, "Just the way you did me in East Jersey."

He shakes his head. "I didn't want to hurt you."

"You didn't."

"No. You don't get it. I *couldn't* hurt you. So if we had to do that… I wanted to make sure you were ready for me. That's why I did *that*."

I need him to be absolutely clear with me. "Are you talking about going down on me?"

He looks pained. "I didn't ask—"

Oh, Chase. My sweet consent king. I remember, the first time we ever had sex, he made me wait until I was sure, then he laid me out, stroking my hair, asking me if I was okay after every couple of centimeters as he slowly worked his dick inside of me—

Wait.

No.

No.

The first time we had sex—the only time we had sex—we were buzzed, wallowing in grief, and found solace in each other. He still made sure I was with him all the way. That part was easy since I not only initiated the fucking, but I pushed him on his back and rode him with wild abandon just the way I offered to do in front of Rex. That way he'd never doubt that I wanted him... because I do.

I want my twin's childhood sweetheart.

The man she promised to marry before she died, and the man who was so gentle with her, I was so jealous when she told me about how she finally lost her virginity to him after our seventeenth birthday, I picked a random jock from my science class and banged him in the locker room during eleventh period.

Chase was always off-limits. Up until the accident, he was Property of Hallie Holden, and there wasn't even a doubt of that. No what-ifs, no maybes. Hallie loved him so much, and I thought he was a great guy, but even if my competitive nature meant I couldn't let her experience something as mundane as sex without feeling what it was like for myself, I never for a moment set my sights on Chase.

Until Hallie was gone and, suddenly, there were a hundred maybes and a thousand what-ifs.

I want him, though I shouldn't, and even knowing he's the last guy on Earth that I should be propositioning, that doesn't stop me at all.

"I want to taste you," I tell him.

He groans. His dick twitches.

I inch closer.

"I want to do what you did to me, to relax me, to make me feel good. Only for you... I want to get on my knees right now and suck your cock."

How's that for making myself clear?

"You... you don't mean that," he breathes out.

Oh, baby. You have no idea how much I mean it. "It's okay. If you want this... just close your eyes. Pretend I'm Hallie."

"Who will you pretend I am?"

Anyone but Chase... and, no. That would be a lie. It'll be Chase, but there's no way I can admit that to him.

So, instead, I murmur, "Does it matter?"

"I should say no. I should lie my fucking ass off. But I can't... so, yeah. It matters." A tiny furrow forms on his brow, cheeks gone taut. "Is it someone in the Grave?"

Ask me what you really want. Ask me if I slept with Maverick during the early days of our journey. Ask me—

I huff out a breath. "I haven't been with anyone like this since... fuck. Since—"

His breath hitches. "Me? In East Jersey?"

I shake my head.

He gulps. "In the Grave? Your living room?"

Fucking hell.

"Yeah." Damn it. I shake my head. "And I let my emotions get away with me then. Maybe that's what I'm doing now… maybe this is a mistake. I'm exhausted. I'm scared. And, fuck it, I'm so horny, it *hurts*. But we don't have to—"

Chase surges forward, cupping my elbows in his hands, nearly knocking the handcuff bracelet against my funny bone. "I want to."

"What?"

"If you're offering, I'm accepting. But I won't close my eyes."

"I look like Hallie, Chase. I'm *not* her."

It's important to me that he understands that my twin… his love… she's gone and she's never coming back.

"Does it matter?" he asks, echoing my exact question from before.

It shouldn't… but it *does*.

So I lie to him as I lower myself to my knees. "No."

I give him a moment to change his mind. To grab his dick, tuck it back into his boxer briefs, and zip up. But he doesn't. Instead, he angles his hips, putting his erection in my reach.

The message is clear. If I want him, I have to take him.

And that's exactly what I do.

Gripping him by the base of his dick, I tug him toward me, swallowing my laugh when my firm hold has him tripping over his feet to get as close to me as possible. I squeeze. He closes his eyes in obvious prayer. That's all the sign I need to part my lips and take him into the heat of my mouth.

Chase throws back his head, muffling his groan by shoving the back of his hand against his mouth.

Oh, baby. We can do a whole lot better than that.

I make it my personal mission to get him to forget about the lurkers. To forget about the threat of rogues coming upon us. I have my matches and my knife. He's wearing his taser. If someone comes upon us before he, well, *comes*, we can take care of it.

Until then, I want Chase's attention on me and me alone.

It only takes a couple of pointed licks, then a very careful squeeze, before he drops his hand, filling the clearing with his sounds of pleasure. I smile around the head of his cock.

Yeah. I knew I could do it.

Satisfied with myself, I turn my attention to getting him to finish before we're interrupted; seeing how long I can keep him from coming will have to wait until we're back at the Grave. He seems to be more than happy to let me do it, too, until his voice reaches my ears.

"Who are you thinking of?" he whispers.

"You."

Does he understand me? With his dick in my mouth, probably not.

I don't think he cares. Just like how I threaded my fingers in his hair, shoving my pussy against his face while he was giving me head in front of Rex, Chase places his palm against the back of my head. Slowly rocking his hips, he fucks my mouth as I do my best to keep up with him.

There's something so erotic about him using me like this. I've never been the type of girl who was happy to drop to my knees and take whatever a guy wanted to give me, but something about Chase… fuck me, I *crave* it.

I clutch his thighs, digging my nails in his jeans, imploring him to fuck my mouth a little harder.

Taking my signal as I meant it, he bucks his hips a little faster. I choke a little—and I *like* it.

I moan around his length. He spits out a curse as the sound does something to his dick. I guess it vibrated against him because any control he had left? It's *gone*.

I'm sucking, squeezing, taking him as deep as I can without activating my gag reflex. It's almost as though Chase knows my limits and, while he keeps on moving, he never takes it too far. I choke, but I don't gag, and when I need a breather, I jerk my head enough to swirl my tongue around the head of his cock.

"Fuuuck." He turns the one-syllable word into three with his sustained groan. "That's it, baby. You know how to make me feel good."

Not really, but I'm trying.

I have no idea why, but I don't stop until he taps me on the shoulder.

It's clear he wants me to withdraw so that he can finish on the ground. And, normally, that's what I would do.

But this… this is different.

I don't release his cock until I've taken every last drop Chase Reynolds has, swallowing it with the most lasciv-ious smile I can give him.

"Sorry," I say, swiping at the corner of my mouth with my thumb, peering up at him through the fringe of my eyelashes. "The lurkers can have your next load, baby. That one was for me."

Chase curls up next to my sleeping bag. It's big enough that he could squeeze inside, and I'd put down everything I left back in the Grave that it's taking all *he* has not to ask for an invitation. Especially after what just happened between us, he's got to think everything's changed.

He would be wrong.

I fucked up. I know I did. I provoked him, and I sucked him off, and I lost my damn mind for a moment and called him by the one pet name that he keeps screwing up and calling me. What was I thinking?

Well, that's easy.

I *wasn't.*

I don't regret doing what I did. Ever since East Jersey, I've wanted to be close to Chase again. It's like we had unfinished business—or that I didn't want him to continue on our journey with the thought in his head that he took advantage of me. I needed him to know that, if it was up to me, I would choose him even without the threat of being tossed to the lurkers hanging over my head.

That's what I did. I offered myself to him on my own, and he accepted. I showed him that—though I shouldn't— I have feelings for him; at the very least, an attraction.

But I can't let it happen again.

So I stay under the sleeping bag, leaving Chase to lie on top of it. I'm wide awake because one of us has to stay up and I'm only hoping that Maverick is enjoying his trip through the woods with way less guilt than I am.

When I hear the crackle of footsteps against the ground, I check my gut. No sign of a lurker, and the heavy steps sound like they belong to a human man and not a ravenous monster wearing a cloak. Only one problem: it sounds like *one* human man.

I sit up right as a shadowy figure slips into the campsite. As soon as he moves closer to the firelight, I make out Maverick—and he's alone.

Huh.

Maverick drops down on the other side of the fire. This time, I stay where I am instead of joining him over there.

I stay up, resting on my elbows. Next to me, Chase shifts, inching closer as though he can sense my movement. He doesn't wake up, though. I don't want him to, either, and I keep my voice low.

"What happened to Veronica?"

Maverick shakes his head. "She moved on."

"Really?" That's surprising. They seemed to hit it off right away, and I would've bet they went off in the woods for a little privacy. Maybe Mav changed his mind, or Veronica didn't think danger-banging in the woods when the lurkers could appear at any moment was a brilliant idea like I did... "I thought she was willing to join us on the last leg of our journey."

Mav snorts. "Yeah. So did I."

CHAPTER 25

averick trails his finger over the weathered map before nodding to himself. "I think we're almost there. Give it another two or three days and we should be crossing over into New York at last."

He folds up his dirt-stained, rumpled map, then shoves it into his pack. I lean back and stretch, yawning as I do so. After a couple of days of monotonous travel and uneventful nights, last night was one of the worst we had. I'm exhausted, and there's still two hours to go until sundown tonight.

We had left the Branch Brook Park where we made camp an hour before sunset this morning. A gaggle of younglings—at least six kids who should've been in a first grade classroom instead of circling the three of us, ready to eat—had attacked us. It was my watch, and my gut failed me. I didn't realize they were there until it was almost too late.

I'm still a badass. In the before times, I wouldn't brag

about burning up three kids. After the Turning, it's different. They're not kids. They're monsters, and I got three of them. Nudging Chase in the shoulder with my boot hard enough to wake him, he came to quickly, realizing the situation and catching the lighter I tossed him.

Chase is a more reckless hunter, I've learned. I'm careful to keep some distance between me and any lurkers, even if that means I have to figure out a way to hunt from further away. I've switched my scavenging from searching for glass bottles to snatching as much hairspray up as I can. Screw firebombs. Give me a flamethrower any day.

Chase? He'll go to a lurker before giving them a chance to attack us—to attack *me*. I don't pretend not to notice, though I've given up calling him out on it. He has this savior complex-thing going on. He'll risk himself to save me, and if I'm the last woman at the end of the Earth that needs him to come between me and a lurker, I let him have this.

Even if I went to throttle him every time he takes an unnecessary risk. He's fast. I'll give him that. He can dart around a lurker—whether they're a youngling or a full-grown monster—flick the lighter, catch the brittle cloak on fire, and bolt before he gets caught in the flames.

Does that mean my heart doesn't catch in my throat whenever he does that? Of course not. It just makes me more determined to kill the bastards so that they can't get their claws on Chase.

Maverick was on the other side of the fire. Before I could jolt him awake, something else got him up. He traded his gun for a pack of matches, igniting a torn piece of cardboard that he waved like a torch before using it to take out the final youngling creeping up behind him.

The younglings didn't trigger my senses. I don't know why, and I can only assume they were new lurkers. Right when I was congratulating us on taking out six more of those freaks, I doubled over as my stomach squirmed so badly, I needed to clench my teeth together to keep from spewing last night's dinner of cold canned beans and stale Cheez-Its all over the ash-covered ground.

At least *eight* more lurkers were coming. Drawn by the fight or the promise of three human meals, it didn't matter that the younglings were piles of ash on the grass or that our fire was still burning. They were coming, and I didn't like our odds.

Neither did Maverick. Though Chase insisted on standing our ground, he refused. The sun would be coming up soon, and if we ran, we could outlast them. Chase tried to argue… until Mav drew attention to how pale I'd gone, and how I was cramping so badly, I'd lost my hairspray and my lighter.

I dropped them.

I dropped the only two tools that could've protected me from a lurker.

That was enough to trigger Chase's protective instincts. While Mav made quick work of packing up our latest campsite, Chase shouldered my pack, then lifted me up, carrying me in bridal-style hold until the pain subsided enough that I made him put me down so that I could walk.

It's the nest. That's how Maverick explains it. From what he heard during his travels on the outside, the nest in Manhattan is so large—and the amount of humans still left to feed on in the city so tiny—that it's spilling over onto this side of the river. Even water doesn't kill the lurkers.

They wade under it, no need to breathe, and emerge in New Jersey, looking to feed.

Two to three days. That's what Maverick just told us. The amount of lurkers coming for us will only increase—and that's nothing compared to trying to make a dent in the nest.

Chase doesn't seem to believe we can. For the last week, they've been arguing back and forth, their bickering taking on a sharper edge. He wants to know how we can kill hundreds and hundreds of lurkers with the supplies we have. While our scavenging has proven to be successful lately—and, in addition to his pack, Maverick carries a stolen duffel bag with everything he thinks he needs—I have my doubts, too.

Not Mav. He insists that he's been planning this for months now, and whether we were there or not, he'd figure it out. He has no intention of dying during this mission, but if we'd rather turn back now…

No. There's no turning back. There never has been.

So we trudge ahead, the rift between Chase and Maverick growing with every step. Meanwhile, the chasm that stretches between me and my twin's fiancé? It's as big as the few inches that separate us as we sleep.

And, if I'm being honest, I think that, more than anything, is why the two men just can't knock it off.

Is it jealousy? Maybe. I don't know what happened between Jen Maverick and Veronica. If Mav has any idea what went down with Chase and me, he's being careful not to mention it.

As for Chase… he's followed my lead. We don't talk about the night we slept together, and we certainly don't bring up how I offered to suck his dick—and then I did. I get the feeling that Chase wants to make sure I offer to do more next time, knowing full well that if he pushes me, the chance of that happening is zero. Same thing when it comes to how closely he watches Maverick when we're traveling. I've caught an angry flash on his features when Mav comes too close to me, and if I show the cop any deference since he, you know, has the map and the compass and the *plan*, Chase gets that same puppy dog look like I kicked him aside.

I want to blame his brooding mood today on getting his night's sleep cut short, too. I at least got my time. Chase and Maverick's were cut by an hour each when the lurkers attacked, but you wouldn't know it by how willing they are to keep moving.

He scowled when Mav stopped long enough to check his map and his compass. Because we're nowhere near any empty, abandoned houses, he decided to see if we were close enough to the Hackensack River to get some water for our supply. Drinking it straight will give me the runs— at best—but if we boil the impurities out over tonight's fire, we'll have something to quench our thirst later.

Now, am I worried about getting dehydrated? It's the first week of October, fall's finally made an appearance, and I wear both my jacket and my sweatshirt around the clock now. I barely sweat, but I do get thirsty. Water is a good idea.

There's more to Chase's frequent disappearances than that, though. It's almost like he's putting some distance between him and Mav, checking to see which of the guys I'll stick by. Who knows? Maybe he's delusional enough to think that, if I do go searching for him, we might have a replay of the other night.

No.

I can't.

And I'm pretty sure he knows it.

Welp. We have to wait for him. Currently, we've stopped in Skyway Park, a thirty-plus acre of greenery in the shade of the old Pulaski Skyway. Following Maverick's map and compass east, he had the idea that we could follow where Route 1 and 9 meet up and take the Pulaski Skyway over the Hackensack and Passaic rivers.

It was a good idea, but that's before we discovered that the Department of Transportation had been doing rehab and renovations to the bridge right before the Turning. While it's sturdy enough for us to walk on, we made it about halfway to the other side only to discover that there's a gaping hole spanning the whole center of the bridge. The edge is charred, splattered with burn marks.

As wide as the bridge and more than twenty feet across, there's no way for us to cross it. We had to backtrack about a mile all the way to the mouth of the highway and jump down from our bridge to the truck route below. Chase, determined and still obviously in some kind of one v. one with Maverick, jumped before we were even sure it was possible. He called for me to jump next, and I did because if he could do it, I would, too.

Too bad it was a way higher jump than I anticipated. I was still a few feet away when I decided that this was the end. I was going to break my neck.

Chase caught me in his arms, stealing my breath as I landed more than a foot off the ground. I barely had enough time to offer a quick thanks before he sat me on the asphalt and started off with Maverick still on the Skyway above us.

He's had a stick up his ass ever since.

Maverick's no help, either. Ever since Veronica vanished on him, he's put his guard back up. We're travel companions with the same murderous goal, not friends, and the older cop has made that perfectly clear.

And that's that. The three of us are still traveling together but, really, each of us is on their own.

"What do you think is taking Chase so long?" I wonder out loud.

I'm curled up in front of the fire, arms wrapped around my legs. Earlier, Chase took close to an hour to find a path down to the river, fill up our bottles, and lug them back to where Mav and I were waiting for him.

By then, Maverick decided to get a better look at his map, plotting another way from our side of the river to New York. There are plenty so we're not worried, and I left him to it while helping Chase build the fire so we could boil the water.

The was shortly before sunset. We've camped in a small clearing that's about a hundred yards away from the shore of the Hackensack River. If lurkers pop their hooded heads out of the water, my sensing ability should give us enough of a headstart to retreat if the roaring campfire isn't enough to send them lurking in another direction.

My stomach is nervous. I can't tell if it's because there's a lurker out there or if I'm just worried that Chase said he was going to find a quiet spot to take a shit in the woods, then take a peek to see if there are any signs of lurkers making a stand in this park before our arrival.

It's been about twenty minutes. Part of me wants to go looking for him. The other part doesn't want to give him hope that I'm coming around. I'll deal with Chase when we get back to the Grave—but that means, first, we have to get back there.

I stand up. "I'm going to go looking for him."

Maverick opens his revolver, checks to see that his last bullet is chambered, then snaps it shut. "He has his taser. He'll be fine."

"That's against rogues," I point out.

"He took matches, too. Don't worry about him. Your sister's man is a good hunter. He knows what he's doing."

Thanks, Mav. I needed the reminder that Chase belongs to Hallie.

I shake my head. "I'll be right back."

Maverick blows air through his nose. "I'll come with you."

"It's fine. Keep the fire roaring. We'll *both* be right back."

I'll make sure of it.

Maverick doesn't argue, and I start in the direction I remember watching Chase take. Not like I expect to find his footsteps and follow them. Nope. My plan is a lot simpler than that. Hoping like hell that we don't have any rogues camping nearby, I'm going to just head toward the river, calling his name.

Turns out, that's not necessary.

I find Chase stumbling toward our firelight almost immediately. His eyes are wide. His face is panicked. His hand is clutching his upper arm, and instead of walking with the athletic grace I'm used to, he nearly trips between one step and the next.

What the—

"Chase!"

His head jerks up, finding me. "No." He stops short, backtracking so quickly that his boot gets snagged on a treeroot and he goes down.

That gives me enough time to reach him. Crouching down at his side, I peer into his sweat-slicked face and nearly moan.

Something's wrong. Something happened out there… and it's not good.

I zero in on his hand. "Chase? What's the matter? Let me see."

He tries desperately to jerk out of my reach. "No, baby, don't—" Grimacing and swallowing back a groan, Chase flops backward before I can touch his hand. He turns away, hiding his face, hiding the pain and the fear and the panic I've already seen, but that's nothing compared to the shiny, dark liquid seeping from between his fingers that I can't miss now.

My stomach drops to the dirt. *Blood.* No. Fuck, no. It can't be.

Can it?

"Is that blood?" I throw myself at him, intent on pulling his hand away. "Damn it, Chase. Let me see!"

"Baby, no—"

I barely even notice that he's called me "baby" twice now. I need to see. I have to know.

I flop on top of him, the last thing Chase would've expected. It works. He goes still, and I pry his fingers off of his bicep.

And that's when I see the chunk of skin missing from the back of his arm.

Everything that happens next is nine months of trauma, of grief, of loss, of a sweet, feisty twenty-three-year-old chick forced to become a killer after watching nearly everyone she loves die.

I fall back, putting some distance between Chase and me. Lurkers start to Turn almost immediately. Once the venom from a bite is introduced into a host, it's a matter of hours before the complete transformation is done. After twenty-four hours, he'll be invulnerable.

Less than that, if I can get an antidote into him, he'll be fine. He'll recover.

He'll be my Chase.

But I know him. He'd sacrifice himself. That, or the lurker bite would overtake him and he'd turn on me and Mav—and we'd have to put him down.

Fuck, no.

I'll take care of this. I'll save him the way I wasn't able to save my brother, my mother, or my twin.

I fall back, but before I do, I snag the taser out of his holster. I'm glad Maverick showed Chase and me how to work it because it's easier than I would've thought to shoot the barbs into Chase's chest.

He was already on the ground. When the taser hits him, he jerks, body spazzing, before his eyes roll into the back of his head. He's out, and as long as he is, he can't eat us.

Here's hoping a lurker's increased metabolism and regenerative properties won't have kicked in to help him shake off being tased…

There's no time to waste. I shove the taser back into the holster, then grab Chase by his boots. Unlike Chase did for me, I can't pick him up and carry him. I can, however, drag his dead weight through the dirt until I'm back at the campsite.

"Help!" I shout, not caring one bit if anyone other than Maverick can hear me. "Now! Antidote. I need my antidote. Get me my pack!"

Maverick is suddenly at my side, standing over Chase. No pack, I notice, and I want to scream at him that there's no time.

"He got bit," he says uselessly.

No shit. "And I have an antidote. Watch him."

"What the fuck happened to him? Xandra... he could Turn and attack us."

Not Chase. He would never. "I tased him. He should be out long enough for me to give him the antidote. It'll work."

It has to work.

I start to rise when Chase shudders. I drop down again. I'm prepared to tase him again if I have to, but when his eyelids flutter and I see those familiar hazel eyes—hazel, not black like a lurker—I know that Chase is still in there.

He reaches his hand out, groping wildly, searching for something or someone, and I can't bring myself to leave his side.

Even when he says, "It's my fault, Hal. I didn't see it. It came from the water... the fire didn't catch on the damp cloak. The stare failed before I could ignite the fucker's skin. It got me... take me out. Put me down. I won't hurt you, baby. I'll never hurt you."

A lump lodges in my throat. "I know."

"I love you."

Tears well in my eyes. "Know that, too."

"Hallie..."

I squeeze his hand. "I love you, too," I tell him. If he thinks I'm my twin and he's dying, it's the least I can do, letting him have these few moments when he's with her again.

"I'm ready. Do it."

Yeah. That part's not going to happen.

"Maverick!" I shout. "Jesus Christ, my pack. Can you grab it for me or not?"

"Hallie... it hurts," grunts Chase. "I'm so sorry..." His eyes fly open again. His back arches as if a shot of voltage has just gone down his spine. Because he's still holding my hand, I'm on this roller coast ride with him, up, then down as he crashes back onto the dirt so hard that it makes me wince in sympathy.

Or maybe that's because he's squeezing the life out of my hand.

"Get away from me," he hisses between clenched teeth. He closes his eyes, screwing them up tight. "Run, unh, save yourself—"

The desperation in Chase's voice, the desperation, the fear, the concern... I've heard it all before.

He sounds like my brother right before he attacked Mom and me.

"Don't be stupid." I snap. "I'm not going anywhere."

Maverick gets up. But he doesn't go to where my pack is nestled next to my rolled-up sleeping bag and the pile of blankets we've been toting around. I want to scream at him to stop dicking around... and that's when he grabs *his* backpack.

Chase is shuddering, grunting and crying out now, but his grip is like a vice—he won't let go of my hand and I don't want him to.

I can follow Maverick as he unzips that secret pouch that used to hold his hat.

"Mine," I tell him. "It's in a sock at the bottom of my—"

My words fail as I watch Mav pull a sock out of his pack. He dips his finger in as he hustled back over to Chase and me.

"Here," he says, pressing a glass vial into my free hand.

There's a lilac ribbon tied loosely around it.

My antidote.

CHAPTER 26

There's no time for me to wonder how he got it or why it was in his pack instead of mine. Chase needs me.

He's shaking, pain wracking his entire body. I'm not strong enough to hold him down, but I give it my best try. I place the antidote on the ground a few feet away from him; safe and sound. Then, yanking my hand free from his since the intense trembles led to him loosening his hold, I climb on top of Chase again. I straddle him, doing what I can to get him to stay still.

If the antidote is going to work, I have to get him to drink it without him accidentally biting off one of my fingers in the process.

I try to pin both of his arms down at his side, careful of his wound at first before I give up on keeping the bloody cut clean and just try to get him to stop moving. Here's hoping that the antidote really will cure everything.

Blood is everywhere. This close, I can't miss the bite. His t-shirt sleeve was cut short enough that it didn't offer any resistance to the sharp claws and fangs of a lurker. It's nasty, but if Chase got away with only one chunk out of him, the antidote will fix him.

I just have to get it in him.

Right when I have him where I want him, his teeth start to chatter so frantically, I have no fucking clue how I'm going to do that. Finally, I let go of his arms—and immediately have to lean back to avoid getting hit in the face when he starts bucking wildly, throwing his arms up in the air as the venom works its way through him.

Hot tears sting my eyes again. I rub them roughly with the back of my dirty, bloody hand. Suck it up, Xandra. We're not going to sit here and watch Chase die.

The plan hits me like a lightning strike, terrifying yet electrifying at the same time.

Leaning over, pressing my tits against his flailing chest, I crush my lips against his. The part of Chase that's still *Chase*, that's still aware what's going on... it responds to me. He relaxes slightly—at the very least, he stops thrashing so violently—and presses his mouth hungrily against mine.

Only he's not hungry to feed. He's hungry to touch. To taste. To kiss.

To fuck.

His hand goes to my lower back, shoving me further against him. I gasp. He thrusts up against me.

I have hope.

If we get out of this in one piece, I'll fuck him. I'll kiss him. I'll pretend to be Hallie until he recovers if I have to... anything to keep Chase Reynolds in this hell on Earth with me.

So while my twin's fiancé's tries to fuck his way

through our clothes, I thrust my fingers through his hair with my left hand, holding him in place. I reach out with my hand and, thank fucking God, I swipe the antidote on my first try. I grab it and try to pop the stopper with one hand.

It's impossible. If I'm going to do this, I need both hands. It would probably help if I could see what I was doing, too. But that means breaking away from Chase and hoping he doesn't start convulsing again.

Somewhere in the back of my mind, I've given up any hope that Maverick will help me at all.

I have to do it. Hoping it works, I jerk away from Chase, a flash of relief running through me when I don't take any of his hair with me when I untangle my fingers from the strands. Sitting up enough to see what I'm doing, I use both of my hands to yank the stopper out without spilling any of the antidote. It's stuck tight and I curse, straining to get it out.

Without me there to occupy him, Chase starts groaning and bucking and growling. I nearly go flying, and it's all I can do to keep the antidote from sloshing out of the vial once I finally do get it open.

Kissing worked once before, and I just hope like hell that it will again. Cooing "baby" to get his attention, I slam my mouth against his, calming him enough that I can scoot closer to his face. Then, lifting the antidote close to his chin, I use the edge of my teeth to bite down hard against his bottom lip.

Chase gasps at the shock of my fierce action and the sudden pain, and he opens his mouth just wide enough that I can shove the vial in between his teeth.

The last drop of antidote oozes out of the glass tube

when the pain from my bite is overcome by whatever is going on inside of Chase. He gargles on the antidote and I rub his throat with my left hand, trying to get him to swallow. I keep the vial in place, holding it tightly with my thumb and pointer finger so that there's nowhere for him to spit it out.

So relieved that he's swallowing, I let down my guard.

My fault.

I never expected Chase to clamp his teeth down right on top of the antidote vial.

I know instantly that one of my fingers is broken, if not both. Slivers of shattered glass are stuck in my hand and Chase's tongue, and I only hope that the antidote will fix that, too. I can't even tell if the shards have cut me because my hand is already coated, slick with blood from Chase's bite mark.

I don't feel any pain, though. Oh, no. That'll come later.

I'm still straddling Chase, but the antidote has accomplished one thing, at least: he stopped moving again, no taser required. His breathing is labored, more of a whimper than anything, but he's alive.

And that's all that matters.

Keeping him between my legs, I shift forward, scooting on my knees until I can reach his face. With the pointer finger on my undamaged hand, I pluck at his eyelid. Yes. Not a single hint of lurker in his gaze. Not a single speck of black ink save for his pupil. They're still the same beautiful hazel shade as they were this afternoon.

The antidote worked. It had to have.

The antidote—

Chase is out. In my limited experience, whenever a survivor was given an antidote, it takes a while for it to do what it's supposed to. The host body needs every bit of energy it has to fight against the lurker venom. It'll win, the antidote will work, but it takes time.

Good. He doesn't need to distract me while I find out what the hell is going on with Maverick.

Climbing off of Chase, I whirl on Mav. "What the fuck were you doing with my antidote?"

I expect him to deny it. I'm a loose cannon with a hair-trigger temper and the ability to build a firebomb and a flamethrower—and I'm furious. I'd deny it, too. Pretend I also had the brilliant idea to sneak around with an antidote tucked in a sock.

That's what I would do.

Maverick doesn't.

Taking a tone that screams "dad dealing with irrational teenage daughter", he holds up his hands in a placating gesture as says, "Xandra… Xandra, stay calm. Getting angry isn't going to solve anything."

Wrong answer.

I dive for the ground and snatch up Maverick's gun before he can even blink. My hands are covered in Chase's sticky blood. One of them is badly damaged, though I haven't come down from my adrenaline high to feel it yet.

But, no matter how much I'm trembling, I don't drop the gun the way that Maverick must have when I appeared in the clearing, dragging Chase with me.

"You had it," I say, my voice shaking before it bursts out as a shout: "You asshole! Fucking answer me! How long have you had it?"

There are times when a survivor's sense of self-preservation really kicks in. When facing down a slightly deranged, undeniably murderous woman fifteen years your junior… one who's covered in blood and unsteadily wielding a gun she doesn't really have any clue how to use… that's a pretty good one.

Facing down the barrel of his own gun, the cop might've thought about lying to me for all of five seconds in an attempt to talk me down like I was a jumper or something before changing his mind. He has to understand that the only way he's going to get out of this without a bullet hole in him somewhere is by telling the truth—

"Since the first night."

—even if it's something I don't want to hear.

"*What?*"

He gulps. His hands are still hovering in the air, though he keeps looking at a place somewhere near my knees. I don't blame him for not making eye contact. If looks could kill, he'd be a dead man right now.

"Xandra," and his voice is so similar to Jack's, I jolt. "Put the gun down. I'll tell you what happened—"

I steady my arms. "No. Truth first. Then I drop the gun."

"You won't like it."

Funny. He said something similar when we were in East Jersey and he was telling me all about his *brilliant* plan to save me from the block.

He's right. I didn't like it then, and I won't like it now. Still, I'm loyal. Trustworthy. If I give him my word, I'll stand by it.

"I probably won't," I agree, "but either tell me the truth and you get your gun back or fuck with me and I'll shoot into the sky."

His fingers flex. That same familiar gesture when he

knows he's outmatched and thinks he can just outlast his opponent.

It didn't work with Rex. He had to waste one of his precious bullets on blowing the old convict away. Now there's only one left, and while I could no more murder Maverick after all these weeks together than take out Chase before he fully Turned, I'll throw that bullet away if I have to.

"The truth, Mav. I want the truth."

"Fine. Jack told me you'd have one. It was his ace in the hole, the reason I was willing to stick around and let you tag along. With an antidote, you'd be safe if…"

"If what?"

He shakes his head. "You started to stir right when I got it out of your pack," he tells me, answering one question, but not the other. He shudders out a breath. "I let the fire go out—"

"On purpose?" I squeal.

"Yeah."

I fucking *knew* it!

His tongue darts out nervously, dabbing at the corner of his mouth. He keeps his head bowed, shadowing his face. "I did it so you wouldn't see me going through your backpack if you woke up, and then I told you I heard something out there when you did."

"But there *were* lurkers out there!"

Slowly, Maverick moves toward me, stepping out of the shadows *he* was lurking in. "I didn't know," he says, and I want to believe him. "I didn't know you could sense them or that they were there. I'm so sorry, Xandra. I never wanted to put you in any danger."

Yeah? Well, he fucked that up, didn't he?

"No. You just wanted to take my antidote and—*why*? If you knew it was for me in case I screwed up and got bit, why did you steal it? To save your own ass?"

For a moment, Maverick hesitates. He doesn't answer me, and I think about pulling the trigger and making the gun useless just to prove a point—until he steps into the moonlight and lifts his head.

I've known him for a month or so. I've often thought he was allergic to eye contact. Whether he was nervous, his cop side made him suspicious, or if his loyalty to the wife he lost meant he never wanted to give me the wrong idea... I don't know. He just rarely looked at me dead in the eye, especially once the sun set.

Until now.

Suddenly, I know why he's always looking at the ground after dusk. Why he makes it a point to avoid my gaze, and why he tends to hide in the darkness when the sun goes down.

His eyes are rimmed with black.

Lurker black.

"It's the worst at night," he confesses.

"What—what the fuck is wrong with you?" My stomach clenches, bile rising as a terrible realization dawns on me. My finger slips on the trigger before I force myself to get back under control. "*You*? You're a *lurker*?"

"I'm not."

"But your eyes—"

"I promise you, it's not what you think. C'mon, Xandra. How can I be? I travel with you during the day, don't I? I sit beside the fire without burning up. I'm not hungry, not like that. I'm no stronger than Chase is. You can kill me right now with a single shot of that gun, if you decide to fire it."

He waits for me to do it. I almost do. Too many months of hunting are ingrained in me: see a lurker, flame a lurker, that's how it should be. But this isn't a match, it's a gun, and if I shoot it, I'm not hunting a monster, I'm killing a man.

But those eyes…

"So," I say after an eternity, ignoring the way he exhales softly; he didn't know if I would do it, either, "you could be—"

"No, Xandra, I *should* have been." He shudders and I see that, apart from the black outline, those sad eyes are the ones I've become familiar with. "Lindsay wasn't the only one who got the Injection. I got it, too… my whole squad did. But I never changed. I never Turned. I don't know why. I thought I'd find some answers if I went off on my own, keeping to myself in case I ever got dangerous. Too many people told me about the New York nest, but nobody could help me. I never really wanted anyone to come with me… if things go wrong, I won't have to worry about living life on the razor's edge. Hell, it's a suicide mission. I've always known that. I only stopped in the remaining communities because it gave me a little taste of home, and the chance to steal an antidote if I can.

"That's what it was all about for me, Xandra. The antidotes. I've never wanted to hurt anyone, but who knows how long I'll be *me*. That rim around my eyes has only grown these last nine months, and I've gotten so cold. So *tired*. I've already drunk three antidotes when it got real bad, and they help for a while… that's all the Grave was supposed to be. Another antidote. No one's ever agreed to leave with me before…"

Until me, I think. And Chase.

Suddenly, I'm reminded of that first day. How Maverick tried to persuade me to stay, how he took me through a lurker-infested neighborhood right after I saw the remains of the graveyard. It started before that, too. He didn't seem all that eager when I volunteered at the high school.

I move two steps back, covering Chase's body with my widening stance.

"You asked me once why I keep that gun. I told you the truth then… but I didn't tell you everything. It reminds me of what I lost, but it's also my safety net. If it happens, if I ever can't control myself and there's no antidote… well, you know. I've got twenty-four hours. It's my insurance policy."

Twenty-four hours. Everyone knows that a lurker is only vulnerable for the first twenty-four hours after they Turn. They can be killed then.

One second. That's all it would take. One second and a quick tug and all my worries would evaporate. I could go home with Chase and nurse him better than Audrey ever would. My fondness for a former cop might even die with him. He would never get the chance to betray us any more than he already has—

The gun seems to triple its weight in my hands. One second stretches into two, and before I know it, a whole minute has passed. I sigh and, turning it around, offer it to him, handle first.

I'm a hunter, not a murderer. And Maverick still is human.

For now.

My action doesn't surprise him so much as it arouses his usual suspicions. Maverick refuses to accept it, taking another step back as if desperate to get away from me.

Desperate, I think, or too ashamed to come any closer…

"Why?" he asks me. "Aren't you frightened? Scared of me? Scared what I can do?"

Am I?

I shrug. "You could've killed me at any point these last few weeks. Before Chase got here, I was alone with you for almost a week. Now, I won't ever forget that you stole from me, but after that… you saved me and Chase from East Jersey. You've partnered with us, and you've killed plenty of lurkers. Knowing how bad you need it, you gave it back so that I could fix Chase. You're… you're something, Maverick Brooks, but you're no monster. I'm not going to shoot you."

"You're not?"

"No."

Honestly, I don't know what's come over me. The Xandra of old wouldn't hesitate to take out a threat. But that Xandra has had to watch too many people she loved die. Mom, Rory, Hallie… Chase was only twenty-four hours away from death. I'm not going to be the one to kill Maverick until I have to. I don't want to be the reason that another survivor dies. I can't take the guilt.

For once I'm going to trust someone else.

I place the gun in the dirt, nudging it toward him with the toe of my boot. Maverick hesitates for a heartbeat before swooping down and picking it up.

"Besides," I add, turning my back on him and praying

that I'm right in putting my trust in this former cop, "I wouldn't have to pull that trigger. I believe you. If you're ever a threat, no one else will get the chance to kill you before you kill yourself."

He doesn't say anything to that, but when I peek over at him again, the gun is hidden from my sight. And, as he turns away from me, so is his face. Though I can't see it for myself, I'm sure his eyes are wide open, awake as they reflect the flames of our night's fire.

He doesn't ask me if he's taking first watch or if I am.

It doesn't matter.

Neither one of us is going to bed tonight.

And then, clearing his throat, he says softly, "James."

I raise my eyebrows at him.

"'Maverick' was the name I earned during my police academy days. But my name… it's James."

I nod at him. "We'll get those lurkers. And we'll find more antidotes. You're one of us now, James."

But if he pulls a stunt like that again, at least I know he's vulnerable for now.

CHAPTER 27

Chase is sleeping, his head in my lap. With my good hand, I stroke his forehead. His temperature is perfectly normal. No fever. He's breathing fine. Teeth are pretty white and as straight as they used to be; no fangs, and his fingernails are the bitten-down nubs I know well instead of claws.

I shouldn't be so worried. I've checked his eyes countless times since last night and nothing's changed. The antidote did its job... I think.

I *hope*.

Twenty-four hours have passed and we're still in Skyway Park. Chase... he hasn't woken up yet. Maverick tells me that it's normal, that the antidote overrides the body and knocks it out because it needs to combat whatever it is that makes a lurker a lurker. I get that. I *knew* that.

But it's one thing to be aware of how an antidote works. It's completely another when someone you love is as good as playing Sleeping Beauty.

Too bad I'm pretty sure a kiss won't be enough to wake up Chase…

Still, it controlled him. A whole day removed from the trauma of thinking I was going to lose Chase, I can marvel over how me kissing him was enough to keep him from Turning quick enough that Maverick and I were in danger. It's like I was his lifeline, and during those terrible minutes, I believed I could be.

What happens now? No fucking clue. I can tell that Maverick is antsy. He says we're so close to Manhattan, he can taste the thick smog and dirt and scent of old piss in the air that used to be old New York.

We don't know what to expect. Maverick's never made it to Manhattan before, and I haven't been since last Christmas, a week before the Turning. We have a ton of people living in New Jersey, but between the number of New Yorkers who received the Injection, how many others were trapped on the island when every exit out was blocked and shut down as soon as the world went to hell, and the lurkers infesting most hi-rises before devouring the survivors… I don't think it's going to be the New York I remember.

I don't know if there will be any survivors at all.

That's what Maverick is banking on. Because, if there's one good thing about having a full day where we didn't march, didn't move, and just lingered around this campsite, it's that I need something to distract me from my worries—and I get that by interrogating Mav about the next stage of his plan.

We're close, right? It's about time I know what's expected of us once we sneak into the city. Are we supposed to just load up on hairspray, matches, and lighters, staring the lurkers down and flaming as many as we can? Between the three of us—and that's assuming Chase is in fighting form—we can probably take ten at a time, but if there's double, triple, even twenty times that?

We'd be fucked, and as boastful of my abilities as I am, even I'm not that cocky.

It doesn't help that I'm not in the greatest shape myself. The pointer finger on my hand is definitely broken. Since last night it's swelled to three times its size, turning a mottled sort of greenish purple where Chase's teeth left an imprint on my skin. He had teased me once when he found out that I carried a pair of tweezers with me in my pack, but I definitely needed them to pick the glass shards out of my hand. It would've been so much easier if I had some aspirin to dull the pain, maybe a hot washcloth like when Jack bandaged up my hand, but I've got neither and I refuse to complain about it. Anytime the urge to bitch comes over me, all I do is take a look at the back of Chase's healing arm and I shut up.

I changed into a spare shirt I snagged from one of the houses we scavenged. My old tank top is so stiff from Chase's dried blood, I can't wear it now, and I tried to wipe some of the dirt and the blood away from his arm. Because he never came back with any water, it's hard to clean, but I managed to knock off some coppery flecks. New skin, raw pink skin, stretches where the bite used to be.

He'll be okay. He has to be. And my finger might give me trouble when it comes to flaming lurkers... but that's now what Maverick has in mind.

Bombs.

Not firebombs, either. *Real* bombs. Well, handmade

bombs that he's been gathering the supplies for in every house we've scavenged since the Grave, but still.

Maverick wants to find a way over the Hudson, head toward the Upper East Side of Manhattan specifically to start, place strategic bombs along multiple blocks, and blow them up. It'll be broad daylight so that the lurkers will be hiding. He expects a majority of them will be lurking in the shadows of the subway system, but there has to be plenty infesting the skyscrapers. The bombs will destroy their individual nests, either the fire burning them or the sunlight if they have to scatter out into it like cockroaches.

How many bombs can he build? He believes he has the supplies to create at least four IEDs, and if it works, we can escape Manhattan and build some more. But, first, we have to go after his first target. To Mav, that's a non-negotiable.

Why the Upper East Side? Of course I ask him that, and I'm actually surprised by the answer—though maybe I shouldn't be.

Tucked in that part of the city, in a tall building with tinted windows, there's a lab. A science lab with ties to the government. His wife was a low-ranking biochemist that worked there for a few months, and was involved in the initial trials of what eventually became the Injection.

That's why he took it. That's why he convinced his needle-phobic wife to take it, too. A cop through and through, he trusted in the government *and* his wife's abilities.

And they failed him.

The National Resilience Institute is a ghost. Maverick believes that every scientist, military personnel, and government official that worked there suffered the same fate as his wife: Turning on New Year's Day. Either it's infested with lurkers or it has information inside that was used to create the Injection that eliminated so many people.

It needs to go.

"What if it has the answer to the antidote?" I asked, stroking Chase's hair. He's still unconscious, and I don't give a fuck what Mav thinks about this thing between me and my twin's fiancé. "Is it worth blowing that up, too?"

"If they could make more antidotes, they would've," was his flat response.

And I get it.

This is about taking out lurkers, of course it is, but at the same time… this is revenge. Maverick Brooks came all this way, went through all of this trouble, sacrificed so much all because he wants to erase the lab that destroyed our lives as we know it—and make sure they can never do it again.

And I'm okay with that.

Thirty-six hours after he stumbled toward our camp, clutching his arm, Chase jolts awake as though he only just fell asleep.

We had to tell him that he made it through *two* nights. It's dawn now, and when he's terrified he still has some lurker in him, I point out that we sat in the sunlight together all day yesterday and nothing happened to him. His arm is back to normal. He needs to piss, to eat, to get clean… but other than that, he's okay.

I try to hide how relieved I am so that he doesn't get the wrong idea, but fuck it. I *am* relieved.

I don't know what I would've done if I had to kill Chase.

Maverick goes with Chase down to the river's shore. When they come back a half an hour later—that I spend stupidly fretting over Chase while I grab a power bar and some stale chips out of my pack so he can have breakfast— with a pair of full steel water bottles eacb between them, Chase has washed the blood from his skin and dunked his head in the iffy river water. I toss him a fresh shirt, feeling flushed when he rips off the bloody one, giving me a front row seat to the view of his muscular, sculpted chest.

Broad and strong, tall yet thick, and without a piece of hair anywhere to distract me from his gorgeous pecs and tapered waist... fuck. He looks even better, and when our eyes meet, I know I'm blushing now.

He catches me staring. Worse, I don't know what he saw written on my face, but on his, I see... hope.

Damn it.

Something's changed. We both can sense it, and whether or not Chase sees his recovery as a new lease on life, he doesn't bother letting me pretend that I don't sense the pull between. He just takes his time in pulling the fresh tee over his head, runs his fingers through his damp hair, then comes over to where I'm sitting next to the food I set out for him.

He crouches down. "Hey."

Nope. Not going to have this conversation. "Here. You haven't eaten in almost two days. Take this. I have some more food in my pack if you want it."

"I'm not really hungry. Not yet."

I know what he's doing. Lurkers are forever starving. By telling me he's not hungry—though I'm sure he has to be—he's just reassuring me that there's no lingering side effects.

I shove the bar at him. It's chocolate and peanut butter, his favorite. "Do it for me. Eat."

Oh, I'm a manipulative bitch now, too. Chase doesn't even hesitate. He rips open the wrapper, then takes a small, dainty-ish bite. I roll my eyes and he laughs. In less than a minute, the entire bar is devoured.

I knew he was hungry.

Once he's done, he takes a deep breath. "So… I messed up. One of those bastards got me."

I knew he would blame himself. "No one's perfect, Chase. And you got it in the end, didn't you?"

A shrug like battling a lurker after it has the taste of your blood is no big deal. "You gave your antidote to me."

I can feel the heat of Maverick's gaze on the side of my face as I speak to Chase. "Hey. Let's call us even, okay? You gave up your antidote for me back in East Jersey."

"I had to. And, I'll tell you what… I'd do it again."

Same, Chase, same.

New York City.

Travel was slow-going the last few days. We already knew that there would be a much heavier lurker presence the closer we got to the nest, but I don't think we realized what that really meant.

We blew past fifty the night before, and none of us got any sleep once we made it to the New Jersey side of the

George Washington Bridge. It was dark out, and though the mile-and-a-half long suspension bridge was clear enough that we could see lurkers approaching from either side, we were basically sitting ducks. Each one of us carried a handmade torch, choosing to continue the march.

On the plus side, we're faster than lurkers. The bridge wasn't wide enough for them to overwhelm us, especially since the portable fire had them hesitate long enough for us to engage the stare. By the time we fought our way across, there were forty more piles of ash to be blown away into the Hudson River, and we landed in the Washington Heights area of New York.

It's been close to a week since Chase was attacked. You'd never know he was bit at all, though I do notice he's part of the reason why it took so long for us to go from Skyway Park to Fort Lee where we reached the GWB. After his recovery, I told him about Maverick's plan. I needed to give him the choice to still come along; knowing Mav's true motivations behind this hunt, Chase needed to decide if that's what he wanted to do. I should've known better than to doubt him. Of course he's going—as long as I'm going, that is—though his determination to get to New York so we can finally start the return trip to the Grave has wavered some.

I could tell that Maverick was disappointed that I laid out all of his cards for Chase. Too bad. He should just be lucky that, for now at least, I decided to keep the fact that he took the Injection to myself.

If his eyes get any worse, or he pales more notably, or gets even hungrier… I'll have to tell Chase. Until then, I don't want to worry him.

And if I tell myself that instead of admitting it's

because I know he'll drag me off this crazy mission the instant I give me a reason to, well… I've come all this way. Maverick might be targeting the science lab responsible for creating the lurkers.

Me? My intentions have always been clear. I'm going to kill as many lurkers as I can or die trying.

Washington Heights is a good hundred blocks from the NRI. In the before times, that might've given me a pause. Why walk when there are taxis, rideshares, and public transportation like buses and subways? Now? After we've walked a million miles just to get to this point, I laugh. A hundred blocks? I can do that in about an hour-and-a-half so long as the roads aren't too damaged.

To my surprise, they're not that bad. It still stings to see the dried blood and char marks everywhere, the bones, the empty cars, and torn asphalt, but there are stretches in front of us that are almost… normal. It's spooky as hell because New York City is never vacant, and it seems like one big graveyard, but with Maverick carrying his primed IEDs in that duffel bag, I'm looking forward to the coming explosions.

Too bad we never get the chance to take them out of the bag.

It's late morning. We should have had *hours* to engage the bombs, place them where Maverick wants, then stand back and watch the NRI implode.

Should have had.

We don't.

The NRI is positioned on 63rd street. When there were only six blocks to go, a sound from our old lives rips through the silence, catching our attention.

A car.

No.

An SUV.

The big, shiny, black vehicle comes speeding down a side street, taking a wide turn, careening down the cross street. My hand goes to my pocket, reaching for my knife. Chase jumps in front of me.

Maverick howls in rage.

The SUV stops maybe twenty feet ahead of us, spitting out six near-identical men. White skin. Dark hair. Black suits. Black shades.

Holy fuck, we've summoned the Men in Black.

One of them—the driver—takes the lead. He's a little taller, a little thinner, and I notice that he has a red tie while all the others have a grey one.

The leader, I'm betting.

"Seize them," he orders.

The five remaining men surge forward in unison, moving impossibly faster than any human should. Two each for Maverick and Chase, one to grab my arm, breaking my hold on my knife. Already they're underestimating me. I immediately promise myself that, if I can get out of this, they'll so regret it.

Maverick starts to buck and fight their hold, but the two silent agents—because they have got to be some sort of agents—standing on each side of him barely pay him any attention. Their eyes are locked on the man in front, and when he nods one time, the agent on the left releases Maverick's upper arm, grabbing his forearm instead. A single powerful squeeze, then a sickening crack, and we all know it's broken.

Maverick doesn't scream, but his face—already so pale, even after so many days spent in the sun as the Injection goes to work on him—is suddenly ashen. He sags in the other agent's hold, all the fight in him gone.

"That's better. We'd hoped to offer you our hospitality without a fight, but if you insist…"

Hospitality again. We escaped Rex and East Jersey only to get caught by a SUV full of government spooks who might not have threatened to feed us to lurkers—*yet*—but they speak in violence all the same.

"Fuck you," I snap, rage roaring through me like a gasoline-soaked fire. "Who do you think you are?"

The man in front whips off his sunglasses. I shrink back in horror, and I know I'm not alone.

His eyes are solid black.

Lurker eyes.

Pale skin.

Extraordinary strength…

"You're some of them?"

Chase says *them* like it's a dirty word, and I don't blame him.

I'm fucking stunned. I can't believe that we've been face to face with nearly a half-dozen lurkers in the sunlight and not a single one of them is trying to eat us. And then I realize something else—

"You can talk? If you're a lurker… how can you talk?"

And that's when it hits me.

The suits. The building. The car… the *eyes*.

They're not lurkers.

They're the people who created them.

CHAPTER 28

His name is Winston, and he's the brains behind Project Phoenix.

How do I know that? While two of his goons return to the SUV, driving off who knows where, the man with the black eyes and red tie instructs the other three to grab each one of us by the nape of the neck, herding us to the NRI building. The glass doors open, as though they recognize the men, and we're marched inside a lab that is sterile and clean, yet smells like caramel.

Not burnt sugar. Not like the rot of a lurker, but close enough.

Because that's what they are. Lurkers who have their wits about them. Lurkers who can talk, who can go out in the sunlight, who can control their hunger. Oh, they get all of the upside. They're fast. They're strong.

They're indestructible.

Because that's what the Injection was meant to do. What the scientists who worked for the NRI had spent years working on.

Project Phoenix. A state-of-the-art medication that, like the National Resilience Institute was instructed by the US government to create, was designed to turn ordinary Americans into superhumans.

Or, as Winston explained after he led us into an empty office, forced us into three of the four visitor chairs before taking the one behind the expensive-looking desk, it was meant to make us, "The perfect blend of human and monster. Strong enough to withstand anything, powerful enough to conquer any who oppose us, and as close to immortal as we can be. Like the phoenix, we would rise up from the ashes of a world on fire and then our administration would rule it."

Fuck that.

I've always hated the government. Not like I'm an anarchist or anything. I just don't believe that, even in the before times, they did enough to help us ordinary people. Hearing that they *planned* the Injection, that they were trying to turn the American population into some kind of supersoldiers... yeah. That doesn't sit right with me at all.

And that's not even counting that they obviously failed somewhere. Project Phoenix was Project Fuck-up as far as I'm concerned, but I know better than to interject. It's probably not a good sign that Winston is offering us all of this information unprompted.

Maybe it's because he thinks highly of himself and this project and just wants to show off.

Or maybe—

"The first trials were done on volunteers in the NRI. As you can see," he says, gesturing at himself, "they were a success. Apart from a newfound intolerance of the sun and bright lights, Project Phoenix did what it was supposed to do."

Then, in case we need any other evidence of how fucking amazing Winston is, he rises from his chair, bends down behind his desk, and, with one hand lifts the whole damn thing two feet off the ground.

That looks like mahogany to me. That sucker's gotta weigh close to four hundred pounds and he's holding it *with one hand*.

Message received. As if one of the other goons snapping Mav's forearm like a twig wasn't proof enough of how impossibly strong they are...

"In case it didn't, some of our finest minds had a backup plan," Winston says, setting the desk back down on the floor. "Unfortunately, the antidote wasn't... let's say, *perfected*." Again, he gestures toward his face, drawing attention to the shades that the agents wear even indoors. "By the time we worked out the bugs on that, the president had insisted that we push through the most recent batch of PP-56"—the Injection, I'm betting—"that was unfortunately... tainted. A sad mistake. When it was designed to go into effect, it... turned."

No, asshole. It *Turned*.

There's that rage bubbling up inside of me. I couldn't give a fuck about the sunglasses-wearing prick standing behind me. I know he was ordered to keep his hand on my neck during our march to the NRI because it would take a twitch of his damn pinkie to snap it. The threat was real. They had us, and we had no choice but to go with them.

He could kill me now. Considering Winston had gone to great trouble to capture us before we could blow up their building—almost as if he knew or suspected something like that could happen as we approached the NRI—he has to have a reason. Add that to how he's still giving us all of this information like a villain monologuing… either I'm safe or I'm dead either way, and I might as well let out some of my rage before it burns a hole in my gut.

"Because of your tainted medicine? Because your stupid fucking president"—who made a big display of taking the Injection on TV, one of the first to do it, and who inevitably became one of the first lurkers to Turn… though, I remember, the white house kept that under wraps until their commander-in-chief chowed down on his press secretary in front of TV cameras and there was no one left to create the spin for him—"released an untested medication to thirty percent of the population? Millions of people died that day!"

The lurkers have decimated America for a half-assed science project?

"Yes," Winston says, and there isn't a hint of emotion in his pale face. No shame. No regret. "The antidotes were too late to save many. And… well… a cage didn't work to contain certain indispensable individuals as it should have. That will have to be adjusted for the next phase of Project Phoenix."

"Next phase?"

Next phase?

He nods, seemingly bored—and I loathe him.

I loathe every fucking monster who had a hand in this.

For what? Fame? Power? Profits?

The powerful men and women at the top of the food chain played with our lives and basically ruined them. Knowing now that the president was kept in a cage after his Turning by men like Winston—men who were strong enough to contain him, then failed, leading to the rest of the world discovering that the president was a lurker… and withdrawing any help they had offered us—doesn't make me feel any better.

Good people died, too, and I will *never* forgive anyone who put this into motion.

"Fuck you."

"Pardon?"

A pair of chilled fingers pinch my neck. I don't care. Way I see it, we're dead anyway. "I said—"

"So what happens now?" That's Chase. As always, he's my knight in shining armor, rushing to my rescue. "Are you going to let us go?"

He might be wearing shades, but there's no denying the scrutinizing look that Winston gives Chase, almost like he's peering through a microscope at an unusual create. "You won't be allowed to leave New York."

"So… what? We're staying here now?"

"Oh? Did I give you that impression? I'm sorry. Of course you won't be staying here."

The goon responsible for Maverick raises his hand; no reason to watch the cop closely considering he's gone silent, sagging in his seat, completely out of it since we were caught by his enemies before he could exact his revenge. No help from him, though I do feel a little bad.

If being snagged by these assholes is bad for me and Chase, it must be hell for Maverick—especially after they snapped his arm, leaving him cradling it against his chest.

Winston nods at the other agent, gesturing for him to come closer. As the other man leans in and whispers in his boss's ear, Winston listens and continues to nod.

"I stand corrected. I guess you could say that this

facility is your new home. You see, I lead the project, but I'm not in charge of any of the science behind it. That's above my pay grade, and I just follow orders from those left to give them. In this case, that's the Doctor. Seems like we're in need of test subjects for further trials for the next phase of the project. You three will do nicely."

Winston rises up, planting his hands against the desktop. "We're done here," he says, addressing our new bodyguards. "Take them away."

They don't shackle us or handcuff us the way that Rex did, but with six more suit-wearing lurkers coming out of the woodworks, flanking us on each side as they lead us underground, I admit that there's no point in running.

There's nowhere for us to run *to*.

They take us down the emergency stairwells. Each level is gloomy and dark, carrying that same sickly sweet smell with it. It's the perfect amount of light to keep these almost-lurkers from wincing, though they all keep their sunglasses on as we're herded down so many flights, I lose count.

My head is spinning. They've moved their formation so that there is at least one agent standing between the three of us. If we try to speak, the one in the back barks at us to keep quiet. I can't say anything to either Maverick or Chase, and that includes any plotting for an escape.

Even hand signals are out. I twitched my finger once, and the agent directly behind me said that if I did it again, he'd break it. Bastard. I already have a broken pointer finger on my right hand. I don't need another one.

Still, I hold out hope that we can get out of this mess before they turn us into a trio of human guinea pigs—hope that lasts until they march us in front of a glass door, pull it open, wait for us to go in, and slam it shut.

I don't need to hear the lock turning to know what this is.

It's a cell.

There thee of us share a small room around the size of Stacey Finch's bedroom back in the Grave. A small stainless steel toilet is in one corner, an even smaller sink perched over it. Two narrow cots—twin-sized if we're lucky—are lined up against the furthest wall, a small gap between them, making the setup look like an equal sign. No blankets, only a sterile white sheet and a single creased pillow.

Two video cameras are positioned in opposite corners. Two of the walls are made of solid grey cinderblock. The third has a white door built into it that is across from the door we entered in through on the fourth wall.

About an hour after we're abandoned in this room, I'm pacing, Chase is whispering assurances under his breath that I know neither of us believe, and Maverick... he claimed one of the cots, lying on his side, giving us his back while still cradling his broken arm.

And that's when a pale woman wearing a lab coat and carrying a clipboard walks in through the same door we did, bringing two suit-wearing agents with her; like the agents, she has on sunglasses. She's about forty years old, give or take, her light brown hair pulled into a low bun.

With the agents' help, she takes blood from each of us, jabbing Maverick's good arm repeatedly until her needle can break through his skin and reach his web-thin veins.

Another small tube contains a hair plucked for each of our heads; my scalp is still stinging from where the sunglasses-wearing technician yanked it from the root.

It's a good thing that I've been in such close contact with these two these last few weeks because when they demand we all fill a third vial with urine, there's no privacy. Having no other choice, we all drop our pants on the spot.

Once she has collected all of her samples, she places them in a black nylon bag—similar to a lunchbox—that one of the agents is holding. That done, she checks her clipboard before reaching into one of the way-too-many pockets on her labcoat. Without a single expression crossing her emotionless features, she pulls out two syringes. One is only partly filled. The other is completely filled.

The medicine inside of it is the same color as piss.

Lovely.

She goes over to Maverick first. "Give me your arm."

"Go to hell," is his rough, grave reply.

She ignores that. Instead, she glances at the nearest agent. "Hold him."

Again, moving much quicker than should be possible, he's suddenly at Maverick's bedside. One shove on Mav's shoulder and the cop is on his back, spitting obscenities that tell me he still has some fight in him. Not enough considering the goon pins him easily, holding him in place for the technician to inject him with the entire full syringe.

"What the fuck was that?" he demands. "More of the Injection that killed Lindsay and ruined my life?"

If this technician was one who worked alongside

Maverick's wife, I have no clue. She doesn't react at all to her name. She doesn't react to *anything* but her clipboard.

She glances at it again, then turns toward me.

"You're next."

I shake my head. "I don't want it."

I wasn't important enough to rate an Injection in the before times. It saved me then… I sure as hell don't want to mess with it now.

Chase steps in front of me.

The technician looks down her nose, finding me anyway as though I don't have a man blocking her path.

"You don't have any choice. This is just a basic healing serum. It'll knit your bones together, fixing that finger of yours like it'll fix his arm. Now give me your hand. The Doctor insists on testing whole specimens only, and he doesn't like to be kept waiting."

Like I care. "No."

Her head tilts enough that I know what'll happen even before it does. The other agent grips my hand before I can blink, presenting my hand to the technician.

She pricks me with the syringe, shooting the tiny amount of serum into my skin.

"There. By the time we get you to the Doctor, it will be healed."

"I'm not going to the Doctor."

That's what I say. I meant it, too, but I knew that, when I came down to it, I'd have no choice about that, either— and I don't.

The technician and her entourage disappeared through that door as soon as she got what she needed. I hated to think what she was doing with our hair and our blood and our pee, but when she returns another two hours later with her precious clipboard, we all find out.

She turns toward Maverick first. Like my finger, his broken arm did heal. He's currently lying on his back, arms folding behind his head, and after he erupted on the technician earlier, he hasn't said another damn word since.

No matter how Chase and I try to get him to talk to us.

He was the planner. The man with the map. The man with the bombs. Everything we had was confiscated by Winston when they caught us—including my pocketknife, though I was allowed to keep my jacket... for now—and I think losing his gun broke him more than failing to blow up the NRI.

Chase has hope. That's just the kind of guy he is. He vows he'll get us out of this, and I want to believe him desperately. This can't be it for us. Back at the Grave... I was going to finally figure out why I can't stop thinking about him.

But we're not at the Grave. We're in New York, and I don't think we're getting out of here anytime soon.

At least, if Winston has his way, we definitely won't...

The technician taps her clipboard. "James Brooks. You have traces of the Injection in your system, but a minimal reaction. The Doctor wants to study that."

Right next to me, Chase startles. I don't know what surprises him more: that Maverick isn't really Mav's name or that he took the Injection but didn't Turn. It's probably not a good thing that I didn't show any reaction to that— he has to know that I *did* know—but before he can do or say anything, the technician turns on him.

"Chase Reynolds. We found lingering lurker venom, plus the initial dose of an antidote. The Doctor wants to reverse the antidote and see if you Turn or if you become one of us. The first class."

What?

They want to make him a monster?

"No—"

She ignores my pained shout. "Hallie Holden. There—"

It's like a record scratch. Hearing my twin's name right after this horrible woman announces that their Doctor plans to fuck with Chase… I can't help it.

"What the… No. You got it wrong. I'm not Hallie. I'm Xandra."

If her face could move at all, she would be frowning. She points at something on her clipboard. It's a computer print-out. "Hallie Holden," she repeats. "Twenty-three. From Madison, New Jersey."

I don't know how they got all that information from my vitals and my fluids, but only two of those three are correct. "Wrong. It's Alexandra Holden."

"Interesting," she says in a voice that tells me that my insistence is more of an annoyance than anything else. "In that case, the Doctor will see you first."

CHAPTER 29

'm watching every inch of every step of this trek through the stark and sterile hallways. There's got to be a way out and with Chase and Maverick locked away in the cell, it's up to me to find it. And I will.

We've gone further on the same floor. I know the entrance to the emergency stairwells is behind us, but as they take me deeper into the bowels of this building, I understand why they tossed us in a cell down here.

Because the large office on the other end belongs to the Doctor.

If he has a name, I don't know it. The nameplate on the door was removed, and when the two agents march me into his office, he doesn't introduce himself. He accepts their monotone greetings—"Doctor", "Doctor"—as his due, then takes the clipboard from the shorter of the two men.

The female technician had scrawled on the print-out in pen before passing it over to the agent. The two men were instructed to bring me to the Doctor while she disappeared through the white door this time. The agents had warned Maverick and Chase to stay put as they led me out, and only the door slamming in Chase's face kept him from coming after me.

Now, alone with a stranger for the first time in a month, I'm afraid.

Scratch that.

I'm *terrified*.

The Doctor could be Winston's twin. A man of indeterminate age, he has the same soulless face. The same dark hair. The same pale skin. The same black eyes. Unlike the other residents of the NRI building, he doesn't wear the shades. It's like he wants you to see the unnaturalness of his gaze while he looks you over. Like the technician, he has on a labcoat.

One word—*Doctor*—is embroidered over the pocket of his white coat. A scalpel, an injection, and a pen poke out through the top.

Under his labcoat, he has on a suit. His tie isn't red or grey.

It's black.

"Take a seat."

His voice is as deep as a canyon. Still no emotion in it, but the rumble leaves me uncomfortable. Though I want to shoot my middle finger up at him—and there aren't any agents around to stop me—that thought gives me pause.

Is the Doctor so dangerous that he doesn't need any backup?

Fuck.

I take a seat.

Unlike Winston's desk, he has a sterile folding table set up between us. Plastic chairs are placed on each side. On top of the table, I see a weird-looking machine. It has wires and paper, a moving part and something like an oxygen monitor… holy shit. It looks like a lie detector test.

If that doesn't freak me out enough, the large black collar he pulls out of his pocket does. It reminds me of the collar I bought for the orange cat that I tried to tame in the before times, only without a jingling bell.

Oh, and the fact that it's *human*-sized.

Once I'm seated, the Doctor zips over to me. I'm still marveling over his speed—especially since lurkers go half as fast as humans—when he quickly puts the collar on me. It's not tight enough that I can't breathe, but it's definitely not loose enough for me to breathe easily. As I gape at him, he hooks me up to the possible lie detector thing.

"What…" I tug at it, panic rising. "What's this?"

He doesn't answer me. Instead, he takes out a small silver button that looks like it could be a car starter, then places it on the table. He flicks another button on the side of the contraption, then stares at me.

He reminds me of the younglings in a weird way. When he stares at me, I freeze.

"What is your name?" he asks.

Stupid question. He has that print-out in front of him, plus the note from the technician. He knows who I am.

Maybe this is one of those initial questions that help tell a polygraph proctor when the person attached to it is lying.

"Xandra— what the fuck!"

I was zapped. A low grade pulse around my neck, coming from the collar he put on me. I told him my name, he pressed the button on the table, and he *zapped* me.

He ignores my outburst.

"Your full name?"

"Alexandra Holden—Jesus Christ! Stop that!"

It was even worst that time. Another shock that made my throat constrict, trying to get away from the pain.

He looks down his nose at me. "You will be shocked every time you tell a lie. You don't want to feel pain? Tell me who you are."

"I did!"

He presses the button.

I scream.

The Doctor waits until I've stopped screaming and I'm only panting in the aftershocks of another jolt.

And then—

"Who is the most important person in your life?"

"My twin."

After glancing at the polygraph, he doesn't press the button. Looks like I finally got one right.

"What is her name?"

"Hallie—God fucking damn it!"

Stars exploded behind my eyes. I taste blood in my mouth.

He really upped the voltage on that one.

His expression is a flat mask, though I see disdain in his eyes as he says, "You know why you're getting shocked, don't you, Hallie?"

I grit my teeth. "My name is Xandra." That time, when the shock comes, I don't give the bastard the satisfaction of crying out. Even if I do almost bite the tip of my tongue off when I spasm in response to it.

"We are very good at what we do at the NRI, Hallie." Hallie. He keeps calling me Hallie. "Identical twins do not share an identical DNA make-up. There are genetic mutations that go beneath the skin. We also took your fingerprints from the urine sample jar you provided Elissa. Yours belong to Hallie Holden."

I don't know how they got my prints, but I don't care.

"She's dead."

"Your sister might be dead. Alexandra is dead. You are Hallie."

"Fuck you!"

He presses the button.

I howl.

For the next ten minutes, he insists that I can't be Xandra. He goes between asking questions that I answer with the truth—that he doesn't shock me for—and then he askes me my name. Every time I answer "Xandra", the pain is almost impossible to stand.

And then I break.

"What is your name?"

I'm crying now. I don't even remember when that started. My nose bled, too; I wiped it with the sleeve of Rory's jacket. My head aches. I want to die.

But I can't.

Not yet.

However, I answer him. I tell him what he wants to hear because, after the trauma he put me through, I don't even know who I am anymore.

"I'm Hallie. Me. My sister Xandra is dead. I'm alive. I'm Hallie." I swallow a sob. "I'm Hallie."

The Doctor leans over and peers at his damned machine.

"And the polygraph says that that is the truth."

Maybe the Doctor isn't as big a heartless bastard as I thought. He opens the door, gesturing for one of the agents that is waiting just outside of it. He comes back with a glass of water and a box of tissues for me. While jotting down notes on his clipboard, he lets me sit and get a hold of myself. I wipe my eyes, blow my nose, and hope like hell that this is another one of my nightmares that I just haven't woken up from yet.

When it becomes obvious that it isn't, I shut down. I go as emotionless as the Doctor. I don't want him to have the satisfaction that he broke me down to nothing, and I just sit there until he finishes what he's doing and tells Hallie that she can go.

That *I* can go.

The last thing he says is that he looks forward to our next session, and I decide then and there to survive this just so I can get the opportunity to snatch the scalpel from his pocket and slit his fucking throat.

As I walk out the door, I ask myself: How can I be Hallie? Hallie was the sweet one. The gentle one. She would never have murderous thoughts... unless the Turning and her beloved sister's death broke her even more than the Doctor did.

I'll kill him. Sure, lurkers are invulnerable. What about the monster that the Doctor is?

I don't know, but it's worth a try.

Another pair of agents, nearly indistinguishable from the others, returns me to the cell. I plod inside, with one of them following right on my heel.

He points at Chase. "You. Come with me. The Doctor will see you now."

My soul cries out. In that moment, looking at him,

seeing his hazel eyes and his sandy-brown hair and that crooked smile… maybe I am Hallie because I love him so much that I ache with it. I want to run to him. To grab him. To hold him close, to cleave him to me, to keep that goon from getting anywhere near him.

My fingers fly up to my face, my bottom lip wavering as I whisper, "No," under my breath. I don't want Chase going anywhere near that bastard. What the Doctor did to me… I can't let him hurt Chase.

I can't let him experiment on him or try to reverse the antidote.

But what can I do?

"Chase, no—"

Maverick gets up off the cot. He looks at me, looks at Chase, then glares at the agent.

"I'm supposed to be next."

What?

The dick in shades seems just as confused as I am. Is Maverick volunteering to go before Chase?

"The bitch who took my blood. She said I was going next. You want to ask her? Or do you want to keep the Doctor waiting?"

Holy shit. He… he is. I know Maverick. I know it when he bluffs; he did that in East Jersey before I could tell the difference. Now… he's buying Chase a little time—and we all know it.

The agent isn't about to question it. I think he must be more afraid of the Doctor than Elissa because he just nods, grabs Maverick's arm, and drags the cop out of the cell.

The moment the door slams shut, Chase is moving. His arms are wrapped around me, pulling me toward him, squeezing me close.

"What did they do to you? Are you okay? Tell me you're okay. God, I love you so fucking much. You have to be okay."

He's careful not to use any name. I don't know why that stands out to me, but as he holds me close, his arms a possessive brand around my back, I hear everything he wants to say… and that I want to hear.

What did they do to me? He doesn't need to hear it, and I can't tell him. Not exactly. It'll hurt Chase even more to know how I was tortured, especially since I'm—

I'm—

I press my head against his chest and whisper one word: "*Baby.*"

That's what Chase used to call Hallie. And that's the same pet name she had for him. Xandra used to tell me it would make her barf, and…

And that was Xandra.

I'm not Xandra.

I pull back, tilting my head up so that I can stare into Chase's stunned yet hopeful face. Fuck. He's fragile. He's so damn fragile, and I did this to him. He wants to believe I said what he thinks I said, and it'll shatter him if he's wrong.

And I know in an instant that this man would've waited an eternity to be my baby again.

"Baby," I say, firmer this time. Then, going up on my tiptoes, I lift my hand, threading my fingers through his hair, and kiss him with everything I have.

Chase groans into my mouth.

"Is it you?" he asks before diving in again, kissing me so deeply, it's like he's touching the back of my throat with his tongue. He retreats just enough to rest his forehead against mine, eyes searching my face for some sign that I'm who he is looking for. "Hallie, baby… tell me it's you."

I nod. That's the most I can get out right now.

"I want to believe it. Fuck. If it's true… okay." He straightens, though he doesn't release me. "When we were twenty, we got caught fucking in my bedroom when we thought no one was home. You were so embarrassed, you swore you'd never tell anyone. Not even Xandra. Who caught us?"

I think back. It's not as easy as it should be—and that's worrisome—but, with a flash, I see Rory's face twisted in a mixture of amusement and horror.

I don't know if I want to laugh or cry at the memory. "You ass. You're trying to trick me. It wasn't your bedroom. It was mine. Rory popped his head in to ask me a question, yelled 'dude' when he saw you on top of his little sister, and I pushed you off of me."

Chase stops breathing for a moment. "I bruised my ass on your floor. The next time I saw Rory, he gave me a box of condoms and a 'do not disturb' sign."

"He did? I didn't know that."

"Because you pretended it didn't happen. You even made me wait two weeks before we had sex again, you were so embarrassed."

I… I remember. A twenty-year-old Chase was so hard up after two weeks, he was begging me for a little affection. I gave in, and we never went more than a few days since—until I forgot who I was and only fucked him once in the last three months.

Something Chase seems very determined to remedy all of a sudden.

One second, he's holding me tight, peering at me like

I'm the eighth wonder of a world that might not have any others left. Who knows? America has been destroyed, but when the news stopped, so did any reports whether or not the lurkers had spread to the rest of the world.

That's one second. The next? Chase drops his head, kissing my neck. His hands go to my ass. I gasp as he hoists me up, guiding me to wrap my legs around him.

I clutch his shoulders as he starts to move. "Chase? What are you doing?"

"I need you, Hallie. You're here… you're *back*. I love you." He carries me easily, but not far. Instead of going to the bed, he backs me up against the nearest wall. Setting me down on my feet, he reaches between us, going for the button on my jeans. "I *need* you."

Holy shit. He wants to fuck me *now*?

I shouldn't be surprised. I've been fighting my need and desire for this man since July. I gave in once, telling myself that would be enough, but when I only became more and more addicted… yeah. I should've known then that something was up. Xandra tolerated Chase. She thought I could do better. No matter what, she never would've made a move on him.

But Hallie? In this life or any other, I would recognize this man as the other half of my soul.

Does that mean I want to pick up where we left off in East Jersey and put on a fucking show for whoever is on the other side of those cameras?

He's got the button undone, my zipper down. Now he's working on his, so determined, it's a little flattering that he needs to fuck me *this* badly.

I feel like I at least have to remind him of the shitty

situation we're in. "Chase! Are you insane? There are cameras in here."

"And? They just put my wife in a cell with me after doing something to help her remember she *is* my wife. They had to expect this. You're mine, Hallie. Before you forget again, I'm going to fuck my wife, and if they want to watch, enjoy the goddamn show."

Technically, I'm not his wife. We were engaged, and kept putting off the marriage for superficial reasons that I can't remember at the moment. Not when Chase has his hand slipping underneath my panties, his breath on my ear as he pants, "Say yes, baby, say yes."

When was the last time we showered? There's ash on my skin, like usual, and this is probably the worst time to forget our surroundings and lose ourselves in each other.

But you know what? You only live once, and there's no promise that I'll get another chance, so…

"Yes, baby," I moan, his fingers brushing up against my clit.

Fuck me. From the moment he said he needed me, my body had already started to respond to him. I can only imagine how soaked I am, and when he shoves my jeans down, peeling my panties away from me, they seem to stick. I'm hot. I'm breathing heavily as he works to get one boot off, then the other. My jeans and panties follow, leaving my lower half completely bare to him.

As Chase hurries to release his dick, not even bothering to undress himself, I shrug off Rory's jacket. I'll keep it, it's mine now—and a reminder of the sister *and* brother I lost —but right now, I want as much of me pressed up against Chase as I can get.

My back is still to the wall. I'm ready to fuck Chase,

and when he whips out his erection, it's easy to see that there won't be any foreplay necessary. Not when there's a chance we can be interrupted at any moment.

Chase is thinking along the same lines as me. Pushing me up so that I'm on the tiptoes of one foot, he grabs me under the other thigh, hooking the other foot around his waist, spreading me wide open. The wall at my back, his chest up against me, he pins me in place right as he uses his free hand to grab the base of his erection and guide the head of his cock to my waiting pussy.

Once we're lined up, he shoves. One thrust inside of me and the only man I've ever loved has found his way home.

For a moment, he just stays there, stretching me out as I take everything he has to offer. He leans his head, nipping my bottom lip until I open my mouth, inviting him in. He kisses me, really kisses me, and as I cling to him again, he begins to move.

Chase fucks me as though he's sure that this will be the last time. There's no quarter, there's no relief. He thrusts up again and again. I take him, moaning his name, moaning how much I love him, and when he grabs my throat, collaring it while holding my head still as I bounce, he kisses me with damp cheeks.

He's crying. Chase Reynolds is crying as he fucks me, and it takes everything I have not to weep in love and loss and relief at the same time.

I think he just needed a few moments to let the tears flow. Not too much later, his face is determined, eyes blazing as he increases his pace. I hop up. He catches me with one hand, both of my legs wrapped around him now.

His thrusts become more shallow as he rocks into me, unwilling to separate completely.

Chase isn't going to last. This was something he wanted for too long, and he wanted it too much. I know him. I know his tells, and I know his body. He's about to blow, and proving that he knows mine as well, he shoves his hand between our damp shirts and slick bodies to rub frantically at my clit, helping me to come without relying on just penetration alone.

God, I fucking love this man.

I throw my head back, smashing it into the wall. It vaguely hurts, but compared to the memory of what the Doctor did to me, it's nothing. In fact, I need this pleasure to replace the shocks and the zaps and the jolts, and as Chase fucks me to a sudden climax, I feel the best that I have in months.

Because of Chase.

Because I love him.

Because I always have.

CHAPTER 30

wish I could say that Chase has a magic dick. That he fucked me back into being Hallie Holden, and now all of my thoughts, feelings, and emotions belong to the twin who really survived.

If only.

My sister's death obviously broke me. Whatever the Doctor did to me only made it worse. I know who I am now, but what does that mean? I still feel like Xandra. I feel strong and determined and ready to kick lurker ass.

But, at the same time, I *am* Hallie. Because only Hallie would curl up against Chase Reynolds, snuggling against his side, feel the satisfied rumble of a man who just fucked the love of his life against the wall before tugging her onto a tiny twin-sized bed with him... only Hallie would hear his heart beat through his chest and know with one hundred percent certainty that it's only ever beaten for her.

Chase...

Ever since the accident, he was so sure I was Hallie.

From the early days, demanding I give her back to him, to all the near slips… calling me by that name, calling me "baby"… I thought he was just trying to turn me into the Holden sister that he lost.

No.

He was trying everything he could to convince me that I'm the one he couldn't bear to lose.

I lay my hands on his chest, teasing his nipple through his t-shirt. My whole life, Chase has been my only lover; I'm the same for him. From the moment we gave each other our virginities when we were seventeen, I've slept with him countless times. He can be leisurely and slow or demanding and quick depending on how bad he needs me.

He was coming within minutes. It's a miracle that he reached between us, getting me off first before he exploded inside of me, but there was pure desperation in every kiss, in every touch, in every thrust until he was panting my name over and over again as he finished.

That was close to three months of having his fiancé close, but unable to touch her without her threatening to chop off his fingers. He must've thought I was coming back to him the one time my body recognized him as mine even though my mind didn't. That night on the couch… I fucked my own fiancé, then tortured myself over it for ages because I thought he was Hallie's.

He is.

He always has been.

And not even being trapped in a cell in the basement of a rogue government agency will stop him from claiming me as his wife.

A tiny grin tugs on my lips. It's not even funny, but I

just changed my mind. When I though that I wasn't Chase's wife yet because we never had a wedding... hell. In the eyes of East Jersey, I belong to Chase. I finally consummated that jailhouse wedding they insisted happened after Chase bartered his antidote for my hand.

He's my husband. At the very least, if we don't get out of here in one piece together, I can die knowing that he's always been mine, too.

It's a morbid thought, and one that Xandra definitely would've had. Shit. It's going to take some time for me to get back in my own head, and I only hope that—as brutal as the Doctor's treatment was—it works. That I remember who I am.

If not, I have Chase to remind me.

I trace a path between his pecs before circling the spot where his heart is with my newly healed finger. No more break, no more cuts from the glass vial... "How long did you know?"

"Hmm?"

He's always been the type of lover to get lazy and dozy and content after he comes. I remember that, too.

That's not going to stop me, though. "About me, baby. How long did you know about me?"

He goes still beneath my questing finger. At first, he's doesn't answer me. His hand caresses the back of my upper arm, fingertips skipping lightly over my burn. While we didn't undress completely for sex, I did shed Rory's jacket. It's currently on the floor, leaving Chase to touch my ruined skin gently.

And then—

"Did Jack ever tell you what happened that night?"

He doesn't have to say *what* night. I know what he

means. "Not really. Just that the firebomb reacted when it found a gas leak. There was a backdraft and it went straight at me and my sister. Only one of us made it. Someone found us, bringing me all the way to St. Matthew's to see if I could be saved."

And it hits me. Something I should've figured out a long, long time ago...

"It was you. Wasn't it? You saved me."

Chase squeezes me closer to him. "I'm so sorry, Hallie. The explosion hit when me and Kev were scouting two streets over. I ran, but Xandra... she got a full blast of it. There was no way she would make it... she was already gone. There was ash, and you... you were unconscious in the street, your arm already blistering from the shot of fire you got." He leans in, pressing a kiss to the side of my hair. "I couldn't help her, but I had to save you. I covered you with that jacket Xandra always wore and I picked you up. Kevin stayed behind to watch for any lurkers while I got you out of there. I carried you all the way to St. Matthew's. You never stirred once." His voice breaks. "I thought you were *dead*."

"I never died," I whisper. "I should have. Xandra was the strong one. She killed the lurkers. She wasn't supposed to die."

His voice breaks.

My heart shatters.

In an instant, I begin to tremble against him. The sobs I've been holding in for close to three months burst free of me like a torrent.

I guess, since I spent all of that time living as if I was my twin, I never got the chance to mourn Xandra—and with the sudden realization that she's dead, I'm not, and Chase was the one to find us after the accident… I *sob*.

When Chase pulls me on top of him, no lust, just support as he lets me cry, I think it finally starts to sink in. Once again, there's no turning back now. The pretense is over. Everything makes so much more sense now. Why I woke up and couldn't deny my attraction to Chase and why, no matter how far I pushed him away, he never got too far. Why Jack called my "Allie"—so close to "Hallie"—before refusing to let me go after lurkers on my own. Why I could sense the monsters approaching once I did, and why I felt so terribly guilty after killing that youngling.

I'm not Alexandra Holden. I'm Hallie Holden—but what does that mean anymore?

Chase rests his chin on the top of my head, holding me close. I don't pull away, though the last three months are a hard habit to break. Deep down, I still feel like this is *wrong*. Chase belongs to a Hallie that doesn't exist anymore.

I love him. I do.

But I'm not sure that can be enough.

Not like I tell him that. And when he starts murmuring against my hair, I just let him.

"I love you, baby. I love you so fucking much. They can't keep us here. We'll take the trip back to the Grave… we'll go home to Jack… and we'll get married at St. Matthew's. No more waiting. We get married, okay?"

"We already are," I whisper.

He pauses. "East Jersey?"

I nod.

"Hell yeah, we're married. You're my wife. I told you,

baby. It's you and me. Hallie and Chase. We'll get out of this. You'll see. Together, there isn't anything we can't do."

He sounds so sure. Damn it. My heart breaks all over again. I just got him back, but how long will it last? The Doctor is another monster. He tore me apart, ripping open my psyche, making me remember who I'm supposed to be —and he did it because I insisted I was Alexandra Holden and my vitals said I wasn't.

Chase's showed that he'd been bitten by a lurker. They want to reverse the antidote.

They want to take him from me.

Xandra would've been strong enough to stop them.

I'm not sure that Hallie is.

I want to believe him. I want to think that there's some way out of this, that love and determination is enough—

—and that's when the white door opens and Maverick is shoved back into the cell.

He stumbles, head bowed. His body nearly drops. Catching himself in time, he plants his palms on his knees, taking in big gulps of air as though he's starved for it.

I push up. Chase hesitates for a moment, wanting me to cling to him, but as I say Maverick's name softly, he knows better than to let his jealousy shine through at this moment.

Maverick doesn't respond.

I shift on the bed. "James?"

His head jerks up, and I see his eyes.

His eyes—

I don't know what the Doctor did to him when they took him from our cell. But, now that he's back, there's no denying that they changed him, too.

Because his eyes?

They're completely black.

The cell smells of sex. Even without his increased sense of smell—if a failed lurker has one—he wouldn't be able to mistake it for anything else.

Throw in our rumpled clothing and the state of the formerly pristine sheets after we got done and sprawled out on one of the cots and… yeah.

I wait for Maverick to point out that something's different about Chase and me. I wait for Chase to ask what the hell is going on with Mav's eyes. I'm sure he hasn't forgotten what the technician said about Maverick having taken the Injection before the Turning, but getting laid seems to have put Chase in a good mood. Instead of going after Maverick, he just wrapped his arms around me, keeping me right next to him as Maverick slumped down on the other cot.

I want to tell him what happened to me. I want to let him know that I'm Hallie. At the same time, I look back on some of our interactions and I have to wonder if Mav… if he knew.

If Jack had warned him before I left that, while I came with an antidote, I also came with way more baggage than even I would've guessed.

Having a mental breakdown and spending the last three months living as the twin sister that I lost in a traumatic flaming… that would definitely qualify.

I'm not better. I don't know if I ever will be. In this fucked-up world we live in, there's a chance that I'll forever carry that baggage, the same way I toted a backpack and sleeping bag all over New Jersey. In the before times, I was going to school to eventually become a psychiatrist. I know better than anyone how fragile a mind can be.

Which is why I let Maverick have his space. Whatever the Doctor did had to have been as bad as what he put me through... I'm almost positive of that. He suffered, and he did that so I at least had one last moment with Chase.

He's still with me. I know we both expected that one of the goons would tell him it was his turn to be taken to the Doctor. Only... that's not what happened. Once Maverick was brought back, they left the three of us alone.

Who knows? It's getting late, and though there aren't any windows, I've gotten used to the rhythm of my body's internal clock. If it's not dark out yet, it will be soon, and I can only imagine that asshole of a Doctor and his creepy team taking a break out of torturing their "subjects" to have a quick dinner.

I don't care. I'm not sure how much time I'll have left with Chase. Already, it seems like I lost so much of it. Now that I know exactly who I am, it's like we have a second lease on life together. I need him so badly that the idea of watching him walk out the door with one of those agents... I cling to him.

No one comes back. On the one hand, that means they don't even bring us anything to eat or drink. We can sip water from the sink in our cell, but I'm sure the guys are hungry by now. Me? I'm so anxious, my stomach is twisting. I never thought I'd miss the way that the lurkers make me feel sick when they're near, but this is so much fucking worse, I don't know if I'll ever eat again.

As I curl up next to Chase, I think about the sensing

ability that I took for granted. It never triggered when I was around Maverick. It's the same with everyone we've come across in the NRI. They all took the Injection, but because they didn't Turn, I don't think of them as a threat.

Great job, Hallie. I can handle lurkers. I've proved myself even as I pretended to be Xandra. The Doctor and his goons? I'm in way more danger than I've ever been.

And I'm thinking that as the front door to the cell eases inward and another agent steps into the room.

Same dark suit. Same grey tie. Same black glasses... at first glance, it seems like another one of the same agents, only with one noticeable difference: it's a woman agent.

She's shorter than any of the others with a thick, curvy build and her dark hair slicked back in a bun even tighter than Elissa's. She walks like she has a pole up her back, and she turns her shielded gaze on each of us in turn.

She looks familiar. Weird that I think that. I'm pretty sure that Maverick is the first almost-lurker I've ever met, but as I stare at her... my jaw drops.

I know *exactly* who she is.

Veronica. What the hell is Veronica doing here?

The flirty rogue that disappeared into the woods with Maverick before heading off on her own... it's her. I know it's her.

What the fuck is going on here?

Well. At least I finally know why Veronica teased me when I asked her why she wore sunglasses. I thought they were blue, but if her eyes are black like Winston's... like Mav's... then I would've known there was something up with her when she called herself a rogue.

But she's not a rogue. She's an *agent*.

I open my mouth, but before I can say a damn word, she clears her throat.

"Get up. All of you."

Maverick's head whips around at the feminine voice. It's one hell of a relief when I see that his eyes... while the rims around the irises are much thicker than they were before, some of the black has faded. There's still some Maverick Brooks in there, and I see pure relief crossing his features as he jumps to his feet.

Chase hesitates. I know what he's thinking. That this is some kind of trap. But she's not here for him. She said for *all* of us to get up, and shimmying out of his hold, I get to my feet. I'm fully dressed now—from Rory's jacket to my boots—and I'm glad that Chase is, too. I grab his hand, tugging him so that he's standing.

Veronica holds open the door. "The Doctor will see you now."

That's what she says. Just out of sight of the cameras as she steps into the hall, she shakes her head and flaps her fingers, gesturing for us to follow her.

Should I? Is she a part of Project Phoenix? Is she a member of the NRI?

Or is there more to her than meets the eye?

She mouths two words, pointing in the direction of the emergency stairwells. Two syllables as she leads us away from the direction of the Doctor's office.

Let's go.

What choice do we have? Sit here and wait for Chase to take his turn with that sadistic prick?

Let's go.

Why not?

I don't know where the other agents are. I have no idea if the cameras in our cell worked or not—though I'm leaning toward not unless they really didn't mind watching me and Chase get busy—but as soon as the four of us reach the hall, I expect it to have been a test. Or a trap. Something.

Nope.

Veronica tears down the hall. Maverick is right on her heels. Chase refuses to release my hand, and the two of us run together toward the stairwell.

Once we're inside of it, Maverick throws him arms around Veronica. "You did it. You fucking did it!"

Excuse me?

Veronica gives him a quick squeeze, then backs out of his embrace. "V told you I would, didn't she? Come on, Mav. You think I wasn't going to get revenge on what they did to my team? For Jules and Lindsay?"

She says all that as she takes the stairs two at a time. I'm confused as all hell, but I'm a survivor through and through. I don't miss a step, and neither does Chase.

Even if I have to ask, "Veronica?"

She shakes her head. "Delilah."

Huh?

"I don't get it."

Maverick chuckles. He's the happiest I've seen him in weeks, all while we're running for our lives through a narrow, gloomy stairwell. "Really, Xandra? I would think, of anyone, you'd recognize a twin when you saw one."

At first I don't get it. That's probably because hearing him call me by my sister's name is a pang I wasn't expecting. As we take the next landing, turning to head up another flight, I can't help but gasp out, "Hallie. My name is Hallie."

Yup. I was right. The lack of any reaction on his part tells me that Maverick was just waiting for me to come to my senses. Oh, well.

"Wait… twin? What do you mean, twin?"

"You met her," Delilah answers. "I spoke to her the other day when I was granted a morning leave. She said you guys were coming and I should keep an eye out for you."

"Veronica runs a collection of rogues," explains Maverick. "I met her on my travels over the summer, and I knew she kept her base around the Pulaski Skyway. It wasn't luck that we found her. I was looking for her."

Of course he was. "But why?"

"Because Delilah is her twin sister."

"I also worked with Lindsay at the NRI," Delilah adds. "She was my best friend. I'm doing this for her."

"Lindsay," pipes up Chase. "Who's Lindsay?"

"Maverick's wife," I tell him. "She died in the Turning."

Chase blinks.

I pat his arm. I know, baby. It's a lot.

Delilah scowls as she keeps an easy lead on us. "Some of us were lucky enough to get the first trial of PP-55. Lindsay… she hated shots. She didn't get it, and by the time she did… she got the bad dose."

"It's my fault," begins Maverick.

Delilah shakes her head. "No. It's Project Phoenix's fault. You know that, Mav. That's why I told you, if you ever come after them, I'll help take them down from the inside." She pauses for a moment, and even with the sunglasses on, there's no hiding the hurt in her face. That... that's an expression. "I lost Jules because of them. Fuck 'em. It's time I finally quit, and I'm taking you guys with me."

I don't understand half of what's going on here. Honestly? I don't care. Somehow, this Delilah has led us through the stairs, shoving open a door that has brought us onto a side street.

A *dark* side street.

No wonder none of the agents have bothered to come after us so far. We're two survivors, an almost-lurker, and whatever Delilah is without a single match or a way to strike a flame. We'll be easy pickings for lurkers—and the burnt caramel smell coming from every direction tells us that they're *everywhere*.

We try. I can't say that we don't. The four of us run, but we only make it two blocks away from the NRI before we run into our first horde of lurkers plodding toward us, their long, ragged cloaks dragging against the asphalt.

Somehow I've gotten disconnected from Chase. Staring at the approaching lurkers, knowing it won't do any good, I take his hand in mine and give it a squeeze. I spare a look over my shoulder at Maverick, at Delilah, and I nod.

The lurkers are closing in. I'm sure the NRI won't be far behind them.

And you know what?

Just then I swear the spirit of Xandra is hovering some-where nearby. A whisper on the breeze causes my hair to whip around me and I can almost hear her, like always—

"Got a light?"

And I grin.

AUTHOR'S NOTE

Thank you for reading *Burn*! I hope you enjoy the first part of Xandra and Chase's story — and will return to the end of the world with the follow-up book, *Phoenix*, coming in 2026!

As I mentioned in the foreword, I wrote the first part of this book more than a decade ago. It was for a NaNoWriMo back in 2013, and the idea was born in the first few days following Superstorm Sandy that decimated New Jersey that year. We went without power for almost a week, and I started to think about what it would be like if it never came back on. That's how *Burn* was born—but then I let it sit on my hard drive up until recently.

I started the rewrite of this story more than five years ago, at the beginning of the Covid-19 pandemic. Because of the talk about a good portion of the population dying and the idea of a vaccine saving the rest of the world, I put it back on hold. As much as this is a passion project of mine, it felt too, too real so I dove back into my fantasy worlds again.

Fast forward to the beginning of this year. In between other projects, I started working on 'Xandra''s story again. And I decided that, with the way the world is now, it might never be the right time to release this story so why put it off? Especially since it felt very timely to write a book when the government is failing us in so many ways.

Hopefully you guys enjoyed this story. It's so different than anything I've ever done before, and it's been percolating in the back of my head for so long that I'm so glad to share this world with you! And if you want to know what happens next, you can pre-order *Phoenix* now!

xoxo,
Jessica

ABOUT THE AUTHOR

Jessica lives in New Jersey with her family, including enough pets to cement her status as the neighborhood's future Cat Lady. She is a full-time writer and an around-the-clock reader who loves all things fantastical and paranormal. After writing for fun for more than a decade, she finally decided to take some of the stories out of her head and put them out there for others who might also enjoy them! She loves Broadway musicals (especially *Newsies!*), supporting her beloved New York Mets, and collecting mugs, e-readers, and everything that comes in her favorite shade of light pink!

JessicaLynchWrites.com
jessica@jessicalynchwrites.com

ALSO BY JESSICA LYNCH

After the Turning

Burn

Ash *newsletter exclusive

Phoenix

Welcome to Hamlet

You Were Made For Me*

Don't Trust Me

Ophelia

Let Nothing You Dismay

I'll Never Stop

Wherever You Go

Here Comes the Bride

Tesoro

That Girl Will Never Be Mine

Welcome to Hamlet: I-III**

No Outsiders Allowed: IV-VI**

Holidays in Hamlet

Gloria

Holly

Mirrorside

Tame the Spark*

Stalk the Moon

Hunt the Stars

The Witch in the Woods

Hide from the Heart

Chase the Beauty

Flee the Sun

Curse the Flame

The Other Duet**

The Claws Clause

Mates*

Hungry Like a Wolf

Of Mistletoe and Mating

No Way

Season of the Witch

Rogue

Sunglasses at Night

Ghost of Jealousy

Broken Wings

Of Santa and Slaying

Born to Run

Uptown Girl

A Pack of Lies

Here Kitty, Kitty

Ordinance 7304: the Bond Laws**

Living on a Prayer**

The Shadow Realm**

Rejected by the Fae

Glamour Eyes

Glamour Lies

Through the Veil**

Forged in Twilight

House of Cards

Ace of Spades

Royal Flush

Claws and Fangs

(written under Sarah Spade)

Leave Janelle*

Never His Mate

Always Her Mate

Forever Mates

Hint of Her Blood

Taste of His Skin

Stay With Me

Never Say Never: Gem & Ryker

* prequel story

** boxed set collection

www.ingramcontent.com/pod-product-compliance
Lightning Source LLC
Chambersburg PA
CBHW071216300726
48975CB00004B/1333